TEASE

ALSO BY SOPHIE JORDAN

THE IVY CHRONICLES

Foreplay

HISTORICAL ROMANCE

How to Lose a Bride in One Night

The Earl in My Bed (Novella)

Lessons from a Scandalous Bride

Wicked in Your Arms

Wicked Nights with a Lover

In Scandal They Wed

Sins of a Wicked Duke

Surrender to Me

One Night with You

Too Wicked to Tame

Once upon a Wedding Night

THE FIRELIGHT SERIES

Breathless (Novella)

Hidden

Vanish

Firelight

TEASE
The Ivy Chronicles

SOPHIE JORDAN

wm

WILLIAM MORROW
An Imprint of HarperCollins*Publishers*

TEASE. Copyright © 2014 by Sharie Kohler. All rights reserved. Printed in the United States of America. No part of this book may be used or reproduced in any manner whatsoever without written permission except in the case of brief quotations embodied in critical articles and reviews. For information address HarperCollins Publishers, 10 East 53rd Street, New York, NY 10022.

HarperCollins books may be purchased for educational, business, or sales promotional use. For information please e-mail the Special Markets Department at SPsales@harpercollins.com.

FIRST EDITION

Designed by Kevin Estrada

Library of Congress Cataloging-in-Publication Data

Jordan, Sophie.
  Tease : the ivy chronicles / Sophie Jordan.
     pages cm
  ISBN 978-0-06-227989-7 (pbk.)
  1. Single women—Fiction. 2. Man–woman relationships—Fiction. I. Title.
  PS3610.O66155T43 2014
  813'.6—dc23

2013048680

14 15 16 17 18 OV/RRD 10 9 8 7 6 5 4 3 2 1

For Lily Dalton and Kerrelyn Sparks, my road trip compatriots

TEASE

Chapter 1

"ARE YOU SURE THIS is the place?" I stepped out of Annie's car into the cold January night. My hand lingered on the passenger door as though I might suddenly pull it wide open again and dive back inside.

The bar looked more like a dockside warehouse than a building. A stiff wind could blow it over. More motorcycles than cars sat parked in front of the tin-walled structure. The place was crowded. There was no real rhyme or reason to the parking situation. No lines or curbs marked where to park. It was just a massive free-for-all.

"Yep," she answered. "This is it. Maisie's." She waved to the red neon sign positioned at a crooked angle. Despite the sweet-sounding name, the bar looked about as innocent as . . . well. Not me.

"You sure there's not another Maisie's?" One that didn't look like it could give you tetanus just by walking through the door.

"Look." She motioned to a nearby Lexus parked between a pickup and a rusted Pinto, her breath puffing like fog from her lips. The luxury vehicle was about as out of place in the lot as we were in our skinny jeans and designer coats. She walked a few steps closer to the vehicle, her boot heels crunching over the snow-covered gravel. "It's Noah's car." Noah. Annie's latest obsession and the reason we were even here.

Nodding, I buried my hands in my coat pockets and fell into step beside her, trying to pretend that I wasn't totally out of my element. I was all about a good time, after all. That was my rep. Nothing too wild for me. Not even a biker bar.

Still, I tried to imagine my two best friends coming here with me. It would never happen. Even if Georgia and Pepper didn't have boyfriends who kept them occupied, this wasn't their scene.

It's not really yours either.

True. I wouldn't find my type here. No one to flirt with. Definitely no one to take back to the dorm. Maybe one of the guys in Noah's fledgling band would qualify.

Sighing, I looked over at Annie just as she parted the front of her coat and seized both of her enormous breasts and adjusted them, making sure her cleavage was optimally displayed within the deep V of her too-small sweater. I was really scraping the bottom of the barrel with her, but there wasn't anyone else to hang out with tonight. Georgia was out with Harris. Pepper and Reece invited me to stay in and watch a movie with them, but that always made me feel a little lonely. Isolated even though I was among friends. They were in love and it was in everything they did. Every word. Every touch. And yes. They were constantly touching each other—my presence the only thing stopping them from getting naked. It was enough to turn my stomach. But hey. Better them than me.

Love was losing control. And I never lost control. I just made it look like I did—hooking up with different guys every week—but I was always fully cognizant of my actions. In charge every moment along the way.

Sighing, I tucked a short strand of hair behind my ear. Even Suzanne, my go-to wing-girl of late, had a date tonight. All my friends had—or were close to having—boyfriends. Considering that was the last thing I wanted, I was stuck with the likes of Annie. Not the nicest girl I'd met in my two years at Dartford but she was the only one available. Since I wasn't the kind of person to stay in and stare at the walls or watch reruns of *Glee,* that left me here. At a biker bar.

The moment we stepped inside, I decided I might have miscalculated what I could handle, because as bad as Maisie's looked on the outside it was way worse inside.

Apparently the smoking ban was ignored here because the air was thick with the stuff. My virgin lungs seized and I coughed. As wild as I got, I didn't smoke. Cigarettes or anything else. The worst thing I put in my body was a Taco Bell burrito. My tearing eyes squinted into the haze.

The average patron was male, over thirty, and sporting a beard and tats that didn't especially smack of quality. Patches that looked gang related decorated their denim jackets and vests. Not that I could vouch for the authenticity of said patches, but I once watched a special on the History Channel about biker gangs and these looked legit to me.

"Annie," I murmured, hovering in the doorway. "Are you sure about this?"

"What?" She blinked. "This is the kind of place all the great bands get their start."

I shook my head, and said in a deceptively casual voice, all the while my eyes scanning the room, "This is the kind of place you get knifed."

I always did this. Watched. Assessed. I might appear carefree, but my mind was always working, always weighing and considering. I had to be this way. It's how I made sure I never ended up in a situation that I couldn't escape. Like before.

She rolled her eyes. "I never thought you would be such a wimp. C'mon. Let's get a table."

I wasn't a wimp, but every move, every decision I made was calculated. I partied at places I knew. Mulvaney's, Freemont's, the familiar frat houses. I only fooled around with guys I knew, too. Even if they were strangers, I knew them. Because I knew their type. They were all the same. Easy to read. Easy to control.

Weaving through tables after Annie, it was clear there weren't guys like that here. No. These guys looked like they'd just been released from the penitentiary. Burly and tattooed with eyes that followed us like hungry wolves. Nobody controlled them.

I stared straight ahead as if I didn't see them. Didn't feel their stares.

We took a table near the stage, sliding off our coats and hanging them on the backs of our chairs. Noah and his band were already performing. They weren't very good, but I didn't think the bar was set very high here. Just the same, I think Noah and his guys would have been better off performing something other than an old Depeche Mode song. The patrons who did pay attention didn't look impressed.

Annie clapped loudly—the only person—as they finished one song and slid into the next. Noah winked down at her.

"Isn't he great?" she called over to me.

"Yeah." I winced as his voice cracked midsong. Even if I could forget that he was singing Depeche Mode in a biker bar, he was dressed in a striped button-down polo and looked like he'd just rolled out of the Gap.

"So how did he get this gig, anyway?"

Annie didn't answer. She clasped her hands together and swayed in her seat. I rolled my eyes and searched for the waitress, hoping she would be making her way to us soon. Mind-numbing alcohol sounded like a good plan.

Tonight was one of those nights I couldn't handle being alone. If I had stayed in, I would just be stewing over Mom and our phone call this afternoon. It happened every time we talked. Fortunately those calls were few and far between. She would heap on the guilt, remind me of what a very bad daughter I was. The only thing that made me feel any better was slamming back a few shots and wrapping myself around a cute guy who knew what to do with his lips—and it wasn't talk.

"I need a drink," I announced, renewing my efforts to spot a waitress.

As the song ended, I managed to snag the waitress's attention and place an order. She didn't even card me. Scanning the room, I was reminded of how I wasn't going to find a cute guy here. "How long is he on for?"

She shrugged. "Dunno."

Discouraged, I slumped in my seat, perking up when the waitress returned with our pitcher. Fortification was in order if I was going to sit through her mooning over Noah. I poured into a clear plastic cup and quickly gulped down the beer, instantly feeling warmer and more relaxed. As I drank a second cup, I squinted at the stage, checking out Noah's drummer. Not bad. A little on the skinny side, but he had good hair. He grinned at me and I smiled back, holding up my cup in salute as he did a less than stellar job on the drums.

I scanned the room surreptitiously throughout the next few songs, nursing my third beer. I'd learned long ago if you made eye contact a guy took it as an invitation. So I didn't make eye contact unless I was issuing an invitation, and there wouldn't be any of that tonight. Not here anyway.

Not even when I spotted *him*.

Holy hotness. A little shiver blew through me as I watched him from under my lashes, careful not to ogle. I drank more, as if that would kill the sudden awareness that shot through me. He was one of the youngest guys in the place, but still older than me. Probably early twenties. He greeted several people with nods and waves, a couple of slaps on the back. My gaze slid over him appreciatively as I drank. The alcohol wasn't helping. I squirmed a little in my chair, everything inside me suddenly humming and alive.

I couldn't stop myself. Couldn't look away. He was *too* good-looking. In an edgy-can't-be-tamed kind of way. In other words—not my type. Still. Looking never hurt. As long as he didn't know I was checking him out.

Propping my chin in my palm, I lifted my drink and finished off another cup. I was definitely feeling good now. A heady euphoria wrapped around me as I checked him out.

He wore a leather biker's jacket, slim-lined and well worn at the seams and elbows. Denim covered his long legs, a chain looping from the front of his jeans around to the back. Biker boots carried him across the bar. Even in all that clothing, he looked built.

His face was flushed and wind-chapped from the cold. His hair looked deliciously windblown. The kind of artfully wild mess—longer on the top and cropped shorter on the sides—so many guys on campus spent a long time trying to perfect. And yet I doubted he did more than run his hands through his hair when he got out of bed. He looked at home here as he settled on a stool in front of the long stretch of bar.

The bartender, an older woman with implausible red hair that bordered on purple, leaned across the counter and pressed a quick kiss to his cheek. Yeah. A definite regular. Just further confirmation that I should stop staring before he noticed me.

Annie elbowed me. "Take a picture, why don't you?"

I tore my attention away and shrugged. "He's cute." I hic cupped. Ugh. Beer always gave me hiccups. An unfortunate side effect.

Did I say cute? Not cute. *Sexy hot.*

"So what are you waiting for?"

I arched an eyebrow at her.

"C'mon. It wouldn't be a Friday night without you hooking up with someone, right?"

I glared at her. Even if there was some truth to what she was saying. Her lip was curled like she was looking at something gross on the bottom of her shoe. Funny considering she was hardly an example of sexual restraint.

"I need to use the restroom." I hesitated, expecting her to stand and join me. I didn't really want to walk around alone in here, but she didn't move. Of course not. She wasn't like Georgia or Pepper, who would insist on sticking together in a place like this. Hell, they would stick close to me in one of our usual hangouts. They were good girls. The best friends I've ever had. I was lucky to have them. Stuck with Annie tonight, that was painfully clear.

I pushed up from the table with a sigh. The room swayed for a bit and I steadied my hands on the table to get my balance. "I'll be back."

Focusing on the neon restroom sign, I tried to walk in a straight line. I mostly achieved this. I think. Ignoring crude catcalls, I made it to the restroom without incident. Two other women stood in front of the mirror applying lipstick.

One froze as I entered, holding the red tube over her lips. "Oh, honey. I think you're lost. You shouldn't be here."

That about summed it up. I nodded and the action made me dizzy, so I stopped and closed my eyes in a long blink. Opening my eyes, I admitted, "I might have taken a wrong turn." A wrong turn that started with getting into Annie's car tonight.

The second woman turned to assess me in my skinny jeans and sweater. "If I were you I'd get back in your car and find the nearest TGI Friday's." She wagged a finger. "This is no place for you. It gets pretty rowdy as the night wears on." She glanced at the invisible watch on her wrist. "You got maybe one more hour."

"Thanks. I'm not staying much longer." At least I hoped not. Determined to convince Annie that we really should go, I used the restroom and washed my hands.

Emerging from the bathroom, I jerked to a stop at the sight of a couple stumbling down the narrow hall. The guy had one hand buried under the woman's skirt, exposing her thong.

I blinked several times as if the action would clear my vision. The man hefted her against him, wrapping one of her legs around his waist as they fell into the wall. Her leg jutted out into the narrow hall, blocking me. *My God*. They were going to have sex right here outside the bathrooms.

They were flailing around so much, her legs scissoring the air. I couldn't pass them. Not without risking getting crushed into the wall or impaled by one of her lethal-looking heels. And my reflexes probably weren't the best right now. Not after four beers. Or was it five?

I eyed the pair, contemplating my move. And that's when I noticed him on the other side of the couple. To be accurate, that's when I noticed him noticing *me*.

He didn't seem aware of the couple between us. He was looking directly at me. His gaze slid over me. There was nothing subtle about it. He surveyed me thoroughly, from head to toe. Like he didn't quite know what to make of me. And I'm sure he didn't. I wasn't typical of Maisie's clientele. Not in my black knee-high boots, jeans, and purple cashmere sweater. And not with the diamond studs in my ears that Dad bought me because he felt guilty about leaving me alone for Christmas while he took his girlfriend to Barbados. *At least he spent New Year's with me*. I ignored the whisper reminding me that he only did that because he broke up with his girlfriend the moment they got back from Barbados.

The guy's eyes settled on my face, and I could see they were a warm, deep brown. He looked even hotter up close. And taller than he had from across the room. Just barely over five feet, it didn't take much for me to feel smaller than everyone else—especially guys—but the top of my head would barely reach Biker Boy's shoulder.

And then I squashed that thought because it would never matter. There would never be a moment where I would stand close enough to him to find out firsthand. I wasn't stupid enough to get tangled up with the likes of him.

Realizing I was checking him out just as much as he was checking me out, I quickly broke eye contact. Heat crawled over my already overly warm face. Even not looking at him, I could feel his stare. We stood there, the couple making out between us with their distracting groans and pants, and I tried to pretend that this wasn't awkward. That I wasn't buzzing and unsteady on my feet and ripe for seduction from a guy who looked like him.

I took another glance. It was impossible not to look at him again.

He didn't quite smile, but there was definitely a glint of humor in his eyes. His gaze flicked back to the couple and then to me again. He was amused. I compressed my lips, determined not to engage with him. I didn't need to give him the wrong idea about me. Like I might be the kind of girl into hot biker boys.

Seeing an opening, I made a break for it. Squeezing past the gyrating couple, I darted forward clumsily on my heeled boots. Biker Boy turned sideways, looking down at me as our bodies came flush with each other. Fortunately the hall was wide enough that we didn't actually touch. *Thank God.* A few inches separated us, but that didn't stop me from noting that, yes, the top of my head barely cleared his shoulder. He was seriously tall. And if I wasn't already drunk, standing this close to him would make me feel like I was.

His brown eyes gleamed down at me in the gloom. I kept moving, feigning disinterest—like I did every time I got the vibe that a guy might be more than I could handle.

If there was even the faintest doubt in my mind that I couldn't control the guy in question . . . then it wasn't happening. Period.

I shuffled along quickly, resisting the urge to look back. He was still watching me. I knew it. The nape of my neck tingled. He was probably wondering what the hell a girl like me was doing in a place like this and how I should get far, far away. Or maybe that was just what I was thinking?

When I got back to the table, I downed another drink. "How much longer, you think?" I asked after a few minutes.

Annie huffed out a breath. "I wouldn't have brought you along if I'd known you were going to be such a nag."

"I didn't know we were coming to a place like this." I looked around, taking the opportunity to search for Biker Boy. I couldn't resist. He was back at the bar now, accepting a fresh longneck from the bartender and talking to a burly older guy beside him.

"A place like this? Listen to you. You're such a princess, Emerson."

I rolled my eyes at her. She was the one wearing body glitter that smelled like peaches. It looked like Tinker Bell had dumped her bag all over her head. I finished my cup and reached for the almost empty pitcher to pour myself another. My head felt comfortably insulated now, fuzzy and warm. Even the band sounded better.

The drummer winked at me and I grinned back at him. Yeah. He would do.

Glancing around the room, my gaze went to Biker Boy again. As though he felt my stare, his gaze swung to me. My eyes swung forward again, cheeks burning. *Way to act disinterested, Em.*

My face grew hot all the way to my ears. It wasn't like me to get all flustered over a guy checking me out. It must be how totally out of my element I was here.

"What's wrong? You look funny. Who do you keep checking out?"

"No one." I shook my head, and then stopped, my fingers flying to my temples as I willed the room to stop spinning.

Annie looked around the room searchingly, clearly not believing me. "Ahh." I stole a glance over my shoulder, following her gaze with a sinking feeling. Yep. She'd spotted him. Who else would I be looking at in this place? There weren't many options. "Him again, huh?"

"What?" I played dumb.

"Oh. C'mon. Don't try to act like you haven't been checking him out. Of course you have. He's the hottest thing in here."

I shrugged and took another sip. "Fine. I noticed him. But he's not my type."

"Loser biker dude or not, he's every woman's type. At least I'm betting between the sheets he is." She giggled and the sound grated on my nerves.

"Yeah, well, I'm not interested in finding out." I took a long gulp. "He's probably in some biker gang."

She twisted in her chair to survey him more fully. "Bet he's good in bed though. Could teach those college boys we're used to a thing or two, huh?" She elbowed me in the ribs. "I wouldn't mind giving him a go."

"Aren't you here for Noah?" I reminded her, annoyed at the level of interest in her voice. Somehow I had forgotten just how free she was with her . . . er, charms. Even my reputation paled in comparison to hers.

"Noah's busy right now." She wiggled her fingers in a little wave at Hot Biker Boy.

"What are you doing?" I hissed, grabbing for her hand and missing. Scowling, I tried again and caught her fingers this time.

"Making a new friend, I hope. What's the harm in meeting him?" She yanked her hand free.

"Noah is watching," I warned.

Annie faced forward again and waved at Noah as if she hadn't just been flirting across the room at some stranger. "I'll just tell him I was signaling him for you."

"Liar," I snapped.

"It'd be good for you. Never thought I'd have to say this, but you need to loosen up."

A shadow fell over our table and a deep voice that sounded like it smoked a carton a day asked, "Looks like you girls need a refill on that pitcher."

Looking up, I felt a stab of both disappointment and relief. It wasn't hot Biker Boy. No, this guy could be his grandfather in a not so kind future.

Annie brought her cup to her lips, her hushed "eww" for my ears alone. She stared straight ahead at the stage, clearly leaving me to deal with this on my own.

"No, thanks, we're g-good." I cringed at the slight slur of my words and set my cup down. I let having a designated driver lull me into a sense of safety. My mistake.

He pulled a chair out at our table and flipped it around. Straddling it, he sank down, his bulging belly pushing against his stained shirt that peeked out from his patch-emblazoned vest. "Well, I can see you're good." He leered back and forth between me and Annie and I wondered if he honestly thought himself even remotely appealing. Annie continued to act like he wasn't even there, staring straight ahead at the stage, bobbing her head to the music. "Real good," he added.

"Look, we're just here to—"

"Name is Walt." He leaned forward, rocking on the front legs of the chair.

I fixed a tight smile on my face. "Walt." Deep breath. "We're really just here to listen to our friends." I motioned to the stage. "We're not looking for company."

He buried his fingers in his thick beard, scratching deep. "Sure you are. A girl that looks as good as you is always looking for company."

I winced, wondering how to explain that I wasn't looking for *his* company.

He brought his chair closer, the four legs hopping over the

wood floor with sharp whacks. Now I could smell his breath, rancid as rotting eggs. This close I could even detect bits of food in his beard. And what really sucked is that he just kept coming closer. The man had no concept of personal space.

"Really, Walt, we're not here for—"

He dropped his hand on my thigh. I gasped and jumped a little as his big, meaty paw squeezed me through my jeans. Peeling his hand off, I dropped it on the tabletop. His friends at the table beside us hooted with laughter.

Even Walt chuckled. "That's okay, sugar tits. You'll warm up to me." He brushed a hand along my short hair. "Never had complaints before."

This guy was all charm. I wanted to ask if these uncomplaining females had been conscious but bit back my reply. "No, really." I slapped at his hand and shook my head, starting to get angry. The skin at the back of my neck pulled tight. I hated that feeling. It reminded me of when I was fifteen and stupid—someone who ignored all the signs and warning bells, dismissing them with the naiveté that nothing wrong could ever happen.

Well, I wasn't fifteen anymore, and I didn't ignore warning bells anymore either. And I was hearing them with old Walt right now.

But no more. I grabbed the pitcher and dumped what was left of it in Walt's lap.

He lurched from his seat with a curse, sending the chair clattering on its side.

Annie laughed, her hands flying to her mouth—not that that did much to cover up her hyena hoot.

I scooted away in my chair, still wary, especially at the sudden rush of red to Walt's face. His gaze jerked from his soaking-wet crotch to the table full of his friends and the color in his cheeks deepened. They were laughing harder now. He huffed like an enraged bull, his chest swelling like he was about to erupt.

The music ground to a halt. Noah hopped down from the stage. "Annie?" He looked from her to me in concern. "What's going on?"

Walt's gaze sharpened and narrowed on Noah. The biker's beady blue eyes brightened as if he was about to devour an especially tasty snack. He stepped up to Noah, bumping his bigger barrel chest into Noah's slight torso and sending him staggering back a step. "These bitches belong to you?"

Annie gasped. Noah's wide eyes shot to me and Annie before looking back at the biker who outweighed him by at least one hundred pounds. Before he could react, Walt swung.

I winced at the hard smack of bone on bone. Noah fell back on the table, sliding along the surface and hitting the floor with a crash of flailing limbs.

Annie screamed. The other three members of Noah's band surrounded him and tugged him to his feet. Instantly Walt's friends shot to their feet and closed ranks.

"What did you do?" Annie snarled at me as the shadow of a half dozen bikers fell over us.

I shook my head helplessly. My stomach pitched and bile surged in my throat.

"Picked the wrong bar," Walt declared, focusing all his

attention on Noah. What little was visible of his lips amid his scraggly beard curved wide. He reached out and gathered two fistfuls of Noah's nice button-down. "Now I'm gonna fuck you up, boy."

Oh. *Crap.*

Chapter 2

NO SOONER HAD THE words left Walt's mouth and it was on.

Shouts erupted and the place broke into chaos. Walt and his crew swarmed Noah and his hapless friends. Annie's screams rocked my ears. Glass shattered and chairs and tables flew. I staggered, getting jostled in the sudden press of bodies. An elbow caught me in the eye. I cried out at the sharp jab and went down, dark spots dancing in my vision as feet stomped all around me. I clenched my teeth against the pain and curved into a small ball, clutching my face.

A hand clamped around my arm and yanked me up. Suddenly I was off my feet and being carried. Blinking, I focused on the guy who was carrying me. *Hot Biker Boy*.

"What are you doing?" I demanded.

"Getting you out of there before you get trampled." I shivered at the first sound of his voice. It was deep and throaty and matched him perfectly. Goose bumps broke out over my skin.

I twisted my head around to assess the chaos. What about Annie? And the others? "My friends!"

He shook his head, his mouth pressed in a grim line.

The image of Annie getting crushed beneath biker boots flashed through my panicked mind. Desperate, I hit his impossibly hard chest. "You have to help—"

"You're lucky I got *you* out of there. I can't carry all of you."

I squirmed in his arms, determined to go back for Annie and the others. I couldn't leave them! "Let me down."

An air horn blared long and hard across the air. The kind that made your ears bleed. Everything fell silent in the buzzing echo of that noise. Everyone froze—even Biker Boy.

"Enough!"

My gaze flew to the owner of that gravelly voice. A man stood on top of the bar, a shotgun in one hand and the air horn in the other. "I'm not having my bar trashed tonight! Next person to throw a punch in my bar is gonna eat a bullet!" For emphasis, the owner swung the barrel of his shotgun around the room. "Understood?"

It was like I'd walked into some old Dirty Harry movie. *This couldn't be real.*

"Oh, it's real, sweetheart." The deep voice rippled through me, leaving gooseflesh in its wake.

Apparently I'd spoken out loud. My gaze snapped back to Biker Boy. His heart thudded strong and steady beneath my palm where it rested on his chest. I jerked my hand away and crossed my arms. "You can put me down. I think everything is under control now." A quick glance confirmed that Walt and his friends were reclaiming their seats, grumbling and looking like chastised children. The rest of the bar followed suit, righting tables and chairs.

"Sure." He lowered me to the ground, my body sliding along his in the most disconcerting way.

I quickly put space between us, stepping back and pressing a hand to my neck where my pulse hammered like it wanted to burst from my skin. I inhaled his clean soapy smell. It was nice. Especially in this place where the odors mostly consisted of sweat and smoke.

He clucked his tongue and peered closely at my face. "Oh, you're gonna have a shiner there."

With a grimace, I touched my tender eye. "I'll just get my friends and go."

"Yeah. That would be a good idea."

Scowling, I dropped my hand and whirled around. Leaving him behind, I found Annie with an arm wrapped around Noah's waist. He didn't look good. The right side of his face was swollen, his eye puffy and sealed shut. His band members didn't look much better as they clumsily gathered up their instruments.

"Let me help." I moved to wrap another arm around Noah, but Annie yanked away.

"You've done enough."

"Me?" I pressed a hand to my chest.

"Thanks to you Noah got jumped."

"Me?" I repeated dumbly.

"Yeah." Annie's face scrunched up, looking almost unattractive. "Get your own ride home."

"Are you serious?" I looked around me. "You can't leave me alone—"

"It's not my problem." She shouldered past me. I gaped at

her, watching as she headed for the door. Granted, I knew that
Annie wasn't the nicest girl. I hadn't liked the way she treated
Pepper last fall when Pepper and Reece were first hooking up.
I'm sure jealousy had been a factor in her catty remarks, but
that was months ago. She'd been decent since. I never would
have imagined she'd leave me stranded like this.

So much for a fun night out.

Noah's band members followed, lugging their instruments
and amps. They didn't even move toward the bar to get paid.
Although a guy who drove a Lexus probably wasn't in this for
the money anyway.

I reached a hand out for the drummer—he was my only
hope—but he just glared at me with one eye that looked like it
was warming up to a nice shade of blue. Clearly they all blamed
me. And they were leaving me here. Unbelievable.

I hurried after them, weaving between tables on unsteady
legs. Someone bumped into me and I had to grab the surface of
a table to keep from falling. The sudden action made my world
spin and I squeezed my eyes in one long blink in an attempt to
quell the dizziness.

"Hey, watch it," a woman's scratchy voice warned.

My gaze lifted toward the door, panicked that they had
already left and I'd lost my chance to change their minds. I
caught sight of their retreating backs an instant before the
doors slammed shut behind them.

With a curse, I pushed after them. By the time I stepped
outside, they were already getting into their cars. Sudden cold
that had nothing to do with the wintry air swam through my
veins. My boots crunched over the snow-packed parking lot.

"Annie!" I shouted just as my foot hit an icy patch and I went down hard. My ass took the brunt of the fall and for once I was glad that it was well padded. I might be petite, but I'd been cursed with a backside that could serve as a flotation device.

Annie heard me. I watched helplessly as she looked back at me before ducking inside the car behind the wheel. Struggling less than gracefully to my feet, I gawked as she started the car and reversed it out of the parking spot. Noah's Lexus followed, his drummer driving.

I stared after the taillights, my teeth chattering. My jeans were wet from my fall. Looking down, I swatted at my thighs, trying to dust off the white powder.

Snow started to fall softly then. Blinking against the wet flurries, I turned and moved back toward the bar, taking shuffling steps to keep from falling again.

My legs felt heavy, every step a chore, but I forced myself to cross the threshold. It was warmer inside at least—even if it smelled like one giant ashtray.

I stayed near the door, scooting along the wall, trying to be inconspicuous. No easy feat when I'd started a brawl not ten minutes ago. I'm guessing I was on people's radar.

Teeth still chattering, I fished my phone out of my pocket and punched in Pepper's name. It rang four times and then went to voice mail. Yanking the phone from my ear, I glared at the lit screen. "C'mon, Pepper." Damn rabbits. I could guess what they were doing. Instead of leaving a message, I poked at the phone several times with my finger, missing the end button before successfully landing on it.

Pink Floyd piped out of the speakers near the stage and everyone looked livelier than they had half an hour ago. No more of Noah's best of the '80s to mellow the mood. It was a miracle they hadn't been booted out of here before I even spilled beer in some biker's lap.

I was on the verge of dialing Georgia—if I could hit the right button. She'd been with her boyfriend since she was sixteen, so they probably weren't having sex. At least certain comments from Georgia led me to believe that they didn't exactly have a rocking sex life. Harris was such a tool. Sad really. Georgia deserved better. She deserved fun and a guy who worshipped her and that just wasn't Harris, but somehow I was the only one who saw this.

"Friends leave you?"

My head snapped up at the sound of the deep voice. The motion threw off my balance. I staggered sideways.

Hot Biker Boy reached out as though to steady me, but I slid farther away, determined that he not touch me. He held up his hand, palm face out, as though to proclaim himself unarmed.

My stare moved from his palm to his face. A face too pretty to be in this bar where it looked like you needed an injection of penicillin if you just brushed up against one of its patrons.

Except he was one of *them*. A pretty-boy biker just seemed like an oxymoron. A giggle started to slip past my lips, but I quickly pressed my fingers to my mouth to kill the sound.

I gave my head a small shake, trying to clear it from the effects of alcohol.

He leaned against the wall just a few inches beside me. "You okay?" he asked.

"Y-yes. Fine. You? How are you? Oh, wait. Me?" I frowned. "Why? Why do you ask? Don't I look okay?"

One corner of his mouth lifted in a sexy half grin. I could have kicked myself for babbling so much. A simple yes would have sufficed.

He angled his head, his deeply set eyes focusing on me with an intensity that I wasn't accustomed to. Like he was really looking past the clothes and makeup and hair to the girl beneath. I squinted. Were those his lashes? Ridiculous. They were longer than lashes ought to be on a guy.

"You *look* drunk," he replied.

I winced. Was it that obvious? "Not really. I've had a few."

He gave me a skeptical look. In turn, I gave him what I hoped was my most sober look.

Shaking his head, he looked out at the bar that was growing just as rowdy as the women in the bathroom had predicted. It seemed like our fight had kicked things off for the night and now things were really hopping.

"You stranded here?"

I looked back at him and lied again. "No." Stranded made me sound so . . . helpless. Even if it was true, that wasn't me. I wasn't helpless.

"Where'd your friends go?"

"They had to go somewhere," I answered, not caring if that wasn't really an answer at all.

"Without you?"

I exhaled. It was a difficult lie to maintain when I stood here alone. Cold. Wet. And more inebriated than I should be considering my designated driver had flaked out on me. I dragged a hand down one side of my face.

He buried one hand in his jacket pocket but didn't add anything else. We leaned against the wall in silence, staring straight ahead, several inches separating us. The heat from his body radiated toward me. I rotated my phone in my hand nervously, waiting for him to go away, unwilling to call Georgia in front of him and reveal just how desperate and alone I was.

One of the women from the bathroom was dancing on top of a table now, waving her arms above her head as she gyrated her hips to the shouts and cheers of men below her.

He spoke up beside me, his voice a rich, deep rumble over the din. "I know you're not stranded or anything." Was that mockery in his voice? "But I could give you a ride home. If you want."

If you want.

I turned to survey him, propping a shoulder against the wall. I looked him up and down, considering every Hot Biker Boy inch of him. He really was beautiful. Dark haired, with eyes not quite as dark, a chocolaty brown. Deep and mesmerizing. Too bad he was everything I could never have. "I'm not going to fuck you."

He swung around to fully face me, his shoulder leaning against the wall. His brown eyes glinted as he looked me up and down, deliberately thorough. In the same manner I had evaluated him. "I don't remember asking," he answered.

I felt my face go hot. His words were as dismissive as I'm sure he meant them to be and my temper flared. "So what?

You're offering to drive me home because you're just a Good Samaritan? Right. I believe that."

My gaze skimmed the long length of him in his leather jacket and biker boots. He was a walking fantasy. If I was into the idea of losing control and having hot sex with a bad boy, he would be an ideal candidate.

One of his eyebrows winged high. "It's just a ride."

Nothing about him screamed safe and yet what he was offering meant I needed to trust him.

"It's never *just* a ride." I tucked a damp strand of short hair behind my ear. No, when I went home with a guy, a hell of a lot more happened than a simple drive from point A to point B.

"Look, princess," he began, all mockery gone, his tone indicating that he had finished playing.

Princess? Affronted, I squared back my shoulders.

"You're alone and drunk in a place you have no business being," he went on to say. "Right now there's a dozen guys watching you, trying to figure out the easiest way to get you on your back."

I blinked, my stomach rebelling. I looked out at the room again, seeing the faces, the eyes. He was right. Several were looking our way. Assessing me.

He added, "You're like a lamb in a pack of wolves in this place."

Yeah. That pretty much summed up how I felt. Not an alien feeling. I'd felt that way before. And I'd vowed never to feel that vulnerable again.

And yet here I was.

"And you're not a wolf, right?"

"Don't worry. I'm not into princesses. Drunk or sober."

I bit back denying that I was a princess. It would be like pleading for him to like me. And I didn't beg for any guy to like me.

"You really want to stay here?" his expression reflected his doubt.

I looked back out at the room. Walt chose that moment to blow me a kiss . . . followed up by an obscene gesture. I quickly tore my gaze away. *How did I end up in a place like this all by myself?*

Clearly I had gotten too comfortable, too cocky, too accustomed to always being in control. One phone call with Mom and I flew off the handle and let myself get into a situation where I was no longer in control.

All this thinking, and too much beer, did not make for a good combination. My stomach couldn't take it anymore. "I'm going to be sick." Whirling around, I pushed out the door. I moved several steps and settled my hands on my hips, throwing my head back and breathing in the frigid air, letting it brace me. The nausea subsided.

I heard him behind me, his solid steps thudding over the slush of snow and ice.

"I'm okay." For some reason the words felt more like an assurance to myself. I glanced back at him. His forehead creased as he watched me, clearly unconvinced.

Sighing, I glanced out at the parking lot again. Snow was starting to pile up on the bikes and cars. Bleakness swallowed me. I just needed to get home. The compulsion to seal myself in my dorm room until I felt like me again rose up inside me like a desperate, living thing. I could forget the recklessness of this night but I had to get it behind me first.

"I live in town," I heard myself saying. "In a dorm. At Dartford."

He chuckled lightly and the sound rubbed like velvet on my skin. "Could have guessed that." His gaze skimmed over me. "C'mon, college girl. Let's get you home."

I hesitated, still thumbing at my phone in my pocket. I *could* call Georgia. Or just take a ride from this guy and be home in thirty minutes. Georgia and Pepper wouldn't have to know how stupid I was for going out with Annie in the first place and drinking too much. I could forget all about tonight and go back to being the carefree party girl in charge of her fate. And the next time Mom called I'd let it go straight to voice mail. I could feasibly go another six months without talking to her. All these less than coherent thoughts chugged through my brain.

He stepped ahead into the parking lot and stopped, turning halfway, waiting for me. My eyes scanned him. He was tall and built. Any girl would want to climb all over him. And he could handle it, too. He wouldn't break a sweat. I squeezed my eyes in a tight blink at the sudden image of my legs wrapped around his lean hips, his big palms holding me up by the ass as I dragged my mouth down his neck. My breathing quickened.

"C'mon. You don't have to be scared. I promise I'm not a sociopath."

Wouldn't a sociopath say that very thing? But it was his: *You don't have to be scared* that got to me. Taunted me. I wasn't scared. *Ever.* I wouldn't allow myself to be. Not again. Lifting my chin, I stepped forward and followed him. He stopped at an old beat-up truck, actually leading me to the passenger-side door.

I gave the truck and him a long look. "What? No bike?"

"It's like ten degrees out."

So he did have a bike. That image of him wasn't totally dashed then. He pulled the door open for me. It was rather gentlemanly, and, I admit, unexpected. Most of the guys I hooked up with didn't get the door for me.

I shoved the comparison aside and climbed inside. He shut the door, the sound jarring. I fumbled for the seat belt, my fingers clumsy and slipping several times before getting a good grip. God. I really was drunk.

I exhaled a deep breath and stared straight ahead, willing myself into sobriety.

It wasn't the first time I'd drunk a little too much, but this was seriously the worst scenario considering I was at the mercy of a strange guy. How many crazy abduction stories began this way?

I shivered a little where I sat and not just from cold. I wrapped my fingers around my knees. *Come on, Em. Pull it together.*

Then he was in the truck cab with me, turning the engine over. It purred to life. He adjusted the heat. The air puffed out cold from the vents.

"Give it a minute," he said. Leaning down, he grabbed an ice scraper from under his seat. Slamming the door shut, he hopped out and scraped the windows free of ice and snow with strong, sure movements.

I watched his face through the glass, and his look of concentration did something to my chest, made it squeeze a little tighter. *Stupid*. I knew that achy little squeeze for what it was, and I couldn't let myself succumb to attraction for him. Square jaw; straight nose; and sensual, well-carved lips aside—he wasn't my type. As if to confirm that fact, I turned on him as soon as he got back inside the truck. "You're taking me straight home."

He gave me a look that told me he was beginning to think I was a freak. "I got that, yeah." Chafing his hands, he blew air into them, not looking at me again as he waited for the truck to warm up. Like I wasn't worth the time, and that made me feel a little foolish.

"Are you a student?" I asked, relieved that the question sounded normal.

He glanced at me. "As in do I go to college?"

I nodded. "Yeah."

He lowered his hands from his mouth. "Do I look like a college boy to you?"

No. Not any of the boys I went to college with at least. "Did you finish high school?"

He made a soft snorting sound. "Yeah. I finished high school."

A beat of silence followed before I asked another question. "How old are you?"

"Twenty-three."

He was three years older than me. And he never went to college. "What do you do?"

The skin along his jaw tensed, a muscle feathering the skin, a hint that I had hit a nerve. "Who said I did anything?" His tone was hard, almost mocking again.

I'm sure that he *did* something—how else did he survive?—but now I'd annoyed him and he wasn't about to share anything with me. I shrugged like I didn't care.

"How about we start with names?" I asked, my voice conciliatory. "I'm Emerson."

"Shaw," he returned.

Shaw. He looked like a Shaw. Whatever that meant. It just fit him. I exhaled through my nose. The air escaping the vents was feeling decidedly warmer now.

"Emerson." He shifted the truck into drive and backed out. "Well. Hope you don't mind me saying so, but you've got some suck-ass friends."

A breath shuddered from my lips. "Yeah. Well. They're not really my friends."

"Guess that's good, but then why were you out with them tonight?"

Because an ugly conversation with my mother sent me over the edge and made me act stupid.

Instead of saying that, I admitted, " 'Cause my real friends all have boyfriends."

The words slipped freely from my lips and I realized I might have been better off if I'd just admitted to a fight with my mother. I almost sounded like I envied my friends their girlfriend status.

"And you don't?" Was he trying to find out if I was available? But he'd already made it clear he wasn't interested in fooling around with me. My gaze traveled over the hands holding the steering wheel. They were big, masculine hands. Sexy, with strong lines and blunt-nailed fingertips. The kind of hands that screamed capable, strong. Hands that would know how to touch a girl.

Blinking, I forced my gaze to the road, my grip on my knees tightening. "No. I don't have a boyfriend. What about you?"

He rolled up to a stoplight and eased on the brakes. "No. No boyfriend either."

I giggled. I couldn't help it. My body relaxed and slipped to the side, sagging against the door. With a hiccup, I turned and watched him from beneath heavy lids. "You're funny." And panty-dropping hot. The insane impulse to crawl across the seat and press my mouth to his neck seized me. Alcohol motivated, I'm sure. That and the fact that it was a Saturday night and I would typically be tangled up with a boy by now.

He considered me with his brown eyes, making me feel all soft and fuzzy inside. The cab of the truck felt warm and cozy. I could doze off right here. "So how come you don't have a boy-friend like your friends do, Emerson?"

"Too much trouble." I sighed sleepily. "A boyfriend would just keep me from doing whatever I wanted to do." Was that my voice all throaty?

His gaze, bottomless and deep, gleamed in the shadows of his truck. He eyed my legs, encased in snug denim. I felt stripped bare under his regard and the sensation wasn't entirely *bad*. "And what kinds of things do you want to do?" His voice dragged over my skin like a physical caress.

Smiling, my head rolled against the back of the seat. I was buzzing, floating in a feel-good state. I felt a little dangerous, untouchable, which was a heady thing. Deceptive maybe, but I felt empowered . . . in control again. "Oh, all kinds of bad things."

And then, because I couldn't stop myself, I stretched toward him as far as my seat belt would allow. Until the tip of my nose brushed his neck. My lips moved against his skin as I spoke, "Things like this."

A small hiss escaped him. I pulled back and looked up at him.

His voice rumbled up from his chest, deep and tight sounding. "Go on then. Show me."

My smile widened at the challenge. I never could pass up a dare and that sounded an awful lot like a dare to me. I brought my face back to his neck and breathed him in. He smelled good. Like soap and winter and fresh-cut wood. No overpowering cologne on him. I nuzzled his neck like I was some kind of purring cat desperate to get closer. And then I licked him. Tasted his warm, slightly salty skin with a small, satisfied growl. I followed up with a moist, open-mouthed kiss on the side of his throat.

His breath caught just above my ear, fluttering my hair. I felt him swallow, his throat working against my lips.

Everything in me felt all melty and liquid-hot. Like my muscles had dissolved into heated butter. I wanted to crawl inside him. Press my body to his until I experienced every part of him. Every line and dip and hollow. All his hardness. My belly tightened, the ache there throbbing deep.

A sudden surge of need shook me to my core. It wasn't like anything I'd felt before and that rattled me. I'd made out with enough guys that I should have felt this way before, but something about this, about him, was different.

I leaned closer, ready to crawl into his lap, but my seat belt locked hard and caught me, keeping me from going farther. It was enough. Enough to bring me back.

Enough for me to remember that I did not fling myself at guys like him. I settled back on my side of the truck, my gaze turning wary as I watched him, his jaw locked and tense, eyes glittering with a predatory light. He looked like he wanted to say something . . . or do something. Like maybe haul me into his lap.

I tensed. I knew better than to tease guys who couldn't be managed. It was a line I never crossed except I just had.

A horn honked behind us. He blinked and turned his attention to the road.

I willed him to hurry, to get us across town so that I could dive into my dorm and forget tonight. Forget him.

He stared straight ahead, one hand draped casually over the top of the steering wheel. "I don't think you're the bad girl you pretend to be. Not even close."

I compressed my lips and watched the blur of lights flash past as we entered the city. No point in arguing. Not unless I wanted to prove to him that I was a bad girl, and I didn't dare do that.

"You're drunk," he announced. "Tomorrow you'll wake up in your warm bed and not even remember my name."

I sank deeper into the seat, bringing my legs up to curl on the bench. The fog of euphoria shrouding me began to fade away. My head was starting to throb, pulse right at the temples. My heavy lids slid shut, instantly easing some of the pressure that was building between my ears. I'd rest them for just a moment. Until he got to campus and then I'd tell him which dorm.

Shaw. His name flitted across my fading consciousness. I'd remember. I'd remember his name.

Chapter 3

IT TOOK PRECISELY FIVE seconds upon waking to realize that I was naked. Well. Mostly. I was wearing my panties and bra. My gaze shot around the room, and my next thought to chug through my mind was even more alarming. *Where the hell was I?*

The bed was big and comfortable. A contrast to my single bed back in the dorm. Not as big as the California king I had back home, but I spent so little time there that this bed felt vast and beyond strange to me. It smelled good, too. Like soap and freshly laundered sheets.

I racked my brain for memories of the night before. Not too difficult. I wasn't so drunk that I couldn't remember. I recalled perfectly Annie ditching me. And I remembered Shaw.

Shaw.

Oh. Hell. He was imprinted on my brain like a fire-burning brand. Shaw, who'd offered to drive me home. I closed my eyes in a slow, pained blink. And I'd accepted that offer. I'd gotten into his truck—in the truck of some hot, dangerous biker boy.

I yanked up the covers and looked down at my body as if I could identify evidence of . . . well. *Sex.*

My eyes burned, tears prickling the back of my throat. My last memory was of sitting in his truck. And—*God*—I had licked his throat. What happened after that?

My body looked the same as it always did. Slightly flaring hips that just barely saved me from looking like an eleven-year-old boy. Less than impressive breasts. Skin too pale, but bearing no marks. Still, I was hardly satisfied. I wriggled around, trying to detect any difference, any physical sensation that might reveal the effects of last night's activities. I mean I would know if had sex. *Right?* Tears pressed hotter against the backs of my eyes as the possibility sank in that maybe I had and didn't even know it. *God.* I was trapped in an episode of *60 Minutes.*

This shouldn't have happened. I shouldn't be here.

My flight instinct kicked in. I needed to get out of here. I scanned the room, looking for my clothes. Bare wood walls stared back at me. I was in a single room, large and airy despite the darkness of the walls. Light streamed in from several windows in the kitchen area. A pair of double glass doors to the left of the bed granted me a marginal view of the outside world. I glimpsed blue skies and snow-draped ground. Morning light glinted off the bare, ice-crusted branches of a large tree just beyond this door.

Silence shrouded me. Only the faint hum of the heater purred softly on the still air. It was as though I were the only person left on the planet. Definitely the only person in this house. Where was Shaw? *Off abducting another girl?*

An overstuffed armchair sat near a fireplace where logs

smoldered and flickered red-gold. My clothes were draped across that chair. Spread out almost neatly.

Wrapping the blanket around my body, I hopped to my feet. The sudden movement made my head spin. I swayed, pressing a palm to the side of my face, as though that could stop the tiny hammers beating at my temples. Instantly I vowed never to drink again. As in never. True, I've made this vow before, but this time I meant it.

I scurried toward the chair, nearly tripping over the blanket dragging at my feet. With a grunt, I grabbed it and whipped the fabric up and over my arm. When I reached the chair, I looked around furtively and dropped the blanket. Snatching up my clothes, I dressed as quickly as I could. Sinking down into the plush chair, I worked one boot on my foot. I was reaching for the next one when the sound of thuds reached my ears.

I froze, my pulse jackknifing against my throat. Everything slowed as those footsteps grew louder, closer, putting a swift end to the otherworldly silence. The door pushed open and Shaw stepped inside the space. Several logs overflowed in his arms. His gaze immediately landed on me. He paused in the threshold. I watched him, immobilized, feeling like a hare caught in the sights of a predator.

Then he moved, kicking the door shut behind him with one booted foot. His big body strode across the cabin and I resisted backing away. He stopped and squatted before the fireplace. "You're up."

I watched as he started stacking wood into a box beside the fireplace. He didn't glance at me as I sat there, still frozen, fingers curled tightly around the edges of my boot.

I moistened my lips, trying to find my voice as I watched his arms pull and flex beneath a long-sleeved thermal shirt. A light coating of snow dusted his dark hair and shoulders.

The ability to speak finally returned. "What did you do to me?"

He stopped stacking wood, his gaze flying to my face. I sucked in a breath. Everything about him right then, in the full light of morning, was *more*. More good looking. More masculine. His eyes brighter, more vivid. The fact that he looked pissed didn't alter the impact in the least. But it made my stomach knot. I squirmed inside at the intensity of his stare.

"I didn't *do* anything to you except take care of your drunk ass."

I swung a finger at the bed. "I woke up in your bed." I waved an arm. "I assume this is your place."

He nodded. "Yeah."

"Did you undress me?"

His jaw locked. "It was that or let you sleep in wet clothes." He arched a dark eyebrow. "You fell. In the snow. Remember?"

Yeah. I remembered that. And licking him. I remember that with excruciating clarity. "Where did you sleep?"

His mouth curled in a cocky grin at this question. "Where do you think?"

My face burned hotter. It didn't take much imagination to figure out where he slept. There weren't any other bedrooms in this cabin.

He turned his attention back to the wood and answered his own question, sounding a little bored all of a sudden. "On the couch."

I snorted. "Yeah. Right." I yanked my boot on the rest of the way and stood. "Let me get this straight. You brought me here. Undressed me. And then slept on the couch?"

He shook his head and rose to his full impressive height, towering over me. "You're unbelievable. You think I'm looking to score with an unconscious girl?" He looked me over slowly, thoroughly, making me achingly aware that I must look a mess with my bed head and rumpled clothes and day-old makeup. I probably looked like a raccoon from mascara smeared under my eyes. "Sweetheart, you're not that irresistible."

I inhaled through my nose. Okay. Maybe I'd insulted him, but he definitely came back swinging. "I'm sorry," I said, not sounding very apologetic and not caring. "Excuse me for panicking at finding myself half naked in a strange bed."

"Maybe you should pick better friends who don't bail on you, so that if you get drunk and pass out you won't wake up in some strange guy's bed. I mean, that's just a suggestion."

Touché. "You're an asshole." It was the best I could do.

He smiled again, but there was no mirth in it. "I've been called worse."

"I'm sure you have." I grabbed my coat off the couch and whirled around, marching for the door.

"Where are you going?" he called.

"Home," I shot back without looking over my shoulder.

"Oh yeah. Cool. How are you going to get there?"

I pulled the door open, stepped out onto the porch, and stopped. The full reality of just how much at his mercy I was washed over me. A winter wonderland stared back at me. The cabin sat back about fifty yards from a frozen lake. Far across the water, I could see other homes and cabins dotting a distant shoreline.

His tread sounded behind me and I whirled around. "Where the hell am I?"

"About half an hour from campus." He cocked that infuriating eyebrow at me. "Long walk, huh?" He looked down. "And those boots aren't made for long-distance treks, princess. Especially through snow."

I bit back my "no shit" response. My hands went to my hips. "How did I end up here? You were supposed to take me to my dorm."

He leaned against the doorjamb, apparently indifferent to the weather. A cold wind blew, buffeted his shirt against his chest. A well-muscled chest. Lean and hard. I could make out the definition of his pecs and the ridged stomach.

"Now how was I supposed to do that when you passed out and I couldn't wake you? Oh, and your license has a Connecticut address so no help there. And your phone? Password protected."

I crossed my arms and glared at him, hating that he was right. I'd done this to myself. It wasn't his fault. Sure, he was arrogant and rude, but I guess I should thank him and count myself lucky that I didn't end up with some perv who would take advantage of an unconscious girl. My gaze skimmed him. I couldn't help it. He was sexy as hell.

"Thanks," I mumbled.

He jerked a hand to his ear as if that could help improve his hearing. "What? What was that? Something semi nice just came out of your mouth? Impossible."

Seething, I bit out a little louder, "Thank you." I sucked in a breath and added in a less angry voice, "It was really decent of you to help me out. I'm sorry if I caused you any inconvenience."

"Inconvenience," he murmured, smiling.

"Would you please take me home now?"

"Not a problem. I live to help spoiled little Greenwich princesses."

The way he looked at me said it all. He didn't think very much of me. The idea stung more than it should have. I was used to guys liking me. At least superficially. And face it, that's as much as I let them see. I never let them get to the real me, the Em beneath the party girl veneer. Assuming they ever tried. Most were content with simply fooling around. No strings attached.

"This morning, can you tell me where you live—princess? Then I can get on with my day because, believe it or not, I have things to do."

I bristled. So he thought I led a charmed life . . . that I was a spoiled princess who teased guys by licking them and then passed out like a pathetic drunk. My face burned. I guess he wasn't that *wrong*. Except my life was far from charmed.

Not that I was telling him that. Who cared what he thought of me? He could think what he wanted.

"Let's go. I don't want to keep you from the things you have to do . . . like plan the next crime wave with your biker gang."

He grinned again, and I realized he was enjoying this. Me

baiting him. Him baiting me. Now that my panic upon waking in a strange place without any clothes on had subsided, I realized I maybe enjoyed it, too.

"Sure. And you don't want to miss your nail appointment."

I cocked my head. "That's tomorrow."

The sound of his chuckle followed me as I turned and walked off the porch. His truck was unlocked—why wouldn't it be all the way out here in the middle of nowhere? I yanked open the passenger door and hopped inside.

He climbed in and started the engine. We sat there for a few moments as it warmed up. I stared out at the frozen lake, marveling at the peacefulness of it. I wouldn't have pictured a place like this as his home. It was . . . nice. Which was weird. He was a biker. Some crapped-out meth house might have been a more accurate image. A stereotype, I knew, but it wasn't as though he wasn't stereotyping me.

I slid him a glance. "You live out here long?"

"It was my grandfather's. He died a year ago and left it to me."

I quickly faced forward again, my hands squeezing around my knees. It was the first bit of anything real we had exchanged beside taunts, and frankly, it made me uncomfortable. But then he made me uncomfortable. Undeniably. From the first moment I saw him.

"I'm sorry," I said, because I had to say something. They had been close. The man had left him his house. Obviously they had been close. "About your grandfather."

He put the truck in reverse and backed out of the property. "He went fishing with a friend, came in, made a sandwich, laid down for a nap, and never woke up. He was eighty-nine. We should all be so lucky."

I blinked against the illogical burn that suddenly pressed against my eyes. Gazing at the strong line of his profile, I wondered at my sudden surge of emotion. I suppose it came from hearing the love in his voice for this man who had clearly meant so much to him. And his grandfather had obviously cared for him. I wished I had that. I wished I had someone. Honestly, there was no family member who overly cared whether I lived or died. No one in my family would lose sleep if anything bad happened to me.

"Still . . . I'm sure it's hard. I'm sure you miss him."

He glanced at me, but there wasn't any of the derision I was coming to expect. No cocky half grin. He looked at me curiously, almost as if he was surprised I could say anything kind. "Yeah. It is . . . thanks."

Nodding, I faced forward again.

He drove us into town with no further conversation. I tucked my hands beneath my thighs and only spoke when we got close to campus, directing him to my dorm.

There wasn't too much student traffic this early on a Saturday and for that I was glad. Stepping out of his truck in front of my building, no one I knew was around. No one to witness me wearing my clothes from the night before and assume I was getting dropped off after a hookup.

One hand on the door handle, I looked back at him. "Thanks. For everything."

It was a weird moment. As anxious as I was to make my exit, I knew I'd never see him again. We didn't move in the same circles. I certainly wasn't going back to Maisie's. Realizing that kept me rooted to the spot, staring at him longer than I should. Kind of like I was memorizing him. A guy unlike any other guy I allowed myself to be with.

"Sure." His eyes looked dark as they held mine. "Stay out of trouble."

I felt my mouth twist into a smile at the irony of some guy I met in a biker bar telling me to stay out of trouble. "I'll try. You, too. Don't get in any more bar fights."

His eyes glinted. "Yeah? Well, you don't start any more."

I laughed once. "Yeah. No worries. That so won't happen again."

"Bye, Emerson."

I closed the door on him and walked to the front door of my dorm. I concentrated on putting one foot in front of the other and ignored that small thread of sensation running through me that told me he was watching.

THE SUITE WAS EMPTY. Not a surprise, but I checked both rooms anyway just to be sure. Pepper had a fabulous new boyfriend. Ever since they'd gotten together she spent most nights at his place. And Georgia had Harris. Not a fabulous boyfriend, in my opinion, but a boyfriend nonetheless.

For once I was glad they weren't around and I didn't have to explain where I'd spent the night. I loved them, but they tended to worry about me. They would love nothing more than me putting my wild streak to rest and getting a boyfriend.

Stripping off my clothes, I slid on my robe and grabbed my shower caddy and headed across the hall to the shower, trying not to shudder at the idea of a boyfriend. Boyfriends kind of wanted you to let them in. Among other things. And that so wasn't happening.

I spent at least half an hour under the hot spray of water before washing my hair and body. I kept thinking about last night. And this morning. Waking in Shaw's bed. Despite his bad-boy edge, he hadn't made a move on me. Sure, the invitation had been there when I'd practically straddled him and licked him like candy the night before, but he hadn't jumped my bones. He hadn't pushed for more or tried to manipulate the drunk girl. And this morning . . . this morning he just wanted to get rid of me.

Turning off the water, I shook my head and reminded myself not to be offended. It wasn't like I wanted him.

After drying off, I reached for my robe and slipped it on. The shower rings screeched as I pulled back the curtain. Suzanne stood in front of the mirror brushing her teeth.

"Hey, you!" she mumbled around a mouthful of toothpaste.

"Hey. How was your date?"

Rolling her eyes, she bent her head and spit in the sink. "Fine until his ex-girlfriend walked into the place with her new boyfriend and then he couldn't stop staring at them all through dinner. Turns out he took me to her favorite restaurant. Nice, right?"

I winced as I inched toward the door. "What a dick."

She nodded. "I would have had more fun going out with you."

"I'll remind you of that the next time you ditch me for a date," I called, halfway through the door.

"Hey!" she called out defensively. "I'd understand if you canceled your plans for a date."

I snorted. "And why would I ever do that?"

"Oh, someday you will. I just know it! When you meet Mr. Right." Her words rang out as I headed into the hall.

Suzanne read too many romance novels. She was starting to believe in them. Shaking my head, I entered my room and made quick work of getting dressed. I dried my hair so icicles wouldn't form when I stepped outside, already knowing exactly where I was headed this morning.

Hair dried and minimally styled, I applied light makeup and pulled on my heavy coat. Tossing a thick scarf around my neck, I slipped on my Uggs.

It was still early enough that not too many people were up and about. I made a beeline across campus for the Java Hut, hoping the caffeine would help my aching head. My stomach grumbled the instant I entered the popular campus coffee shop. It was practically impossible to get a seat during the week. At the moment the line was relatively short, only two people in front of me. Sorority girls from the looks of them and the Greek letters emblazoned on their butts.

One of the baristas spotted me. "Hey, Emerson!"

He was familiar. I think I fooled around with him at a party last semester.

"Hey!" My gaze flicked to his name badge. "Jeff."

He grabbed a cup from the stack. Pen in hand, he scribbled my name on the cup. "What do you have?"

"Cappuccino."

The girls in front of me shot me a not-so-nice look, clearly not appreciating my drink order coming before theirs.

The cashier shot them an apologetic look and started to

punch the keys until Jeff stalled her with a hand on her arm. "I got this," he murmured while sending me a wink.

The cashier shook her head and turned to the two sorority girls. "What can I get for you?"

With a last withering glare for me, they stepped up and ordered.

I smiled weakly at Jeff. "You didn't have to do that." Really, I wished that he hadn't.

"I wanted to." He shrugged. "Small perk of the job. Buying a drink for a cute girl."

"Thanks," I said, because at this point it would cause more of a scene to resist.

"So how've you been? You have a good holiday?" he asked as he began frothing milk for my drink.

"Yes, thank you."

"Awesome. Went skiing. My uncle just bought a place in Vermont. Only a few hours from here. Lets me use it anytime. You ski? You should come with me one weekend before the snow melts. There's a hot tub." He lifted his eyebrows suggestively and I knew just what he was imagining we could do in that hot tub.

"Um. Maybe."

"Cool. You still got my number?"

Had I ever had it? I nodded.

"Well, don't be afraid to use it." He sealed the lid on my cup, and leaned across the counter toward me, bracing his hands on the marble. "You didn't call me back when I called you last time."

I accepted the cup, fidgeting with the edge of the cardboard sleeve uncomfortably, unsure how to respond. Most guys were happy with a fling. Sometimes they called, but they never cornered me about it like this when I didn't call them back.

He winked and held up both hands. "Hey, it's cool. I'll call you later."

I smiled and nodded like that would be good. "Thanks for the drink."

Turning, I walked across the wood floor, sipping from my steaming cup. I'd meant to order a muffin, too, but no way was I turning around for another dose of awkward.

Stepping outside, I tugged my soft scarf high against my chin and turned in the direction of the art building.

"Em!"

Looking up, I watched as Georgia trotted across the street, tugging Harris after her.

"Hey," I greeted her.

"Hi," she replied in her sultry Alabama accent, cheeks flushed from the cold. "What's up? Where you headed?"

"I'm going to work in the studio."

She nodded. "What'd you end up doing last night?"

I hesitated. Now would be the moment to tell her that Annie ditched me, but then that would lead to the topic of how I got home . . . and where I spent the night.

I settled for: "Went out with Annie."

Georgia pulled a face, revealing just how little she thought of Annie.

"Bet ya'll had fun." Harris looked me up and down, his lip curling ever so slightly, and I wanted to kick him. I knew he thought I was a slut. Annie, too. I could read his dirty thoughts as he considered me. He was probably picturing Annie and me taking on half the football team or something. Judgy little bastard. I didn't get why Georgia didn't see it. I guess she was blinded by the fact that they'd been together since her sophomore year of high school. I knew his type though. He was happy to keep his pretty girlfriend, but he was always looking at other girls . . . leering at me. I had no evidence of him cheating, but I'd be surprised if he didn't enjoy the offerings to be had at one of his fraternity parties when Georgia wasn't around.

Georgia buried her hands in her front coat pockets and rocked on her heels. "Well, what are you doing tonight?"

I shrugged. "No plans yet."

"Pepper mentioned a party."

"We have that dinner party, Georgia, remember?" Harris reminded her.

She angled her head, frowning. "No."

"At the home of my dad's friend. The president of First National Bank, remember? I'm hoping to intern there."

"Oh." Her shoulders slumped in disappointment. One look at her face and I knew she wasn't interested in going.

"I can go alone, but I told you about it a month ago, Georgia." He paused, letting that sink in. "They're expecting me to bring a date."

She nodded. "No, of course. I'll go. I said I would."

I took a long sip of my cappuccino, further committed to the idea of staying single as I observed their little byplay. I wondered how much longer Georgia could tolerate him, and then reminded myself it had already been four years. Some habits were hard to break—including, it seemed, a sucky relationship.

Georgia looked back at me. "Well, sorry, but maybe you can go to that party with Pepper and Reece."

I shrugged. "Yeah. Maybe." It could be fun. Pepper and Reece didn't do too many parties. Most of their time consisted of staring into each other's eyes and other activities that I wasn't privy to—rightfully so.

"C'mon, Georgia. It's cold. I'm going in." Harris let go of her hand and entered the Java Hut. I watched Georgia as she stared after him. She looked troubled. The smooth skin of her forehead creased.

"You two okay?" I murmured.

She snapped her attention back to me. "Yeah. Sorry about that."

About what? That her boyfriend was an asshat? I shrugged like it was no big deal. It wasn't my place to tell her who she should and shouldn't date. I'd tried that once with my own mother and it didn't go over too well.

"Harris is just stressed. He's got a big test coming up. And he's looking for an internship for the summer."

I nodded like I understood.

"Want to go to breakfast tomorrow? It's been a while. We'll get Pepper to join us, too."

It had been a while since the three of us had one of our breakfasts. I missed those mornings. Maybe I'd even tell them about Mom pressuring me to attend Justin's wedding.

But then you'd have to tell them about Justin. I mentally shuddered at that idea. I didn't want to think about my prick of a stepbrother much less talk about him. Some things were better buried in the past.

"Yeah. That would be great."

She gave me a quick hug and disappeared inside the Hut. I set a brisk pace across campus, eager to get to the studio and lose myself on the canvas . . . the only place where it felt safe to let emotion run free. Where I could let myself lose control.

Chapter 4

I LOST TRACK OF time as I worked. A few other students worked in the studio, intent over their projects, but silence was an unspoken rule in this place. It was a large room. Larger than any classroom save for maybe the few stadium-style ones on campus. Floor to ceiling windows allowed natural light to pour in. Every once in a while I would glance up and gaze out at the lawn of flawless white, tapping the end of my brush idly against my chin as I soaked up the serene sight, letting it feed my soul.

The studio was my church. A holy sanctum. Wild Emerson who guys only saw as a toy to play with for as long as I would allow it didn't exist here. The wrecked fifteen-year-old who went to her mother expecting help and support? She didn't exist either.

It was just me here. Where I could be real. It was freedom. Peace. On the canvas there was no threat, no risk in letting myself go.

I dipped my brush in various colors, mixing and blending until achieving just the right shade of blue. I worked the colors

on my canvas, not even thinking, just going with it. Flowing.
Being.

It was always like this. I never deliberated. I just did. Whenever I sat back to observe the end result, it was almost like I was
seeing it for the first time.

My phone hummed on my workstation, beside me. Blinking, I looked up and noticed long shadows creeping in from
outside. Looking down, I read the text:

Pepper: Where r u?

Setting down my brush, I wiped my hands on a well-used
towel and picked up the phone to type back.

Me: Studio.
Pepper: Wanna go out? Party tonight.

For a moment, I hesitated and actually contemplated saying no. But then I'd be stuck in my room all night, alone. Even
though I could study for my upcoming art history exam, I
didn't relish that.

Me: Sure. On way to room.

Standing up, I gathered my brushes and palette. I walked
to the sinks in the back of the room and rinsed everything off.
Once my supplies were clean, I took them back to my station.
Untying my smock, I lifted my gaze to my canvas and froze.

I had been vaguely aware that I was creating something

inspired from the winter wonderland currently going on out-side, but this was totally unexpected.

The scene was plucked straight from this morning. A pair of glass-paneled doors that looked out at a snow-covered world and cerulean blue sky. Just the hint of a bed with rumpled blue sheets.

Clean lines. Bright colors. Very modern in theory. My heart was in this, which only made me wonder why I would have painted this scene. What was I telling myself?

The only thing more shocking would have been a portrait of Shaw himself. Clearly he was still on my brain. Standing back and observing the canvas, I shook my head. Maybe I'd prime over it. Start over. Use the canvas for something else.

I glanced down at my phone. It was almost six. My stom-ach twisted and growled. I pressed a hand against my belly, certain it was devouring itself. A painful reminder that I hadn't eaten all day. Slipping on my coat and wrapping a scarf around my neck, I nodded at Gretchen a few stations down working on an elaborate collage. She worked with a lot of textiles. She paused amid ripping up what looked like old curtains to wave good-bye to me.

I hurried from the building and started across campus, burrowing into my coat as my boots crunched over the snow-packed ground. It felt like the temperature had dropped ten degrees from this morning.

When I entered my room, it was dark and empty. Georgia was already gone, but I could hear Pepper's and Reece's voices floating from the other side of the suite. Our adjoining door was partially cracked so they probably weren't making out in there. Still, I knocked once before peeking inside.

"Hey!" Pepper grinned brightly, untangling herself from Reece's arms. He sat in her chair, looking his usual hot self. Dark blond hair cut close to his head. His body lean and hard as he lounged there all relaxed looking, totally at home in Pepper's room. Tattoos crawled out from beneath one of his short sleeves and down his toned bicep.

The guy actually looked pouty when she left him to approach me. Like he wanted nothing more than to haul her back in his arms.

She snatched two sweaters off the bed and displayed them. "Which?"

I assessed and pointed at one. "The black one."

"You think?" She stared critically at the black cashmere.

"Yes. Looks great on you." I waved hello at Reece. "Hey, Reece."

He smiled at me. "Hey, Em." Unlike Harris, he never made me feel like a second-class citizen. And he never leered. At me or any other girls. Except Pepper, of course. The guy was genuinely nice.

"What's the plan?" I asked. "I hope it involves food. I'm about to pass out."

She frowned at me. "Have you been painting all day?" She reached for my cheek and wiped at what I guessed was a smudge of paint. "Did you even stop to eat?"

I shrugged.

"Why don't I run out and get us a pizza while you two get ready?" Reece rose from the chair. "I know how long it's gonna take you guys."

"Good idea." Pepper nodded and said almost coyly, "Gino's?"

He reached for the hem of her sweater and tugged her closer. "Would I ever get pizza anywhere else?"

He dipped his head to kiss her.

I looked away, not much into voyeurism. Gah. If I didn't love them so much I might puke.

"I'll call it in as I head over. Be back in half an hour." The door clicked shut after him and Pepper just stood there hugging her sweater to her chest and looking so in love I wanted to both hug and kick her.

"Earth to Pepper."

She looked back at me still wearing that silly grin. "Sorry."

"No. You're not." Smiling, I shook my head. "Staring at you two, I almost have hope."

She dropped down on the bed. "That you'll meet someone? Of course you will. When you meet the right person. When you're ready."

And there was the heart of the matter. *When I was ready.* She didn't understand that I never would be. How could she understand? I had never explained it to her and I wasn't about to start now. Talk about dragging down the evening.

I dropped on the bed beside her. "So where are we going?"

"Well, one of Reece's friends is having an engagement party."

I groaned. "An engagement party?" Were people our age actually already starting to get married? Every time I turned around I was hearing about engagement parties and weddings. It was the beginning of the end. I couldn't even contemplate it. Soon I'd be spending my weekends attending bridal showers. And then baby showers. Shoot me. "That sounds . . . fun."

Pepper rolled her eyes. "Well, don't sound too excited."

This talk of weddings made me think back to my phone call with Mom. I'd already missed the bridal shower for Justin's fiancée. It was a week ago. I didn't even know the poor girl Justin was marrying, but Mom made sure I got an invitation. I missed it. Just like I was going to miss the wedding. This party tonight already felt like a bad idea. It was making me think of Mom and Justin way too much.

I grabbed an extra pillow and propped it behind my head. "Isn't there something more fun to do? You know. Like attend a funeral wake?"

She swatted my arm. "It'll be fun, Em. There's supposed to be a band." I must have still looked unconvinced because Pepper added, "It's not like an actual wedding or anything. No four-string quartet. It's at a house. Should be pretty casual."

"Okay," I reluctantly agreed.

I pushed up from the bed and waggled my eyebrows. "Guess I better take a shower. Never know. I might meet someone worthy of a hookup."

Pepper shook her head. "You're so bad."

"I know," I called over my shoulder, suddenly feeling a little more like myself as I stopped in front of my closet, determined to find the perfect outfit for a night out.

THE HOUSE WAS JAM-PACKED by the time we arrived. For an engagement party, it had to be mostly friends of the bride and groom because everyone was relatively young. No parents or grandmothers looked on from a buffet table loaded with casseroles. Furniture had been removed or pushed against the walls.

A band was set up in the living room. Guests milled throughout the house and spilled outside onto the back porch. Several heat lamps were scattered across the covered porch, warding off the worst of the cold. These were locals. Friends Reece had grown up with. Salt of the earth types. They weren't the Dartford college crowd, and I tugged self-consciously on my diamond earrings, wishing I had left them at home. And maybe my designer jeans, too. I stood out where Pepper and Reece blended in.

Reece led us through the party, searching for the happy couple. When he found them, he introduced Pepper and me.

"Reece, she's adorable!" Beth, the bride to be, a girl he went to high school with, exclaimed. She squeezed Pepper's hand. "Maybe we'll be getting an engagement announcement from you next, huh?"

I looked away, acting interested in the crowd. What was it with happily married (or soon to be married) people wanting you to join their ranks? There must be some kind of secret recruiting agreement.

The bride and groom soon moved off to greet other guests and accept well wishes. Reece left us in the living room to get drinks from the makeshift bar in the kitchen.

"Not bad, huh?" Pepper called over the music, looking around. "There are some cute guys here."

I nodded. "Yeah." She was right. Several even tried to catch my eye as I looked around. For some reason I wasn't feeling it tonight. Which was a shame since my hair was actually doing what I wanted it to do.

"Uh-oh, but watch out for this one. He's trouble." I followed the direction of Pepper's gaze. A guy so hot he could be on the cover of *GQ* was making a beeline for us. He swept in and grabbed Pepper around the waist. She squealed as he swung her around.

"Logan!" She punched him in the chest. "Put me down!"

"I can't help myself. You're always with that asshat boyfriend of yours. I see my chance and I gotta take it."

"Isn't that asshat your brother?" I asked dryly.

Logan turned his hundred-watt smile on me. "Emmmerson." He released Pepper and stepped closer to me. "You're looking . . ." He paused and I waited for the cheesy line. I'm sure he used them, but it didn't matter. He was so hot he could say whatever he wanted to girls and they threw their panties at him anyway. It didn't matter that he was eighteen and still had a few months left of high school. The guy had college girls chasing him.

"I'm looking what?" I prodded.

"Conveniently alone tonight."

"Conveniently?"

"Yeah. Convenient for me. You're usually surrounded whenever I spot you. What's up with all these losers?" He motioned out to the room. "They haven't closed ranks around you yet? Their loss."

I laughed. I couldn't help it. He was good. Funny. Not just hot but in possession of an actual personality, too. I should have expected as much. He was Reece's brother, after all. There had to be more to him than looks.

"So how about it, Emerson?" He draped a nicely muscled arm over my shoulder. Impossible not to notice that. The guy was ripped. An athlete through and through. I think Reece had said Logan had a bunch of college baseball scouts after him. "Are you going to finally give me the time of day?"

"Better watch out," Pepper warned. "You'll get eaten alive."

"Hey." Logan pressed a hand to his chest. "I'm hurt. I'm not that bad."

"I'm not talking about you. I'm talking about Em. She's a man-eater."

"Thanks!" I swatted at her while jerking a thumb at Logan. "And what's he?"

"Um, I'm going to go with not a man-eater," Logan offered, nodding his head sagely.

"No. Just a man-hoe," I retorted.

He pressed a hand over his heart. "Ouch."

I propped one hand on my hip. "Am I seriously saying anything you don't know?"

"I guess not, but does that mean you don't want to make out?"

Pepper giggled, clearly enjoying herself too much. I mock-glared at her. "Need I remind you that last fall you wanted this guy to coach you on foreplay?"

"Emerson!" Her face turned bright red. "That was before I met Reece! And I thought Reece was Logan, too, remember?"

Logan was laughing now. "That story will never get old."

Pepper crossed her arms and glared at him. "Yeah, your brother just loves it. Why don't you tease him about that?"

"I'll pass for tonight. Save that reminiscing for a special occasion like his birthday. Better yet, I'll bring it up in the toast at your wedding some day."

Pepper punched him in the arm.

I shook my head, grinning. He really was appealing in a carefree let's-just-get-naked kind of way. Too bad he was Reece's brother. He might be one-night-stand material, but he was off-limits. Even if he wasn't Reece's little brother, he was still in high school. That might not bother the majority of girls at Dartford, but I preferred my guys to be over eighteen.

The back of my neck suddenly prickled. The volume in the room took a sudden dip. The band played on, but the conversation seemed to have come to a stop. I looked around. Several people were turned, staring in the direction of the door.

The smile slipped off my face. Shaw was walking into the house.

Hot Biker Boy Shaw.

I blinked, trying to reconcile the sight of him here. I'd been doing my best to forget about him and last night. Hard to do when less than twenty-four hours later he was right in front of me.

He looked relaxed, a mild smile fixed to his face as he nodded and shook hands with several people.

What was he doing here?

Even though he carried himself confidently, with a wisp of a smile on his lips, something told me he didn't want to be here. It was in his eyes. There was a certain guarded edge to the dark depths.

"Well, look at that," Logan murmured.

I glanced up at him to see that he was staring at Shaw, too.

"Who's that, Logan?" Pepper asked, following his gaze.

"That's Shaw, Beth's cousin. He graduated with Reece.

Joined the Marines right out of high school with Beth's brother, Adam."

"Oh. Why do you look so surprised to see him here then?"

"Just kind of surprised he came here tonight."

"Why?" I asked, trying not to act too interested. "Beth's his cousin."

"Yeah, Beth's his cousin." Logan looked unusually somber. Unusual for him anyway. The guy was all flirt. I hardly ever saw him serious like this. "But Adam didn't make it back. He got killed over there, and ever since Shaw got back, he's been laying kind of low."

I sucked in a sharp breath and looked back across the room. Shaw had reached Beth by now. They stared at each other, neither one making a move, and the phrase Mexican standoff drifted to my mind. She didn't grab and embrace him as she had done to Reece. Hell, as she had done to everyone tonight. The tension was palpable even watching from this far away.

"Does she blame him for her brother's death?" I asked. That hardly seemed fair, and for some reason my protective instincts stirred, which was ridiculous. Her brother was dead. She was entitled to her feelings. And what did I know of the situation? Shaw Biker Boy was not mine to protect.

"I don't really know. All I know is that hardly anyone has seen Shaw since he got back. I heard he's living out on the lake and working at a garage across town."

I could confirm that he was living on the lake. I didn't know about him working at a garage, but he liked to hang out at biker bars. I wondered if that was new for him, too. I mean

I doubted that he hung out in biker bars when he went to high school with Reece, but what did I know?

I watched Beth's lips move, but still no hug was forth-coming. Shaw's face looked tight, strained around his mouth. Beth's fiancé said something then and pulled her away. Shaw was left standing there alone, but not for long. Several people came up and greeted him. Whatever the tension between him and Beth, it didn't extend to others. I continued to watch him, not missing the tension that lined his shoulders even as he talked to people. This wasn't easy for him. Being here. He didn't want to be here, but he had come. Why?

Then Reece was at his side. The two shook hands, Reece even forced one of those guy half hugs on him, which Shaw awkwardly returned. They talked for a few minutes and then Reece was nodding toward Pepper. Toward us.

"Oh, look, they're heading this way."

My pulse spiked against my throat. My first impulse was to run. I hadn't mentioned last night to Pepper. How was I going to explain how I'd met him?

His eyes landed on me as he and Reece made their way across the room. His expression gave nothing away, but his eyes widened ever so slightly.

Then they were standing in front of us and I didn't have time to hide . . . or think up an excuse to give to Pepper when he revealed that we already knew each other.

Logan and Shaw shook hands first. "Good to see you, man," Logan greeted him.

"Last time I saw you I think you were about this high." Shaw held his hand up to his shoulder.

"Yeah, thankfully that growth spurt kicked in."

Reece made the introductions. "This is my girlfriend, Pepper, and her friend Emerson."

He shook Pepper's hand but his eyes were on me. Honestly, they'd been sliding to me even while he talked to Logan.

I held out my hand, prepared to let the cat out of the bag and admit that we knew each other, but I froze at his words.

"Nice to meet you, Emerson." His warm hand enveloped mine and I felt the spark shoot straight up my arm to my chest. Every finger burned an imprint on my skin that I'm sure I would feel hours from now.

"You, too," I managed to get out from my suddenly constricted throat.

"Glad you came tonight," Reece said. "I heard you were back in town, but didn't know how to get in touch with you. I haven't seen your mom around—"

He slid his gaze to Reece. "She remarried. Moved to Boston." And then he looked back at me, his gaze deep, probing. I pretended great interest in my drink.

Reece nodded. An awkward pause fell on our little group.

"He seems like a nice guy," Shaw volunteered, mostly, it seemed, to fill the gap. "Works a steady job at least and cares about her. Better than my old man ever did." He smiled but it looked a little pained on his face. I had the distinct impression that this whole encounter was painful for him.

"Well, that's great. Your mom was so nice. She made the best cookies. I'll always remember she had them waiting for us after soccer practice."

Shaw shook his head with a low chuckle. Just the sound of it made my skin shiver. Which was kind of lame. Since when did a guy's laughter do that to me? "She just got those from the bakery at the grocery store." His eyes held mine as he uttered this. "The day-old cookies were always free for employees." It was like he was trying to convey something, trying to make a point. What? That he was different? That we were from two different worlds? I already got that point. I got it the first time I laid eyes on him, and it had nothing to do with the fact that his mom worked at a grocery store and my mom wore Chanel.

Pepper looked between us curiously. Apparently our stare-down wasn't going unnoticed.

"I'm going to get a fresh drink," I announced, shaking my nearly empty cup. I wasn't in the mood to drink tonight. I still felt the effects of last night a little too much, but it was an excuse to depart from the group.

I pushed through the crowd and stopped at the bar, signaling to the bartender. Unsuccessfully, it seemed. He was under siege from happy partygoers.

"I'll get him," a voice beside me volunteered.

I turned to face a cute guy. He wasn't quite as preppy as a Dartford boy, but close. With his carefully groomed hair and sweet dimples, he was definitely safer than the guy I'd just left . . . the guy I was spending way too much time thinking about.

Determined to shake off my funk, I smiled coyly. Pepper called it my man-eater smile. Well. Boy-eater. Boys, I handled. Men, less so. But this boy was right up my alley, so I gave him all my attention and let him signal the bartender like I was too helpless to do it myself.

Encouraged, he grinned at me again, leaning close enough for our shoulders to brush. "What do you want?"

"Hm." I glanced along the bar. Not too many choices. Beer. Wine. A margarita machine churned behind the bar, too. "A margarita."

The frazzled-looking bartender appeared and Pretty Boy ordered our drinks. I took a moment to look around the room. Reece and Pepper were still talking to Shaw. As though he felt my stare, Shaw looked over at me. I jerked my gaze away just as Pretty Boy accepted the drinks from the bartender.

"Cheers." He toasted his beer against my frothy cup. "I'm Jonathon."

I finished my sip and answered, "Emerson."

"So, Emerson. Are you friends with the bride or groom?"

"I'm a friend of a friend of the bride," I said.

"Ah. So you're kind of crashing the party then?" He winked at me. "A bad girl, huh?" His gaze skimmed over me appreciatively, his eyes lingering on my hair, assessing the magenta strips layered in with the dark strands. What? Did colored hair mark me as a bad girl or something? I stopped myself from rolling my eyes. It was such a stereotype.

"Do I look bad?" I teased back, trying to get into the spirit of flirtatious banter. It was my forte. Something I could turn on and off as easily as flipping a switch. It shouldn't feel like pulling teeth.

It shouldn't.

I peered over Jonathon's shoulder. I couldn't help it. Shaw

was here. A guy I never thought to see again, but he was here. Even from across the room, I was hyperconscious of his presence. Normal, I suppose. I spent the night with him and we didn't so much as kiss. I was . . . curious. That's all. The crowd shifted and I lost sight of him.

"You looking for someone?"

I shook my head. "No," I lied and tried to fight the memory of waking in his bed. Of clean cotton sheets and the crackle of a fireplace. I lifted up on my tiptoes, peeking through the press of people.

Pepper was laughing at something Reece said. Shaw was wearing that already familiar half smile. A body bumped me and I sank back down on my heels to keep my balance. The house was even more crowded than when we'd first arrived. With people pressed tight as sardines, it felt as suffocating as the busiest club. If this was just the engagement party, I couldn't imagine what the wedding reception would be like. I hoped the venue was bigger.

Jonathon set a hand on the bar and leaned in, snapping my attention back to him. His mouth brushed my cheek as he answered, "Oh, yeah. Well. You look like a bad girl." His fingers reached up and toyed with a short strand of my hair. "I bet you get really freaky."

"Me?" I tsked. "Not really. I'm actually pretty boring."

"No way. You're too sexy for boring."

Speaking of boring. Jonathon didn't get any points for originality.

"You might be surprised." My gaze strayed back to Shaw. It was as if he knew I was searching for him. His eyes were already trained on me. My face grew hot. The idea that he was watching me get my flirt on made me decidedly uncomfortable. His eyes seemed so knowing. Smug, almost. Like he knew I was only humoring this guy. Humoring myself. Like he knew the games I played with boys like this. Boys I didn't give a rat's ass about.

No longer feeling like flirting with anyone tonight, I faced Pretty Boy. "If you'll excuse me, I see my friend."

"What? Where are you going?" He grabbed my arm. "I thought we were having fun."

I smiled and lied as I slipped my arm free. "I was, but my friend had this ugly fight with her boyfriend and she needs me tonight." It was easier to say this than wound his ego with the fact that I wasn't interested.

I started weaving my way back to Pepper, but I paused when I saw it was just her and Reece. No Shaw. Had he left? And why did I care? I wasn't returning to see him.

I turned in a small half circle, scanning the room.

"Looking for me?" The voice at my back made me jump. If my cup was full, I would have spilled it all over myself.

I turned to face Shaw, trying to look calmer than I felt. More composed. "Shaw?" Was that breathy little squeak my voice?

He didn't smile. His face didn't reveal anything as he looked down at me, his sharp gaze roving over my features like he could see something there beneath the makeup and the smile I pasted on my face like a well-worn mask.

Then his question sank in. *Looking for me?* God. Is that what he thought? "I-I wasn't looking for anyone."

"It looked like you were."

Okay. So I was looking for him, but I wasn't about to admit that. He'd told me in no mincing terms the night before that I was entirely resistible to him. Not irresistible. *Resistible.* I hadn't forgotten about that dig. I didn't have any desire to come off as some desperate, clingy girl all hot and bothered for him.

He looked back at the bar where Jonathon stood looking decidedly unhappy after me. "Your admirer looks disappointed."

I shrugged. "I just met him."

"In other words, you don't give a shit about him."

Was I supposed to care about a guy I exchanged five sentences with? Why did it feel like whatever answer I gave would be wrong?

"You give a shit about every girl you flirt with in a bar?"

"I don't lead girls on."

Was he judging me? I laughed, feeling my temper stirring. Maybe I flirted and made out with my share of boys, but my reputation was more exaggeration than truth. Mostly.

I looked the long length of him up and down, clinically assessing him in all his brooding hotness. And I wasn't the only girl looking at him. Others were checking him out, too . . . hoping he noticed them back.

Was he telling me he was so different from every other guy I'd ever met? I had rarely come across a guy who didn't want to use me for his own needs. I knew there were exceptions. Pepper's relationship with Reece had shown me that, but I wasn't so arrogant as to think I was special enough to attract the exception.

I crossed my arms over my chest. "So every girl you sleep with becomes your girlfriend? Is that what you're saying?" Silence met my question. I smiled humorlessly. "I didn't think so. You and I aren't so very different."

His gaze flicked back to the bar where Jonathon stood, still looking after me. "I bet you're one of those girls who likes to tie guys up in knots and leave them begging."

I stepped closer, letting my body brush against his. This close, I had a perfect view of his mouth—the well-carved lips slightly parted with a breath. "Careful, Shaw, or I might think you're actually jealous."

My words elicited a grunt. I couldn't help tossing them out at him even though I knew they weren't true. I didn't affect him that way. He'd said so himself. I knew when a guy liked me, and this one didn't. And yet here I was. Taunting him like I wanted something.

Like I wanted him.

He turned away and started cutting through the crowd. Annoyed, I followed him, not realizing until he cleared the front door that he was actually leaving. Without even responding to my taunt, he was just walking away? I get that he didn't like me, but c'mon. He didn't have to be a dick about it.

I followed him down the porch steps onto the walkway and called after his back. "Why didn't you let my friends know you already knew me?"

He turned around. Several yards separated us. "I don't know you, Emerson." He said that like it was the simplest reason, but there was also a ring of something else in his voice. That he didn't even *want* to know me. That stung a little.

Which was dumb. It wasn't as though I was trying to win him over or something. I knew better than that.

"You know what I mean," I said.

He stepped forward, his biker boots crunching over the snow as he closed the distance between us. He stopped right in front of me, his hands buried in the pockets of his leather jacket. I shivered, achingly aware that I'd left my coat inside and was freezing my ass off out here.

"You had this panicked look in your eyes." He tapped the side of his head once. "It didn't take a genius to put two and two together. You thought you'd seen the last of me. I get it. You didn't want your friends to know you were slumming it with me last night."

I worked my lips a little before finding my voice. "That's not it at all." I shook my head.

He shrugged like he didn't care either way.

"I was embarrassed," I admitted. "But not because of you. I didn't want my roommates to know I passed out and had to rely on some stranger to take care of me. God, they'd stage an intervention."

He considered me for a moment.

"Not my finest hour, I know," I added, scuffing the ground with the toe of my boot. And then we just stared at each other. Him looking at me. Me looking at him. Like we were trying to figure each other out. I doubted I could ever do that. This guy . . . a boy who'd been to war, who'd seen people die all around him, was not like anyone I had ever met. He'd lost his cousin, and when he returned home it wasn't to family and friends waiting for him. Not from what I had just seen anyway. Beth looked almost ill at the sight of him. His mother was gone, remarried, and he'd told me yesterday that his grandfather died a year ago. Probably while he was stationed over there. Had he even come home for the funeral?

"What's your last name, Emerson?" he asked.

"Wingate."

Dark eyes with gold shards flecked throughout drilled into me. "You're trouble, Emerson Wingate."

Funny. That's what I had been thinking about him since we first met. And yet here I was. Talking to him. Baiting him. Even though I felt like I was skating on thin ice around him— one sudden move and I'd go plunging under—I was here.

"I know. I'm not your type, right?"

The air felt suddenly thick and I wished I could grab those words back, stuff them down my throat. I actually sounded like I was fishing for him to say he liked me. That he cared.

For a second I had forgotten *he* wasn't *my* type—I was so focused on him. On the fact that he found me thoroughly resistible. I'd let that little fact get under my skin. *Stupid, stupid, stupid.*

With him, I couldn't be in charge, and I needed to never forget that.

"I don't have a type." His deep voice rumbled across the few inches between us.

I nodded dumbly, humiliated, but relieved that he wasn't going to protest and play along with me by insisting I was his type. "But if I did, it would be you."

I gawked at him, shocked. If he didn't look so displeased at his admission, I'd think he was complimenting me. Or flirting.

My phone rang and I pulled it out, grateful for the distraction. I cringed when I saw it was my mother. I pressed the mute button.

"No one you want to talk to?"

"Just my mother. I don't need to talk to her."

"Not close with your mom?"

I shrugged. "Are you close with yours?"

"Yeah. She raised me all alone. My dad was never around, so it was just us and my grandfather growing up. I haven't seen her much since I got back. She married and moved to Boston." The corner of his mouth kicked up and my heart gave a stupid flutter. I just got an almost smile. "But I take her calls at least."

I bit the inside of my cheek, resisting the urge to defend myself and explain just how different my mother was from the kind of mom who baked cookies and made her kids lemonade. My mom was the type who stood by as her daughter was hurt and then insisted she forget it. She wouldn't have worked a job and raised me all on her own. She wouldn't have made such sacrifices.

"Aren't you the good son?" The words came out scratchy and a little raw. I couldn't help it. Thinking about my mother put me in a bitchy place.

"So why don't you take her calls? What'd she do? Cut your allowance?"

"Ha." I crossed my arms. "You really don't know me."

"Well, now I'm intrigued. Tell me about life in your ivory tower, princess."

I inhaled through my nose, almost tempted to lay it all out there. Just so I could wipe that smirk from his face. But that lasted only half a second. In five years I hadn't told a soul what happened. Why would I begin now?

Why would I begin with him?

"Why are you even still talking to me right now?" I snapped.

"You're the one who ran out here after me."

"And you're still here. Why? You don't like me."

"I didn't say that."

"Oh, that's right. If you had a type, I would be it. What does that even mean?" I angled my head and uncrossed my arms, propping my hands on my hips. "I'm fuckable but not anyone you'd want long-term? That it?"

He didn't even flinch at my bald language. Nor did he rush to denials either. "You're . . . interesting."

I laughed. "Is that what you call it? Maybe you're just hard up, soldier boy? Fresh off the boat and—"

"I wasn't in the navy." His voice got all flinty, but I kept going. Kept talking even when a part of me warned that I should just shut up.

I shook my head. "Tomorrow you won't even remember my name, my face—"

He stepped closer, eyes scanning me. "Emerson Wingate. Dark hair with reddish highlights. Bright blue eyes." His gaze dipped, roaming over me. "Hundred ten. Hundred fifteen pounds. Your hands . . ." He plucked one of my hands up, pressing his palm flush to mine. He considered our kissing palms, my hand so much smaller than his own. The tips of my fingers barely passed his middle knuckle.

"Beautiful hands." My chest tightened at his deep voice

washing over me. "Slender. Fine-boned but strong. Like they play an instrument. Piano maybe?" His eyes locked with mine. A dark eyebrow arched in question.

"I-I paint," I admitted.

He smiled as if he had just solved some kind of puzzle. "You paint," he echoed and continued, marking characteristics like he was reading off a chart. "Skin smooth. Pale. A tight little body perfect for tying guys up in knots."

My eyes shot to his face and I yanked my hand away from his. I rubbed my palm against my thigh, still feeling his touch there. "Go to hell."

"Temperamental." He gave me his half smile. "See? I'll remember you."

And then he was gone.

I stared after his retreating back, his figure dark against the mostly white landscape, broken up by only concrete and vehicles.

I exhaled, unaware that I had been holding my breath. I told myself I was glad that he was leaving. Glad that I wouldn't have to see him again.

Turning, I headed back inside the house, wrapping my arms tightly around myself as if that might somehow make me feel less cold. And less empty.

Chapter 5

I WAS GRATEFUL WHEN Monday rolled around just so I could distract myself with the routine of the week. There was no expectation of me going out. I didn't have to work so hard to be the me that I had created ever since I started here at Dartford. Friday loomed ahead like a visit to the gyno. Something you didn't want to do, but you knew you had to. If I didn't party it up on the weekends, if I stayed in, then everyone would think something was wrong with me. That I was sick or depressed. And nothing was wrong with me. I worked hard to convince everyone—myself included—that nothing was wrong with me. I was happy. Really.

My week ran its normal course. I still barely made it on time to classes, slipping in and finding my desk at the last second possible. I dodged my mother's phone calls. The afternoons I spent in the studio, losing myself in my work so much that I sometimes lost track of time.

On Friday afternoon I was working at my station, wishing it were still Wednesday so I didn't have to go out. I sighed, blowing at the strand of hair that dangled in my face. I had agreed to go with Pepper and Reece to hear a new band. Suzanne was joining us, too. Georgia had some lame event with Harris. Some future "Douches of America" banquet.

"That's really good," Gretchen said, stopping by my station to comment. "Not your usual . . ."

I blew at a magenta-dyed streak that dangled in my face. I had pulled the short strands back with a kerchief, but it always kept escaping.

"Good is not my usual?" I joked. "You wound me."

"No." Gretchen shook her head, staring intently at the canvas. "It's personal somehow."

Her words forced me to stand back and consider my work in a way I never did while I was laboring over it. When I'd returned to the studio on Sunday, I had a stern talk with myself, deciding that just because I was painting a scene from Shaw's house didn't mean anything. I was an artist. I seized inspiration when it arrived. I didn't need to examine the source.

The door had taken on a richness. There was a lushness in the browns that made it leap to life. The glass was like crystal, winking with light. I marveled that I had somehow achieved that effect. It took me hours playing with a lot of blues and yellows. The snow visible through the glass bled out beyond the door like this amorphous cloud of pristine white. And there, in that fog of snow, was a face. Almost ghostly. The features vague and indistinct. Except for the deeply set eyes. They seemed to stare back at you, intense and probing.

When had I done that?

"No," the single word escaped me on a breathy exhale. My shoulders slumped.

"What? Something wrong?"

Oh. Hell. No. I was not painting *him*. I wasn't doing that. I wasn't some lovesick stupid girl pining after a hot boy. *I* didn't pine. Pushing up off my stool, I grabbed the offending piece by the edges, determined to add it to the stack of canvases that we recycle.

I was almost to the dozen or so canvases leaning on the far side of the room, Gretchen trailing after me, when Professor Martinelli's voice stopped me in my tracks. "Emerson, what do you think you're doing?"

Still clutching the canvas that was almost as tall as me, I peeped around the side. "Excuse me?"

Professor Martinelli swept into the studio, her many bracelets jangling. I never understood that. Those things would distract me while I painted, but she was never without at least a dozen bracelets on each arm.

"I was going to recycle this and start on something new . . . I have a fresh idea," I babbled, "something that has really been nagging at me—"

She pointed an imperious finger at me. "You will put that canvas back at your station and finish it."

I opened my mouth to protest, but she cut me off. "This is the first piece that you've done that has shown any true inspiration. I'll not have you toss it aside."

I didn't know whether to be flattered or annoyed. I'd been a student here for two years and she had never reacted to anything I'd created like this before. Grumbling under my breath, I carted the canvas back to my station and pretended to work for another half hour, feeling Professor Martinelli's gaze on me. I didn't want to storm out right out after she told me to put the canvas back. She might very correctly think I was annoyed. When enough time had passed, I washed my brushes and cleaned up at my station.

Dusk had fallen. Night came on fast in the winter. I walked along the sidewalk, mindful of the ice patches. Once inside my building, I chose the staircase over the elevator. My steps rang out over the concrete. I kept hearing Professor Martinelli's voice in my ears. And then I saw those eyes. Shaw's eyes. It's like I was possessed . . . and someone else, the "possessed" me, had painted those eyes.

At my door, I fumbled with my keys, but it was suddenly yanked open. I looked up, expecting Georgia, but it wasn't her. It wasn't Pepper.

It was my mom.

THERE WASN'T MUCH DIFFERENCE in her appearance now at age forty-eight versus how she looked when I was nine. Except her face looked kind of waxy. She'd had some work since I last saw her. And her hair was longer. She wore it in a sleek braid down her back with several shorter layers escaping to frame her face. I squinted. I'd never seen her hair this long and I suspected it was due to extensions.

She never seemed to change outwardly. Or, for that matter, inwardly. When I was little she used to do the whole PTA-room-mom-thing. But once she and Dad divorced, she stopped pretending. She stopped trying to be the best mom on the block. She moved to Boston and began her quest for husband number two.

And she found him in my stepfather.

She looked me up and down, her nose wrinkling. "What's all over you? You're a mess."

"Paint," I replied. No greeting. No hug. This was normal.

"You always did have a unique sense of . . . style." Typical passive aggression. When she wasn't being outright aggressive.

I stepped past her into my suite. "How'd you get in here?"

"Your RA. I told her I was your mother and she let me in."

I'd have to talk to Heather about that.

"What are you doing here?" I dropped my bag on the floor and sank down on my bed.

"You're not returning my calls."

Wow. She must be desperate to come here. "I already told you. I'm not going."

"Emerson, would you stop being so selfish for one moment? You're family. How's it going to look if my own daughter doesn't attend her stepbrother's wedding? You already missed the showers. I want you at the rehearsal dinner *and* wedding."

"No."

Her lips compressed and she crossed her arms. The action pulled her shirt dress tightly across her upper body and I marveled at how thin she was. Thinner than the last time I'd seen her. She must be down to four saltines a day.

"You know the embarrassment this will cause me. You just want to hurt me."

Shaking my head, I stared at her. She really thought this was about her. About me wanting to hurt her and not what might or might not be comfortable for me. "It hasn't once crossed your mind that this isn't about you?"

She stared at me, blinking in something akin to bewilderment. "What do you mean?"

"Justin," I spit his name out like it was venom in my mouth. "I wouldn't go to his wedding if you held a gun to my head."

"Oh!" She tossed her hands up in the air. "This is still because of that misunderstanding."

I surged to my feet. "There was *no* misunderstanding."

She held up a hand as if to ward me off. "You were always guilty of an overactive imagination. You flighty artist types—"

"Mother!" I snapped. "I imagined nothing."

"Fine!" Mom grabbed her bag from where it sat on my desk and marched toward my door. "Cling to your bitterness and this ridiculous agenda you have against Justin. You haven't even seen him in five years. When are you going to grow up and move on, Emerson?"

"Oh, I've been quite grown-up for some time." The hard realities of my youth had guaranteed that.

"Don't call me. Don't text." She stabbed a red-nailed finger at her chest. I almost laughed and reminded her that she was the one who called and texted me. "Not until you learn to accept me. You never have. Not since I married Don."

"That's not true. I don't have a problem with Don." Honestly, I didn't. I met with her and Don several times a year for dinner. Even joined them for Christmas one year in Paris— true, I felt safe doing so because Justin was spending the holiday with his new girlfriend, his current fiancée, a girl I've obviously never met but who had my boundless pity.

"When you're finished behaving like a spoiled child, call me." She slammed out of my suite.

I stared at the door, my chest heaving as though I had just run a marathon. A soft knocking at the adjoining door had my head turning. Pepper peeked in the room, her eyes brimming with concern. Great. She'd heard that.

"You okay?"

I nodded.

She stepped inside the room, rubbing her palms over her thighs. "That your mom?"

I nodded again. "Sorry, I didn't introduce you two." My voice cracked a little. I swallowed. "As you heard, we're not on the best of terms these days." Years, really.

She sank down beside me. "Want to talk about it?"

I shook my head. "No." Rising from the bed, I started searching through my closet, stuffing my emotions way down deep where they couldn't get out. "What time does this band start? I could use some fun. And a drink."

Make that a few.

Chapter 6

THE BAND PLAYED LOUD and fast, the drummer going wild with the sticks. Sweat trickled down my neck as Suzanne and I danced hard. Bodies hopped all around us. The place was hot and jam-packed. People bumped around me. Guys I didn't know grabbed at my hips. I didn't care. I just danced, stopping only occasionally to make my way to the booth where Pepper and Reece sat and take another drink from my whiskey sour.

Pepper watched me with her face all scrunched up with worry. She'd looked at me that way all night. Which only made me want to drink more. Until that look on her face didn't register. Every once in a while she would glance at me and whisper something to Reece. Slamming my glass down, I made my way back out onto the dance floor to Suzanne.

My goal was drunken oblivion.

I didn't know at what point in the night Shaw showed up, but when I flipped my head and spotted him in the booth with Reece and Pepper, I stopped dancing. My dancing partner at the moment didn't stop, however. He continued to bump against me, his hands roving over my belly, sliding under my shirt to palm my stomach.

Shaw stared across the crowd at me. I stared back until the guy with his hands all over me spoke into my ear. "You're so fucking hot. How about we get out of here?"

Snapping my gaze off Shaw, I turned until I was facing the guy pawing me. Typical frat boy. He wore his hat backward. Greek letters emblazoned across his chest. "I want to dance!" I shouted over the crazy loud noise.

"We could dance back at my place."

"No." I shook my head, and resumed dancing, indifferent to him.

He stuck close, dancing with me and Suzanne, trying to infiltrate.

"Who's that?" Suzanne called, nodding toward our table. I followed her gaze. Shaw was talking to Reece now. "Friend of Reece."

"Holy hotness," Suzanne murmured. "I'm going in." Smoothing her hair back from her sweaty cheeks, she made a beeline for the table. I pretended not to watch, not to care, and kept dancing.

A new guy moved in, taking her place. I had frat boy behind me and the new guy in front. New Guy gripped my hips and thrust his pelvis in time to the music. I watched the table from beneath my lashes. Suzanne shook hands with Shaw. He was talking to her and I felt a stab of panic. Did he like her? She was pretty. And likable. Obviously. She was my friend. Suddenly annoyed, I pushed out from between my boy sandwich and headed for the bar.

At the bar, I looked left and right. I didn't have long to wait. A guy squeezed into the space beside me. "Hey!"

"Hey," I returned.

"Chad."

"Emerson." We shook hands, his hand holding on to mine longer than necessary.

"You alone?"

I waved back in the direction of my table. "Came with some friends."

"Yeah. Cool. Me, too. Great band." He nodded at the stage. I forced myself not to yawn at the small talk. I just wanted a drink.

"Saw you on the dance floor."

I leaned in a little. "Yeah?"

"Yeah. You're the hottest girl out there."

Ah, the brilliance of flattery. I flattened my hand against his chest. "Well, how about you buy the hottest girl on the dance floor a drink?"

His eyes flared with excitement and I knew in that moment he thought he was getting laid tonight. Boys could be so dumb.

"Sure. What'd you have?"

"Whiskey sour."

He waved the bartender over and ordered our drinks.

"So are you like a professional dancer? You've got some moves."

And the flattery kept getting better. Or rather, cheesier. Our drinks arrived and I took a long sip from my glass. "Nope."

"You a student? At Dartford?"

I nodded.

"Me, too. I'm an econ major. Figure it will help for law school—"

"Chad?"

"Yeah."

"Let's drop the small talk. You don't care about my major and I don't care about yours."

His eyes widened. "Wow. You're to the point."

I nodded and lifted my glass in a sloppy little salute. "Yes. I am."

"I can get to the point, too." He leaned forward so that his mouth brushed my cheek. "I'd like to fuck you."

I stifled a wince and pulled back to look at him. "That's supposed to shock me, I guess?"

His eyes glittered. "How about it?"

Suddenly everything felt bleak inside me . . . as if this was the most I could expect out of life. That there would never be anything more than this. A father who loved me as long as I led my own life, independent from him, never demanding anything other than money. Not his time. Not his affection. A mother who could never love me more than herself. And guys eager to use me and toss me aside afterward.

I downed the rest of my drink and signaled the bartender for another. The bartender returned and lined up two shot glasses in front of me and Chad. I gripped the cold glass, ready to shoot the liquid, let it burn out every other feeling until I was comfortably numb inside.

"You've had enough." The deep voice cut through my fog of bitterness.

Turning, I narrowed my gaze on Shaw, standing there. Up

close and personal. I'd been thinking about him all week—hell, I'd been painting those eyes that were staring at me right now. Still, the reality of him was so much more than what I'd re-created on canvas. Those melting dark eyes blazed down at me, and I read the judgment there so clearly. The tiny hairs on my arms prickled, ready for a fight.

"You're not the boss of me." God. I sounded like I was ten years old. I could do better than that.

He actually had the gall to pluck the shot glass from my hand and plunk it down on the bar. Not only that. He slid it away. I'd have to stretch across the counter to even reach it. "About this I am."

I glared from the glass back to him. "Give it back."

"Why? Just so you can get shit-faced and let some guy you don't give a crap about paw all over you?" He held my gaze as he growled this, not even glancing at Chad.

"Hey," Chad objected, but I didn't even glance at him. I was too busy glaring at Shaw and letting the hot emotions swirling through me gain momentum. I hugged those feelings close and stirred them to a boil. It was better than how I was feeling before. His sudden presence had erased those cold, bitter feelings. Now there was just fury at him for daring to tell me what to do. He wasn't even my friend. He didn't even like me.

"Jealous?" I sneered. "Why? You seemed to be having a good time with Suzanne."

God, now I sounded jealous. *Of my own friend, no less.* It must be the alcohol. I wasn't thinking about what I was saying.

His nostrils flared. "You're not getting drunk."

"Newsbreak. I'm already there." Well. Close anyway.

Although he was definitely killing my buzz. "Look. I get that you're Reece's friend and you probably think I need looking after, but really. I'm fine. I don't need babysitting."

As if I hadn't said a word, his deep voice rumbled across the air. "You definitely don't need another drink."

I inhaled sharply. Who the hell was this guy? It was none of his business how much I drank. Or who I let paw me. "Go to hell," I flung out.

A muscle popped in his jaw and I knew he didn't like that. Gratification swept through me.

He jerked his head in the direction of the doors. "C'mon. I'm taking you home."

I scanned the crowd, searching for my friends. Suzanne, Pepper, and Reece were watching us with great interest from the table. "Thanks, but I already have a designated driver."

"Hey, man," the guy beside me inserted, reaching across the bar to grab the shot glass and bring it back in front of me. "She can make up her own mind." He lifted the glass up for me to take.

I smiled sweetly at him. "Thank you, Chad."

Shaw leaned slightly forward, bringing himself eye level with Chad. "Get your hand out of her face before I break it."

Chad slammed the glass back down on the bar and surged to his feet, squaring off in front of Shaw. "C'mon, mother-fucker," he challenged, which really sounded kind of ridiculous coming from him in his powder blue polo. "You want to mess with me?"

Shaw sighed heavily and closed a hand around my arm like Chad had not called him an ugly name. Any other guy would have lost his cool.

"Let's go, Emerson," he stated, clearly unthreatened.

Even though I resisted the idea of him deciding when it was time for me to go home, I really didn't relish the idea of starting a fight in the middle of a bar. Thanks to Chad, people were already watching us. From the corner of my eye, I could see Reece pushing his way through the crowd toward us, Pepper and Suzanne fast behind. I didn't want to get my friends involved in a fight either. What if one of them got hurt?

Besides. I nodded and slid off my stool. I wasn't one of those girls who got her rocks off on two guys fighting over her.

Though Shaw wasn't really fighting over me. He was just doing what he thought he had to because I was Reece's friend. Because he was Reece's friend. He was a Marine. He probably thought it was his mission to save the world. One drunk girl at a time.

I let him pull me from the bar. We had only walked away two steps when Chad clamped a hand on my arm and yanked me back.

"She doesn't want to go—"

Shaw moved so fast then I didn't even process it until it was over. Until Chad was on the ground. In one smooth, ninja-fast motion, Shaw popped him in the mouth.

Chad went down, his hands cupping his face. I gaped and started to crouch down to help him when Shaw grabbed my hand and hauled me after him. "C'mon." We passed my friends. Shaw nodded once at Reece. "I'm taking her home."

Reece nodded in silent understanding. Pepper gaped and looked ready to say something, maybe protest on my behalf, but Reece turned and led her and an equally shocked Suzanne away.

I tugged on his hand. "Are you crazy? You just hit that guy—"

"He had it coming." His fingers tightened around mine as he pulled me out the back exit and into the parking lot. The music died to a heavy throb on the frigid air. My ears rang from hours inside the decibel-shattering din.

"How's that? He was trying to protect me from you—"

Shaw swung around, his eyes blazing. "Get a fucking clue, Emerson. He was standing near our table the whole time you were on the dance floor."

I pulled my hand free with a violent yank. "So?"

"He was telling his buddies and anyone standing nearby all the dirty things he was going to do to you."

I blinked and swallowed, pushing down my disgust that some strange guy had been talking trash about me before he even approached me at the bar. That was no shock. I knew just what kind of guy he was the minute he opened his mouth. I was more bothered by Shaw "rescuing" me. What made him think I needed rescuing? I could handle myself. I had been doing it forever.

"Oh, aren't you the noble knight," I mocked. "News flash. I didn't need your help back there."

"Sure as hell looked like it to me."

What? Did he think I was going to let that guy take me home and act out all his perverse fantasies on me? The very idea that he thought that way of me only made me angrier. Contrary to what all of Dartford thought, I wasn't a slut.

But isn't that what you want people to think? That you're tougher, stronger, more experienced? I can't be offended that they all believe the image I created. Including Shaw.

I took a deep breath and reached for my composure. Determined to not let Shaw rattle me, I shrugged. "So he was talking shit. Like guys don't do that."

"Not to you," he growled. "You might not think you deserve more respect than that, but I do. You deserve better."

Stunned, I couldn't think of anything to say.

Reclaiming my hand, he resumed hauling me through the parking lot, weaving us through the cars. My mind reeled. *What was that supposed to mean?* He thought I deserved better? Like what? I wasn't Pepper or Georgia or Suzanne. I wasn't a nice girl looking for a fairy-tale ending. That wasn't in the cards for me.

I lifted my face and inhaled the biting-cold air, trying desperately to cool the heat firing my cheeks as he led me toward his truck.

"Contrary to what you think," I got out, staring at his back, "I don't need rescuing."

He laughed harshly then. We were almost to his truck. I spotted it through the cars. Without breaking stride, he tossed over his shoulder, "You, sweetheart, need rescuing in the worst way."

I stared at his back, wanting to hit something. *Him.*

He led me to the passenger side and yanked open the door. Jerking his head, he snapped at me, "Get in."

Neanderthal. I crossed my arms over my chest, not budging. "What's that supposed to mean? I've survived just fine for almost twenty-one years before you came along."

His gaze flicked over me and that glint of scorn was back in his eyes. "That's debatable."

I flinched. It was as if he saw right into me . . . saw that I was a girl hanging on by a thread. How did he know that about me? *How could he read when I managed to fool everyone else?*

Again, I felt judged. Like he somehow found me lacking—which I knew was in direct opposition to what he had just said, that I deserved *better.* But that summed up how he made me feel. Confused. *Lost.* Low one moment and high the next. I didn't know where I was going with him, which was a definite first. It was scary and exhilarating at the same time, but mostly scary.

"Get in," he repeated, his voice hard.

"I don't have to do what you say. And I already have a ride home."

"Yeah, and they're having a good time out. Their night shouldn't end just because of you. So stop being selfish."

The truth of that statement flayed me. Which was probably the desired effect. I felt guilty.

I lifted my chin. "Who said I'd bother them? I'll find another ride." Unable to take it anymore—take *him*—I whirled around. I didn't make it two steps before he caught me up in his arms.

That was all it took. I fought, struggling against him. His arms circled and held me prisoner. The memory shouldn't have flashed before my eyes, but it did. It was there. Inside me, consuming everything. That feeling of helplessness. Of being trapped.

Wild animal sounds escaped me. I growled and snapped my teeth, actually trying to bite him.

"Emerson, stop! Emerson!" Still holding me, he carefully lowered me down, setting my feet back on the ground.

"Easy, Emerson. I won't hurt you." His voice faded as he caught sight of my face. Air sawed past my lips as I stared out at him through my wild tangle of hair.

I felt them then. The hot slide of tears. *Shit*.

His arms loosened around me without entirely letting go. Still, it was enough room to move my arms between us. I dashed at my cheeks with shaking hands, feeling like the biggest idiot. I knew I needed to keep my distance from him. From the moment I'd spotted him, he threatened my careful control. And now look at me. I was *crying*.

"What? What do you want from me?" I whispered feverishly. "Why are you here . . . why are you doing this to me?"

Why couldn't he just leave me alone?

He loomed over me. So close. Too close. Looking down at me, he shook his head. "I don't know."

Mortified that I was actually crying in front of him, I shoved free with a choked little sound and spun around again, sniffing back tears.

"Emerson." He said my name on a breath that I felt right at my nape. My skin turned to goose flesh. Part of me wanted to turn around but I held myself still.

His large hands fell on my shoulders and rotated me around. Standing face-to-face again, his hands dropped. He dragged one hand through his dark hair, sending the strands flying briefly before settling back into place. We just stared at each other in a silent communion. It was strange. There were no words, but something was happening, something passing between us. It sounds like a cliché, but I'd never felt anything like it before. Not with any other guy.

His hands lifted and slid over my tear-soaked cheeks, holding me almost tenderly. He looked troubled. There was no other word for it. "I don't know what it is you do to me."

I do something to him?

His voice continued, a dark little whisper rushing over my lips. "But I'm not going to fight it anymore."

As his warm mouth came down on mine, a jolt that felt like electricity shot through me. Along with that, a thousand thoughts chased through me as his lips pressed to mine, softer and more persuasive than I would have imagined possible from this hard-looking guy.

I could just step back. I could say one word. *No.* I could turn and walk back into the bar. He wouldn't stop me. Not this time. I knew that.

All of these options presented themselves to me in a single flash, but I took the only option I could. The only one there was.

I kissed him back.

Chapter 7

THE INSTANT I SOFTENED against him, everything changed. His lips went from soft and tender to hard and demanding. From gentle and seeking to needy and desperate.

And I was right there with him. I wrapped my arms around his neck and stood up on my tiptoes, plastering myself against his chest. I felt a growl rumble up from his chest. He dipped for a second, wrapping his arms around me and lifting me up off my feet.

I gasped and he took advantage. His tongue swept inside my mouth, tasting me everywhere, stroking my tongue, tracing over my teeth. With every lick of his tongue he pushed me closer to the edge.

My world jarred with motion and I knew he was walking me somewhere, carrying me like I weighed nothing at all. I didn't look up. I didn't care. I buried my hands in his hair and devoured his mouth, his lips, his tongue. I broke away and nibbled down his throat. I caught his earlobe between my teeth and his gasping hiss was my reward.

He staggered and bumped a vehicle. The sudden peal of a car alarm had us jumping apart. I slid down his hard length, releasing a shaky laugh. I ran a trembling hand down my face, my fingers lingering on my lips.

His hand joined mine on my face, his eyes glittering at me in the dark. His chest lifted with heavy breaths. He was just as affected as I was and this made me melt even hotter inside.

What was happening to me? I'd kissed my fair share of boys but I'd never felt anything like this before.

His husky voice fanned my lips. "I love the sound of your laugh."

"You do?"

"Yeah." He nodded. "You should do it more." He took my hand and pulled me after him.

I followed in silence, my feet moving quickly. This time I didn't protest as he escorted me to the passenger side. I had a few moments alone inside his truck as he circled around to the driver's side. I shook my hands wildly in the air in front of me, hoping to release some pent-up energy and calm my racing heart. It didn't work.

He opened his door and I tucked my hands under my thighs, trying to appear calm. In the driver's seat, he gripped the steering wheel and looked over at me. It was all it took. All semblance of calm was lost.

His hand closed around the back of my neck and hauled me across the seat to him. Our mouths collided. My fingers curled into his shirt, fisting the thermal cotton fabric. His chest felt hard and solid against my fingers. Even that turned me on. Not that his scorching lips didn't already.

He kept one hand at the back of my neck, tugging me closer as his other hand dipped to my ass, guiding me on top of him. I obliged, straddling him, hungry to get closer, gasping at the hard ridge of his erection rubbing directly between my thighs.

Voices and laughter penetrated dimly, but I didn't care. We were in our cozy little world inside his truck, lips locked, bodies melded. Nothing else mattered. I jumped slightly as a fist bumped our window. "Get a room!" A group hooted with laughter as they walked past, presumably on their way to their car.

I pulled back with a sharp breath and stared down at him. Everything about him left me feeling dazed and stunned. His eyes gleamed up at me in the darkened cab. His hand slid from my neck, fingers threading through my hair, holding the strands back from my face.

He was mind-numbingly hot, but it was more than that. It was in his eyes, the intense way that he looked at me. Nothing about this was familiar. Nothing about the way we were with each other was like anything I had experienced. I was not in control. Of him. Or me.

"This is crazy," I whispered.

He stared at me for a long moment, still holding the hair back from my face. The pulse of his palm beat against my cheek, in rhythm with my own racing heart, and it was as if I felt his life entwined with mine. Fanciful, crazy thought, but there it was.

His hand on my backside tightened and he dragged me closer until I felt the hard bulge of him directly between my

legs. It made me gasp, but I didn't pull back. In fact, I closed
my eyes and arched my throat, letting myself sink against that
delicious hardness.

"Where do you live?" His voice sounded hoarse and I recognized the feral sound for what it was. Need. For me. I guess
I wasn't so resistible after all. This sent deep female satisfaction
pumping through me.

I gave him the address and crawled off his lap. He started
the engine and turned on the wipers, clearing the thin sheet
of snow. The side windows were fogged and I knew we were
responsible for that. I hadn't even noticed how cold it was while
I was in his arms.

We slid each other long glances as he followed my direc-
tions and drove to my building. It was a shorter drive than last
time, but still long enough for me to think. For my breathing
to calm. For his hot glances to make me even more nervous.
When he was kissing me it was impossible to think. Impossible
to feel nervous. But now I could.

My phone buzzed in my pocket. I fished it out.

Pepper: U ok?
Me: Yes. Headed home
Pepper: Ok. Have fun
Me: Thx

Have fun? Did she think I was having wild monkey sex with
Shaw? He was Reece's friend. She was probably matchmaking
in her head, plotting a slew of double dates.

By the time we reached campus, I knew what I had to do. I

knew I had to say good-bye and make a break for it. Before this got any crazier and out of control.

"You can just drop me off right there." I motioned to the front of my building. If that wasn't clue enough that I was calling it a night, then I didn't know what was.

"I'll take you to your door," he replied, his voice even and calm. Without argument.

"Really? You don't need to do that." I blinked as he pulled into a parking space.

He put the truck into park and killed the engine. He turned to face me, one arm sliding along the back of the seat, his fingertips lightly brushing my shoulder. "Five minutes ago we were all over each other. You couldn't get enough of me. Now it's like you can't get away fast enough."

I swallowed, unaccustomed to a guy calling me out so directly. "Don't take it personally. That's just what I do."

He angled his head to study me and the motion reminded me of a predator evaluating its prey right before he devoured it. "What? Show a little interest and then bail? That's what you do? There's a word for that, you know."

Against my better judgment, I asked, "Yeah? What?"

"It's called a cocktease."

I flinched. That accusation had been laid at my feet before. A few times. Annie called me that when I would fool around with a guy and then not go all the way. Yeah. She sucked. "What's wrong? Can't handle a little rejection? Maybe I just don't want you."

"Right." He grinned like I had just said something amusing, and that annoyed me.

Before I could respond to that bit of arrogance, he got out of the truck and went around to my side. Still wearing that infernal grin, he opened the door for me. I slid down, careful not to touch him.

I led the way, punching the code to open the front door. He stepped in after me. "You're walking me all the way to my door?"

"Yep."

"Fine." I stopped in front of the elevator and punched the button to my floor. Crossing my arms over my chest, I sent him a guarded glance. "You're not getting laid."

He chuckled. "I've never met a girl to go hot to cold so fast."

"Yeah, well, you just called me a cocktease. I don't want you to have false expectations."

"Understood." There was a wealth of laughter laced in that single word.

The elevator dinged and we stepped off. And came face-to-face with Annie. I hadn't seen her since she'd ditched me at Maisie's.

"Emerson, how's it going?" she greeted me, looking not the least guilty.

"Annie," I returned.

Her gaze skipped to Shaw, sliding over him appreciatively. "Well, I can see you're having a good night, Em." She pulled back her shoulders. It was a move I had seen her do countless times. It thrust out her double Ds. She stepped closer, totally invading his space as she held out her hand. "Hi, I'm Annie and you look familiar." She wagged her finger at him playfully.

He stared down at her hand, his face cold, and I knew he remembered her. The fact that he didn't even accept her hand filled me with satisfaction. His gaze slid over her, but it wasn't in a way that made me think he liked what he saw. Quite the opposite. That was a definite change. She never had any problem winning over guys. Annie's smile vanished and she dropped her hand.

"You look familiar, too," he replied. "You're the *friend* who left Emerson stranded at Maisie's." The way he emphasized "friend" made it clear what he thought of her.

Her mouth parted in a small O of surprise. She took a small step back, relaxing her shoulders. "Yeah, well." She turned a tight smile on me. "You're just moving up in the world, Em." She looked Shaw over now with decidedly less appreciation. "Hanging out with all sorts of interesting people."

I nodded, staring at Shaw. "I'm definitely keeping better company these days."

He smiled at me and a strange fluttering erupted in my belly. I looked back at Annie. Her cheeks flushed. With a sniff, she stepped around us and punched an elevator button. Still feeling her eyes on me, I slipped my hand around Shaw's and led him down the hall. I swiped my door card and entered my room, releasing his hand.

My desk lamp glowed, saving the room from total blackness. Avoiding his gaze, I removed my jacket and hung it up in my criminally small closet, taking my time with the mundane task, struggling to slow my racing thoughts. I didn't usually bring guys back home with me. It was letting them into my world. I fooled around plenty, but I didn't want to wake up star-

ing at some guy who should have taken the hint and left hours
ago. And the thing that scared me the most in this situation
was that I could see myself not wanting Shaw to leave. Assuming he wanted to stay over. *Oh. God.* Would you listen to me?
It was like I was a love-struck teenager. Nothing was going to
happen because I didn't want it to happen. It was as simple as
that.

Finally, when there was no delaying it further, I looked up.
"Thanks," I breathed, motioning to the door. "Annie . . . she's
a real bitch."

"I take it you're not hanging out with her anymore." He
shrugged off his jacket and tossed it on my swivel chair. This
only made my chest tighten. So he was staying. At least for a
little while.

I nodded, maybe a little too fast. "No. Not anymore." Was
that high-pitched squeak my voice?

"Good." He approached me with slow strides. With his
long legs, it took about three steps for him to reach me in the
small space of the room.

I held myself utterly still as he tucked a short strand of hair
behind my ear. Even my lungs froze, unable to move air in and
out. This close, all I could think about was kissing him again.
The taste of him still lingered on my lips, and I just wanted to
grab him by the back of the neck and slam my mouth over his
again. *God.* I was a wreck around this guy.

He grazed my cheek with the rough pad of his thumb.
"She's not the kind of friend to have your back."

I nodded again. "I-I know."

He was so close now. I could make out the tiny gold-brown

flecks in his eyes. "Do you want me to go, Emerson?" His voice was deep and low. He didn't even need to speak. This close I could have read his lips.

I dragged a deep breath into my lungs through my nose, but that was a mistake. It only brought the clean, heady male scent of him in.

"N-no." *What was I saying?*

"You don't sound that convinced."

Because I wasn't. Being around him I didn't even know myself anymore.

He dropped his hand from my face and stepped away. I leaned forward, chasing after that hand, almost falling. I staggered a step and stopped myself. He turned his attention to the suite, surveying it. His gaze trailed over Georgia's side, rife with pictures of her family, Harris, me, and Pepper. Even her dog from back home graced his very own frame. It was easy to know which side was hers. Mine was less identifiable. Mine was just . . . *less*.

Naturally, I had a lot of color. Several bright pillows and my floral bedspread that looked like some kind of Georgia O'Keeffe painting. Postcards and posters of various art— some of my favorite pieces. There was only one picture. It was of me and Pepper and Georgia last year at Christmas. We had all piled onto Santa's lap at the mall. And that was it. No family pictures. It would be a lie to have them and pretend I had a real family.

I'm sure he noted the lack of family pictures. It was in such opposition to Georgia's side that showcased a great family. Even Pepper had a grandmother who loved her . . . and a father who had adored her before he passed away. She'd just drawn the short straw when it came to her mother.

I had parents, but I might as well have been an orphan for how alone I felt in the world.

"I guess this is your side?" He motioned to my purple and red floral bed.

I nodded, my heart constricting as he sank down on it. He spent his time studying my postcards and posters. He didn't even look at me. I frowned. One minute he wanted to devour me and the next? Not so much.

I rubbed my perspiring palms against my thighs as he stared at a picture I had taped to the brick wall. I'd drawn it one day during my Biology class last semester. I was bored out of my mind. I had to take the course to meet my degree requirements, but I spent most of the time staring out the window. It was a simple pencil sketch on notebook paper.

I remember that day. It was still warm and nice outside. There had been a girl studying on the quad, her boyfriend across from her, their hands laced lightly together between them as they studied, heads bowed over their separate books. I didn't know them, but there had been something so natural and intimate in the pose. So sweet and innocent. Even the cynic in me had responded and had ripped out a piece of paper and quickly started drawing them.

"You do this?" he asked, a hint of wonder in his voice.

I nodded, feeling a giddy sense of pride.

"It's amazing."

I sank down on the bed beside him, my hands clutching the edge of the mattress. "I'm a studio arts major."

He faced me. "You're really good. Is that what you want to do? Be an artist? Well, you are, clearly," he amended. "But when you graduate?"

I sighed. "I'll probably end up going into marketing somewhere. Maybe a design firm, but . . . yeah, the dream would be to paint."

"Then that's what you should do."

He said it like it was the simplest thing in the world. Smiling, I pulled one of my pillows into my lap and plucked at the fringe. "I need to actually get a paycheck."

He snorted. "You mean you don't have some fat trust fund? Daddy won't take care of you indefinitely?"

My smile slipped. Yeah. Dad would keep paying my way. I was his only child and he seemed to have an endless supply of wealth, but I didn't want that. I couldn't keep accepting his money. It didn't feel right. He paid my way because he had more money than he knew what to do with. You didn't run a Fortune 500 company and not take your responsibilities seriously. And that's what I was to him. A responsibility—the remnant of a marriage he would rather never have happened. I was an obligation that he would never shirk. He'd take care of me as long as I asked him to, but not because I was "Daddy's girl" or because he loved me to the point of overindulgence. I'd met my fair share of Daddy's girls here at Dartford. But I wasn't one of them.

My silence—or maybe my expression—must have answered for me. Shaw's gaze moved on, skimming other scraps of paper that I'd pinned to my wall. His long, blunt-tipped fingers stalled on a sketch I did of Pepper and Reece locked in an embrace where I gave them multiple hands. They were like some sort of human octopus, with hands all over each other.

He laughed. "That's an accurate depiction."

I grinned. "I amuse myself sometimes."

"I can see that." Humor danced in his eyes and he looked at me with something akin to appreciation. The way his eyes slid over me warmed me inside. It wasn't the kind of look I usually got. It wasn't lust filled. He looked at me like he *liked* me.

I toyed with one of my short strands of hair, twisting and tucking it behind my ear. Useless. It sprang free again to dangle over my eye. "Those guys need to lock themselves away for a month until they get it out of their systems."

"You think a month would be enough?" His gaze roamed my face, his gravelly voice rubbing over me like the drag of satin on my skin. Skin that suddenly felt overly sensitive. "I could see how some people might need longer than that." He was staring at my mouth now and my face went from warm to hot.

Butterflies erupted in my belly. I tore my gaze off him and looked back at the sketch of Pepper and Reece. Now I'm pretty sure we were talking—or at least thinking—about something else. Definitely not Pepper and Reece anymore.

I suddenly had a vision of us together. With a whole lot less clothes on. I swallowed and took charge of the conversation again, determined to get my mind out of the gutter. "Pepper wasn't as amused when I offered it to her. She thought it was creepy."

"I think it's funny."

"Thanks." I smiled again and curled my hands around my

knees. The fabric of my purple tights felt smooth under my palms.

"You should paint," he reasserted with a swift nod. "Don't go take some job in a cubicle. That would be a crime."

"And what about you?" I asked. "You were in the Marines. Are you finished with that?"

"I'm still in the reserves, but after two tours, I'm done." His face was impassive as he said this. It was hard to tell what he was thinking. He traced one finger along the slope of a tree that I had sketched when I was home for Christmas. It was an enormous beech tree right outside my bedroom window. I imagined it was the kind of tree a teenage girl would have shimmied down to sneak out. If her parents cared about her comings and goings and bothered with a curfew, that is. Neither of my parents ever cared. I never had a curfew. I came and went as I pleased. Got myself to school. Ate whatever the cook prepared for me. Sometimes Agnes even stayed and ate with me instead of her own family. Out of pity.

While Dad was away in Barbados over the holidays, I hung out at the house and sketched the tree. It was something to do. A break from reruns of *Top Chef*.

He still stared at the picture, but he looked far away, like he wasn't here with me anymore, and I wondered if mentioning the Marines had pulled him away.

I moistened my lips and decided to press for more information. "You lost your cousin over there . . ."

Suddenly he was back with me again. His sharp gaze swung to me, alert. "Guess you would have heard that. No keeping something like that a secret."

I smiled almost apologetically. "Logan told me at your cousin's engagement party."

He nodded grimly. "It's the Marines, right? Some come home. Some don't. We knew that before we went over there. I lost three in my unit in the first tour . . . and then I signed up again because I was determined to make it matter. To make a difference."

I pulled my knees up to my chest, unsure what to say. I wasn't used to dealing with this kind of stuff. To talk to guys about anything serious. "You did."

He grunted. "How do you know that?"

I opened my mouth, realizing that I didn't. There wasn't anything I could say that supported the claim, but I just knew. Looking at him, I knew. He had done something with his life. He had lived. He had worked for something bigger than himself.

And that's how I knew.

I was in trouble. Everything that set him apart from the other guys was what drew me.

Maybe it was this giddy realization. Maybe it was because I still had alcohol buzzing through my system, but a sudden, heady impulse seized me.

Turning, I faced him. Whatever he saw in my face made him freeze. Watching me like he was the prey—for a change—I rose up on my knees beside him. Holding his gaze, I pulled my sweater over my head and tossed it to the floor.

His eyes darkened, traveling over me. I ran a hand over my dark pink bra, lightly caressing the lacy cup.

"What are you doing?"

"C'mon. You act like you haven't seen me in a bra before. I think you've seen me in less than this."

I slowly settled onto his lap, slipping my knees on either side of his hips.

"That was different. You're conscious now."

I smiled coyly, angling my head to the side. I pressed a finger to his lips, enjoying touching him, enjoying the sensation of that mouth that I knew could kiss me until I was quivering and useless for anything else. "Can you let me do this?"

"Be in charge? Something tells me you're used to that." His eyes glinted at me, but he didn't make a move.

I took that as acceptance. Smiling, I lowered my head and pressed my open mouth to his neck. I licked and sucked at the salty-clean taste of his skin. I felt him sigh, his breath rustling my hair. Sitting back up, my hands dove for the hem of his shirt. I tugged it up. He lifted his arms, helping me pull it over his head. The sight that greeted me punched the air right out of my chest.

He was lean and hard. His torso cut and defined. My gaze dropped to his abs. Screw six-pack. I counted. *Was that an eight-pack?*

A large tattoo covered the skin of his left pec, crawling up onto his shoulder. My fingers chased the pattern of an eagle atop a globe and anchor. I recognized it as the Marine insignia. The name Adam was etched into the anchor, including the years of his birth and death. My chest tightened at further evidence that this guy was different. Special.

His breathing sawed roughly from his lips and when I lowered my mouth to his chest, it kicked up a notch as I laved my tongue over him.

His hands came up to circle my ribs. I allowed that. Until they crept up to my breasts, and then I grabbed his wrists.

"Nuh-uh," I murmured, smiling down at him as I pressed his hands to the mattress.

He stared up at me in frustration. "I want to touch you."

"I do the touching. Just relax." I pushed him back on the bed beneath me. Sitting over him, I felt empowered. Maybe I could have him, after all. Maybe he was someone I could control. I knew my game. Knew what worked. He wasn't going to hurt me. I could handle the situation. Handle *him*.

I took one last glimpse of his face, the dark, gleaming eyes fastened on me, before lowering to his chest. I kissed the broad expanse, using my tongue and teeth on the firm flesh. Gentle, butterfly kisses. Long, open-mouthed moist ones. I lavished him with my mouth and hands. His jaw, his neck. I fanned my breath in his ear before biting down on the lobe. He tensed beneath me with a groan and I knew I was getting to him. I felt drunk and it had nothing to do with the alcohol I had consumed tonight. I was high on him.

He tried to kiss me and I dodged his mouth. I was already perilously close to losing my resolve when it came to him. I needed to avoid his kisses. They turned my brain to mush.

"Let me kiss you," he commanded, arching his head off the bed toward me.

I pushed him back down with the flat of my palm and trailed a finger down the center of his chest. "No kissing."

"Emerson." His eyes flashed at me. "I want your mouth."

"Oh, you're going to get it," I promised silkily.

"On mine," he qualified.

I just grinned. "I promise you'll enjoy wherever . . ." I kissed his collarbone. "I . . ." The pulse point on his neck. "Kiss . . ." The center of his chest. "You . . ." My lips trailed down the center of his chest, skimming warm, taut skin.

His hands drifted back to my waist, the rough palms caressing the exposed flesh above my waistband. It was tempting to let his hands remain there, but I moved them back to his sides.

"Let me touch you," he growled.

I tsked my tongue and dropped my hands to his jeans. My fingers closed expertly around the snap and tugged the denim open.

"Emerson," he said, warning thick in his voice. "You won't let me touch you . . . kiss you . . . this isn't—"

"Sssh," I admonished, dragging the teeth of his zipper down with a slow, gratifying sing, exposing the tented front of his boxers. Without touching him, I pulled the slit in his boxers wide, exposing him to the air.

He sprang free. I bit my lip to keep my gasp from escaping at the bold, beautiful sight of him. He was hard, jutting forward, ready for me. I blew a warm breath gently over the tip of him.

"Fuck, Emerson," he choked out.

"No," I softly reprimanded, kissing him just above his navel. "None of that, remember?"

"You need to stop," he growled, his body quivering beneath me.

I touched the tip of him with one gentle fingertip. "Why?" I taunted, looking at him from beneath hooded eyes. He stared at me, a muscle feathering along his locked jaw. "Don't you want me to kiss you here?"

"Not like this."

I pouted. "Like how then?"

"I don't need you giving me a blow job."

My pout turned into an actual frown. What guy didn't want a BJ? "I bet I can change your mind." I lowered my head, but his hands circled my arms and pulled me up before I could make contact.

His eyes glittered, looking almost angry. "What are you doing?"

"Apparently nothing you're into," I snapped, trying to pull my arms free of his grip, but he held fast, each of his fingers a burning imprint. I felt the strength of him, the power of him, tightly restrained beneath me.

"What's the matter? The only way you'll let me close is if I play by your rules?"

His words were right on the mark. I nodded, stung by his rejection of what I was offering. "You catch on real quick."

"Maybe I have a few rules of my own."

My heart skipped at the dangerous glint in his eyes. Immediately, I sensed the tables had been turned. He had taken control of the situation—or was trying to.

"I think we're done here," I said, managing to sound cool.

He shook his head at me slowly and I was reminded of the first time I'd seen him and the realization that this guy wouldn't be so easy to control. I immediately told myself to keep my distance then. Too bad I didn't listen to myself. Now I was in the exact situation I didn't want to be in. *Trapped*.

I knew he wouldn't *hurt* me. That wasn't my fear. My fear wasn't him. It was me. It was *in* me. It was losing control, giving someone else power over me.

His fingers flexed around my forearms. His eyes dipped to assess me in my pink satin bra. "We're just getting started. It's my turn now."

Chapter 8

SHAW'S MOUTH COVERED MINE and what I didn't want to happen did. My brain turned to mush. He had a way of kissing me that consumed me, that melted my bones and made me pudding in his hands.

I still had some resolve left in me. Just enough to squeeze my hands between us and shove at that brick wall of a chest. He moved the barest inch. I was able to tear my lips away. I opened my mouth to demand that he stop and get out of my room, but suddenly he flipped me over on the bed.

On my back, I gasped, speech lost at the sensation of his big body over me, between my splayed thighs. His hand flexed on my thigh, beneath my skirt, searing me through my tights, and I found myself wishing I wasn't wearing tights so that I could feel his palm on my bare skin.

He took advantage of my open mouth and claimed my lips in a kiss again, his tongue colliding with mine. His weight felt delicious, pinning me to the bed without hurting me. A dazed fog rolled over me, obliterating all thought, all logic. There was only sensation.

His lips ate hungrily from mine. *Devouring* is the only word. When his hands found my breasts and cupped them through the bra, liquid heat coursed through me. He kneaded the small mounds and I parted my legs wider, inviting him without words.

He sank deeper between my legs. My skirt was hiked up to my hips, my purple tights a barrier that kept us from direct contact, but I still felt him there, his erection hard and probing, rubbing against me, pushing and prodding as if he could reach gratification that way. I didn't see how. The pressure and friction of him there drove me mad. I wanted more. I wanted it harder. Deeper.

I dug my fingers into his biceps and bucked against him, grinding my pelvis to his.

"Shit," he cursed, breaking his mouth from mine. Before I had time to mourn the loss, his hand was yanking one bra cup down, pulling the strap tighter across my shoulder. His warm mouth closed over my left nipple, taking the entire tip and pulling it deep into the wet warmth of his mouth.

I cried out and arched. It was too much, and it only got better as he turned his attention to my other breast. He laved that one with his tongue, too, sucking it deep into his mouth.

His name tore from my throat.

"That's it," he encouraged, looking up at me, his face even with my breast, his dark eyes promising more. "I want to hear you."

I shook my head no. It was the most I could manage. I couldn't actually spit the word out. Not if it meant he would stop. Because I didn't want this to end. I actually might die if that happened.

His slipped both hands beneath my skirt and seized the waistband of my tights. Sitting back, he pulled the tight fabric down my legs. Alarm bells went off, but they weren't as loud as the rush of blood in my ears or as strong as the clenching ache between my legs.

His rough palms settled on me then, rasping against my naked thighs. "Oh, God," I moaned.

He came back over me, his bare chest pressing flush with me. I felt his erection then through the thin fabric of my panties. My face burned, mortified to know he must feel how wet I was down there. And all because of him. All he needed to do was push the thin fabric aside and he could slide inside me.

The very idea thrilled and terrified me in equal parts. I couldn't let that happen. Right now, with the core of me aching and throbbing, it might feel like I wanted him to do that, but I didn't. My mind knew better, even if my body didn't.

"I meant it," I gasped as he rotated his hips and pushed directly against a sensitive spot that threatened to make my eyes roll back in their sockets. "I'm not having sex with you."

He dark eyes feasted on me as he continued to rub against me. "Did I say I expected you to?"

"N-no." But it sure felt like where this was going.

I pushed against him, whimpering at the hard outline of his cock, unable to stop, unable to keep myself from seeking fulfillment, wanting him to fill me so badly it practically hurt.

His hands slid under me, palming my ass through my panties, grinding his erection against me even more intimately—if that was even possible.

"Oh, God," I moaned, quivering in his hands.

"When we have sex, it won't be a surprise." His voice eddied through me, deep and dark, a current of heat that shot right between my legs. "You'll know it's coming. You'll want it. Mind and body. You'll beg me to make love to you. I'll make sure of that, Emerson."

Make love? No way. "What makes you think—"

"There won't be any doubts or accusations after the fact," he continued as if he hadn't heard me. "In fact, we're not going to do it until you ask me for it."

I attempted to snort, but the sound came out like a choked gasp as one of his hands slid around to cup my mound. He used the base of his palm to press up into the core of me and my head flew off the bed with a sharp cry.

"For tonight, I'm just going to make you come." I shook my head wildly on the pillow. I was already close to doing that. "Something tells me you don't get off that much. Doubt half the guys you waste your time on even bother to make sure you're satisfied."

Understatement of the year.

He lowered his head, licking my bottom lip as he spoke, low and deep and sexy into my mouth. "Not tonight, Emerson. Tonight I'm not stopping until you scream. Until you see stars."

His words sent a trickle of unease through me. He wanted to take care of me? Give me pleasure? Without satisfying himself?

He tugged the panties that shielded me to the side, one finger slipping along my moist heat—and I forgot everything else. I practically came out of my skin. I had never felt anything like it. He stroked me expertly, his finger burying deep and then pulling out, circling that really sensitive pleasure point, inching closer but not touching. I writhed, panted, small incoherent sounds bubbling up from my throat.

"Please," I begged, hating myself—*him*—for making me want this so badly. It was clear to me that he could have me. If he wanted sex, I couldn't resist. He could take me now.

He finally gave my body what it craved. His thumb landed on my clit and pushed down, rolling it in a swift circle at the precise moment he eased a second finger inside me.

I arched off the bed with a shriek. He moved his fingers, thrusting inside me with deep, slow drags. He caught my lips in another searing kiss, drinking the sounds from my mouth as he worked his hand against me, his thumb pushing and circling, his fingers working in and out of me.

"You feel so good, Emerson. So warm. So tight." I brought my hand between us, reaching for him, determined that I push him to the edge the way he was pushing me. My fingers brushed him, but he dodged out of the way and seized my hand.

"No touching, remember?" His gaze pinned me.

I growled my frustration but soon gave up. I couldn't even think with the intense sensations he stoked in me. The deep, twisting pressure built and my head fell back on the bed again.

"C'mon, baby," he murmured against my mouth. "I know you want to let go."

I shook my head, denying it. Denying him. Myself. I couldn't let go. Ever.

I never had.

And then his lips were gone. His chest lifted off from my chest. Blinking, my head came up off the bed, bewildered.

"What are y—"

All speech fled on a strangled shriek as his mouth landed expertly down *there*. I tensed and shoved at his shoulder. His lips closed around that nub and sucked, his tongue laving the sensitive pearl until I fell back on the bed with a low, keening moan.

Pleasure exploded inside me, centered directly where his mouth was fused to me so intimately. My orgasm washed over me in waves. Hot ripples that seemed to go on forever as he sucked me into his mouth.

I buried my hands in his hair and tugged hard on the ends, not for him to stop but for him to *never* stop. His hands slid beneath me, gripping my ass and bringing me up closer to his mouth. His mouth kept working its magic until the last shudder left me.

I fell back on the bed, panting, chest heaving like I'd just finished a marathon. He came up over me, grinning in the most smug, satisfied way. He looked sexy as hell with his arms braced, one on either side of me, his biceps flexed taut to support his weight.

"That was hot," he murmured. He lifted a hand and traced a finger down my cheek to my mouth. If possible, his eyes grew darker. Unbelievable or not, the simple stroke of his finger over my bottom lip brought the intense ache between my legs back and I wanted to go another round with him. I clamped my thighs together as if I could somehow assuage the throbbing there.

His voice continued in a deep purr. "Aren't you glad you let me do that?"

Let him do *that*? I guess choice had been involved. He was no sadist. I could have stopped him at any time. He would have listened to me. And that made me even more enraged at myself. Because I should have stopped him.

I shoved at his chest, pushing him off me. I sat up, pushing my skirt down with fumbling hands and sliding my bra straps back in place. "You should go."

The smile slipped from his face. He stared at me, his expression unreadable, but there was something there in his eyes. Surprise, maybe?

"Really." I nodded, my voice coming out less shaky. There was that at least. I sounded in control even if I didn't feel like it. "Just go."

I searched the bed for my shirt, grateful for the excuse not to look at him. Finding it, I pulled it on over my head. From the corner of my eye I could see he was moving now, straightening his own clothing, tucking himself back in his jeans and yanking the zipper up with angry motions as he muttered indecipherable words under his breath.

He was mad. Good. So was I. And I needed to stay mad. Nurse my anger so that I didn't let him weave another spell around me again.

He faced me. "I should have known better than to get involved with some spoiled little princess."

I flinched before reminding myself that this was for the best. Let him think that. Then maybe whatever this thing was between us would just die. I inhaled thinly through my nose and tried to ignore the sudden ache in my chest that that thought ignited.

I needed to stand my ground. Let him think whatever bad thing he wanted to about me. Because I couldn't handle another repeat of what just happened between us and still keep my distance. At least emotionally. The last thing I needed was to fall for a guy like him. For God's sake, he was a Marine. Not exactly an easy-to-manipulate kind of guy.

"That's right," I agreed. "You should have known better. But now you do." I lifted my hand and performed a small wave. "So bye-bye."

He stared at me, his eyes hard. "You're a real piece of work."

I smiled, telling myself he was no different from any other guy I kicked from my bed. *So why did I feel terrible? Why did the disgust in his eyes tear at me?*

Then he smiled, slow and almost sinister. He approached almost stealthily, sinking back over me on the bed. I fell back, flattening a hand against his chest as if that could ward him off.

"Go ahead," he whispered in a lethally soft voice. "Pretend I don't get to you."

"You don't."

He cocked his head sideways, studying me like I was some bug beneath a microscope. "You know what I think?"

I shook my head. "I don't care."

He continued as if I hadn't spoken, and suddenly his hand was there, inching along the inside of my thigh. I gasped, incredibly turned on despite the voice in my head telling me to stop him. My body knew him and responded, arching under him.

His deep voice rippled across my skin. "I think that deep inside you're dying for someone like me. You've been waiting for a guy to come along and shake up your world and touch you the way you've been aching to be touched." His fingers rubbed against the damp crotch of my panties. "Do things to you that all your pretty college boys can't do." With a quick yank, his fingers were right there, playing against me, parting me, teasing at my entrance and working me into a frenzy beneath him. I fisted the covers and thrust against his hands, opening myself wider for him.

I didn't understand it. How could he elicit such an immediate response from me? Other boys had tried what he was doing, but there was only him. Just Shaw. I was ready to go again, but instead of his mouth and hand, I wanted *him* there. That hardness pressing against my thigh. I wanted our bodies locked and rocking together.

He thrust a finger inside me, then followed with a second, stretching me, filling me, plunging deep inside me where some hidden, indefinable target existed. It was indescribable. Even better than before, and something told me that every time with him would be like that. Better. More intense than before.

I cried out, grabbing his shoulders as his voice continued to lash me like hot wind. "Do any of them make you feel like this?" His fingers stilled, poised just at the mouth of my entrance, stalling my pleasure, torturing me. "Answer me, Emerson."

"N-no." I beat a fist on his shoulder.

"Tell me," he commanded.

"None of them do this."

"Do what?" he pushed, just barely moving his fingers inside me.

"Make me . . . come." And I was so close. *Again.* That tightly coiled spring in my belly was about to snap.

He smiled slowly. "Good. " His hand left me then. "Remember that." He pulled back from me and stood up.

For a moment, I could do nothing but blink, astonished and bewildered. He looked down at me, his sexy mouth curving almost grimly. But there was satisfaction there. He was pleased with himself . . . as if he had just proved something.

Cool air wafted over my exposed skin and it dawned on me that I wasn't moving. I remained sprawled before him with my skirt bunched up around my hips, my girl parts on display. And I hated him right then.

Mortified, I sat up, shoving my skirt back down. "Get out!" The words launched out of me at missile speed.

He grabbed his shirt from where he'd dropped it on the edge of the bed. He moved with unhurried movements, collecting his jacket where he had discarded it on the chair.

"I never want to see you again." My voice trembled on the air with barely suppressed emotion, and I hoped he did not mistake the sound of it for fear. That would be humiliating, and he had already humiliated me enough for one night.

He paused at the door. Still bare chested, he turned to look at me, apparently unconcerned about stepping out of my room partially dressed.

I stood up from the bed and turned my back to him, trying to dismiss him from my sight if not from my mind. Crossing my arms, I fixed my gaze on the blinds and waited for the sound of the door shutting behind him.

"Don't think this is over, Emerson."

I swung around at these words, my eyes snapping to him, startled by the determination I heard in his voice. He stood with one hand on my doorknob, the other one clutching his crumpled shirt. The line of his shoulders was rigid and tense, and I knew I wasn't the only one angry. He looked huge in the cramped space of my suite. Even now, looking at the sculpted expanse of his chest made my face flush hotly.

I lifted my chin. "Well, I say this is finished." Whatever *this* even was. It was too complicated, too full of emotions and feelings that I'd never felt before. That I never wanted to feel. "We are done."

"You keep telling yourself that, princess." He pulled the door wide open. "See you later."

Then he shut the door, plunging the room into muffled silence . . . leaving me staring after him, wondering what precisely in the hell had just happened.

Chapter 9

THE NEXT MORNING I woke to the smell of coffee. Espresso, to be precise. Wafting deliciously close to my nose. I crept one eyelid open to find Pepper standing in front of me, holding a large-size cup from the Java Hut.

Georgia sat propped in her bed across the way, already cupping her drink in both palms. I barely remembered her coming in the night before. It must have been late though because I had stared into the dark long after Shaw left me.

Georgia smiled at me. She had one of the sweetest smiles. Natural and unaffected. She really was the modern southern woman. Sophisticated but still clinging to a certain gentility and wholesomeness that eluded the rest of the female population of Dartford. I could well imagine her waltzing at all those high school cotillions her mother made her attend. "Pepper brought us coffee."

"Hmm." Pushing myself up on one elbow, I accepted the proffered cup. "You're an angel."

"Not really." Pepper settled in the beanbag chair in the corner, plunking her own drink down on the floor, near her feet. With her free hand, she rattled a brown paper bag. "Scones?"

I nodded and she tossed me one, which I managed to catch without crumbs flying all over me.

Pepper continued. "I'm just dying to know what's going on between you and Shaw."

Georgia turned interested eyes on me. "Shaw? Who's Shaw?"

"No one," I mumbled. The chocolate chip scone was still warm as I bit into it. "Yum. This is delicious." I chased the flaky goodness with a drink. Heaven.

"Who's Shaw?" Georgia repeated.

"Shaw is a guy that Reece went to high school with. Just back from the Marines."

"Oh." Georgia's eyebrows, several shades darker than her blond hair, winged high over her expressive eyes.

I wagged my scone at her. " '*Oh*' nothing. It's not like that."

"Is he hot?" she asked, looking back and forth from me to Pepper.

I squared my shoulders. "What difference   "

"He's smoking," Pepper interjected.

I glared at her. "You have a boyfriend."

"What? I can't look? It's hard not to notice something like that. He either is or isn't. And yeah, he definitely is."

Georgia nodded, absorbing this as she rose to investigate the bag of scones. She selected a scone and sat back, crossing her legs Indian style. She was still wearing her pajamas with little red Santas even though Christmas was over. She probably grabbed them because they were her warmest pair.

"So this Shaw, Reece's old high school buddy . . . is hot."

I nodded once, reluctantly.

"And you left with him last night," Pepper chimed in, as if I needed reminding. If I inhaled I could still catch a lingering whiff of him on my bed.

"Where'd ya'll go?" Georgia asked, her soft Alabama accent rolling through me like warm honey.

"Here," I said, my voice so low even I had a hard time hearing myself.

Georgia lowered her cup and leaned forward. "I'm sorry. What was that? It sounded like you said 'here.'"

"I did. I brought him here."

Pepper and Georgia both stared at me in stunned silence.

"What?" I snapped. Taking another bite of my scone, I took turns staring at each of them.

"Well, you hardly ever bring anyone here."

"Like never," Pepper agreed, nodding, her wild mane of hair moving around her like some fiery nimbus.

"Well, I did." I wasn't about to explain that he gave me little choice in the matter. "Not that it's going to become a habit or anything."

"Tell me more about this Shaw." Georgia got that narrow-eyed, considering look. I thought of it as her "parent" look. Which was okay considering my parents didn't really care one way or another about the company I kept. It was nice knowing she had my back. Even when I didn't want her there.

A business major, she was the pragmatist among us. Steady as the tide, she never flip-flopped her majors. It was like she knew who she was, where she was going, and with whom. As much as I didn't like Harris, I couldn't help thinking how comforting it must be to be with the same boyfriend since you were sixteen. To have that kind of familiarity. To know that you can drop your guard around him and be yourself. To have that trust.

I shrugged. "He enlisted after high school. Served two tours. What else do you want to know? He lives in a lake cabin his grandfather left him. His mother remarried and is living in Boston."

"So what's he do now?"

"Reece said he works in a garage," Pepper answered. That he's an awesome mechanic and he's saving up to start his own custom shop."

I looked at her, unable to hold back the question even if it revealed my interest—and how little I still didn't know about him. "He is?"

"Apparently he's really into bikes."

Maybe that's what he was doing at Maisie's then? Rubbing elbows with a potential clientele?

"So he sounds interesting . . . ambitious," Georgia said, nodding again.

I couldn't stop annoyance from pricking at me. I didn't need Georgia's approval of a prospective boyfriend. Not that he was a prospective boyfriend. He wasn't a prospective anything as far as I was concerned despite his confidence that he and I weren't finished.

"Why does this feel like an intervention?" I asked before taking another sip.

Pepper blinked and pressed a hand to her chest. "When

did best friends talking get reduced to being labeled an intervention?"

"Yeah. We just want to hear about your new—"

"He's not my new anything," I cut Georgia off quickly. Setting my half-eaten scone down, I scooted off the bed. Holding my cup in one hand, I approached my closet and pulled my robe off the hook.

"What are you doing?" Georgia asked.

"I need a shower."

I felt their eyes on me as I gathered up the rest of my things. When I turned to face them, I sighed. "Oh, c'mon. Why are you guys looking at me like that?"

"Wow." Georgia shook her head. "You're actually running away rather than talk about a guy with us. I've got to meet this Shaw."

"I knew it." Pepper grinned like she had just won some prize. "You like him."

"Wrong. I just need a shower. I still smell like a bar."

"We'll just be waiting here when you get back." Pepper snuggled down into the beanbag chair like she was settling in for a good long stay.

"When I get back I'm going to the library to study."

Georgia made a sound that was halfway snort and halfway laugh. "Oh. I know you've got it bad now. You're running to the library."

Pepper's eyes rounded. "Do you even know where the building is?"

"Oh, now you're just being shits." I grabbed my shower caddy and yanked open the bedroom door. Their laughter followed me, but so did the knowledge that they weren't entirely wrong.

I was running. Not just from them though. I was running from myself. From the echo of Shaw's voice in my room. The only problem was that even away from my room, I could still hear his voice.

Chapter 10

I HELD TRUE TO my word and went to the library. I actually had a paper due in Medieval Art History the next week, so I was able to knock out the first draft, which left me feeling totally guilt free when I surfaced.

It was dark by the time I emerged from the building. I walked down the snow-powdered sidewalk, wrapping my cashmere scarf several times around my neck, shielding my mouth from the wind. My phone vibrated and I dug it out of my bag.

Pepper: Where r u?

Me: Headed back to room. Where r u?

Pepper: At Mulvaney's w/ Reece. Join us?

My fingers hesitated over the keys. Crash their date? No thanks. I typed back.

Me: Think I'm just staying in.

Pepper: Kidding?

Shaking my head, I glanced up to make sure I didn't walk into someone. Or a wall. The sidewalk stretched before me. Not a soul out.

Me: I'm fine. Just tired
Pepper: U need 2 eat
Me: I ate

The lie seemed easier. I would just grab a granola bar or cook up some popcorn in the microwave.

Pepper: Ok. Walk to class together in the morn?
Me: Sure

I didn't bother to inquire if she was sure she would be spending the night in her dorm or even be around to walk to class together. The answer seemed obvious. She spent almost every night with Reece. I wouldn't be surprised if he put a ring on her finger before graduation. Yeah, she was young, but there was something about them . . . about her and Reece together that made me believe they were in it for the long haul. The real deal. For some people it happened, I guess.

As happy as I was for her, it also hurt to know that nothing would ever be the same again for us. No late nights munching popcorn. No me dragging her away from studying to watch TV or go get a pizza. Those days were gone.

Pepper hadn't brought the subject up, but we would have to put in our rooming requests for next year. I wondered if she wanted to even room with me and Georgia again. Since she and Reece hooked up, she practically lived at his place. Why not save the money and make it official by moving in with him? Pepper wasn't like me with a father paying her way. She was forging her own way on a combination of student loans and scholarships. She worked, too. Babysitting gigs and part-time at a local daycare. Why should she waste money on a dorm room she hardly used anymore?

The idea that I might be losing her as a suitemate gave me a sharp pain in the chest. I rubbed at my sternum as if I could rid myself of the feeling. It was selfish of me. I should only be happy for her.

The night was quiet as I passed the quad. A white blanket of snow stretched across the lawn. Students, eager for the sun— and girls eager to show off their bikinis—would be sunbathing there in late spring regardless of the lingering chill in the air.

"Hey! Em!"

Looking up, I spotted Annie walking toward me. She was dressed to go out in a miniskirt and thigh-high boots. Her overcoat was open at the front to reveal a sweater that exposed her belly and a winking belly button piercing.

"Hi," I greeted.

She wiggled her fingers at me like nothing was amiss between us. Like she hadn't abandoned me at a biker bar. "Guess where I'm going tonight?"

I looked her up and down and resisted saying something snarky. Instead I settled on civil. "Where?"

"I happened to get an invite . . ." Her voice trailed off. She wiggled her eyebrows at me in a clear attempt to entice me to take a guess.

I stamped down my impatience. "Where?"

She leaned forward and held a hand up to her mouth and whispered loudly, "The kink club."

I blinked. "You got an invite?" I didn't know why this surprised me. I guess it was a hit to my ego. I had a reputation as being a wild party girl. How was it no one thought to invite me?

"Well. I met someone who is a regular. I'm headed to her dorm now. She can bring a guest. Who knows? Maybe they'll let me join and then I can bring a guest." She waved a finger at me suggestively.

A few months ago I'd be all over the suggestion of this. Now? I forced a smile. "Well, have fun tonight."

"Oh, you better believe I will. I'll give you a full report. What are your plans? Seeing that sexy beast from the bar again?"

I smiled weakly. "Uh, no."

"No?" She shook her head, waiting for me to elaborate.

"I'm just staying in."

She giggled. "No, seriously."

I nodded. "Seriously."

"Oh. Well. That's different. Have . . . fun."

"Night."

She sashayed past me. There was no other word for what she was doing with her hips.

For once, I didn't care that staying in was in direct opposition to the image I had created for myself. Even party girls needed a night off now and then. My phone buzzed in my pocket. I fished it out and frowned at the message staring back at me from an unknown number.

What are you doing?

I hesitated and then typed.

Who is this?

A single name popped up on the small screen.

Shaw

My heart jumped to my throat.

Me: How did you get my number?
Shaw: Pepper

Traitor. *Of course.* Shaking my head, I typed back.

Me: I have plans
Shaw: Break them

My fingers locked, poised over the keys, heart hammering at his words—at this connection to him through this little box in my hands. I shouldn't have been so surprised to hear from him. He'd said I would. But he hadn't even waited a day, and that only made my heart trip even harder.

Me: I can't

Okay. So the word *won't* would be more accurate, but the

end result was the same. Suddenly, my phone rang in my hand. I jumped a little, staring at the number I knew was his. He was *calling* me?

I answered the phone and brought it to my ear. "Hello?"

"Have you eaten yet?"

No greeting. Just straight to it. That was him. Direct. No games. Most girls would love that. Except me. I was a girl who played games. Who counted on them for protection.

"N-n-yes."

"You're a terrible liar."

I sucked in a breath, walking slowly, freezing my butt off. I was almost to my dorm, but I couldn't walk any faster. It was like my brain couldn't walk and talk at the same time. At least not when I was talking to him.

He continued. "You got to eat, right?"

Not with *you*. "I have plans."

"I'm sure you do, but you can still eat with me before you head out for your wild night." I rolled my eyes at his assumption. "Where are you?"

I frowned. He said that like he knew I wasn't home at my dorm.

And then I understood why as I rounded the corner of my building. I stopped dead in my tracks. Shaw was leaning against the front of the building just near the front door. Talking on his phone. Talking to me. He hadn't spotted me yet. He wore a small, sexy smile on his face as his voice rumbled in my ear.

"C'mon. I know this great burger place. Let me take you there."

Was he asking me out? A shiver rolled through me. Excitement? Dread? Maybe a bit of both. I didn't do dates.

He looked up then and caught sight of me. And then more shivers. He lowered his phone as I walked up to him. There was no choice. He was in front of my building.

"What are you doing here?"

Smiling, he reached across the space separating us and tapped my phone. Realizing I was still talking into it, I fumbled to put it away, feeling like an idiot.

"I came to take you to dinner."

"Like a date?" I couldn't help it. I said the words as if he'd just declared he was taking me on a safari or something equally outrageous.

"If going out for food with me is a date, then yeah." He studied me closely, the building's perimeter lights hitting the angles and hollows of his face and making him look only hotter. "But if you don't like that word, then fuck it. Call it something else."

A smile flirted on my mouth. "Look, Shaw, you're a really nice—"

He threw his head back and laughed, and that only made him look sexier. And not nice at all. He looked delicious and dangerous in the best way. A bad boy who would know how to make a girl scream. Again, in the best way.

I stopped and glared. "What's so funny?"

"You're about to give me the same tired brush-off you give every guy who trails after you."

A pair of girls I vaguely recognized from my floor approached the door. They looked us over—well, they looked

Shaw over. Their eyes heated with appreciation and speculation as they gave him the once-over. A sudden possessive urge to touch him, mark him as mine, seized me.

I waited for them to enter the building before responding to Shaw's accusation. "That's not true." Okay, maybe it was, but I wasn't admitting that to him.

"Yeah. It is." He stopped laughing and leveled his dark eyes on me. They glinted in the near darkness. "Because I'm not a nice boy, and you know it. That's why you won't go out with me. You're too scared."

He might as well have waved a red flag in my face. "I'm *not* scared."

"No? Prove it." He nodded toward the parking lot where I assumed his truck waited. "Let's go eat."

"This is ridiculous—"

"Chicken."

I felt my eyes widen. "Oh my God. Does this really work? Do girls really go out with you if you dare them into doing it?"

He shrugged. "It's not a dare. Just stating the facts. You're scared. And I haven't asked a girl out since I've been back, so I wouldn't know. But they never said no in high school."

I snorted. "I'm sure they didn't." I could just imagine him and Reece together in high school. The girls must have been throwing their panties at them both.

Well, not this girl. After last night I knew he was hard to resist, but the key was to never end up alone, on a bed, with him again. Should be easy enough to manage.

"Fine. No big deal. It's just food."

He nodded, looking supremely satisfied. "Sure." And yet he looked like he had just won a skirmish.

"I'm paying for my own meal though."

His smile slipped. Feeling as though I'd won this round, I turned and headed toward the parking lot, leaving him to follow.

Chapter 11

HE WASN'T KIDDING. IT was the best burger I had ever tasted. I groaned after my second mouthful. Juice from the meat, bacon, and cheese ran down my chin. I grabbed a napkin to swipe my chin and cover my mouth in an attempt to hide the indelicate display.

Shaw watched me, his eyes intent on my face, and I worried that I was making a pig of myself in front of him and probably turning him off. And then I reminded myself that that wouldn't be a bad thing. Putting Shaw firmly in the friend zone would be a good thing.

Okay. So the idea was kind of crazy given that last night he had given me a mind-blowing orgasm. He would have given me two if he hadn't decided to punish me and leave me hanging right on the precipice of number two. I would never be able to relegate him to friend. But then it didn't matter how *I* viewed him. It was how *he* viewed me.

"I can't tell you how impressed I am that you went for the Death Burger."

I took a sip of my Coke.

"You're not one of those girls who orders a salad in a burger place."

I rolled my eyes. "I never let a guy's presence dictate what food I eat."

I looked around the diner as I dipped a French fry in ketchup. The place was definitely a dive with its peeling floor tiles and cracked picture of Elvis behind the cash register. "I've never been here before."

"Not surprised. Ask Pepper. I bet Reece has brought her here. We used to eat here a lot in high school."

He sat with one arm stretched along the back of the booth, his long-sleeved shirt stretched temptingly across his broad chest. The cut of his muscled pecs was visible beneath the fabric and my mouth dried a little. I looked up at his face, trying to avoid the sexy distraction of his body, but that only presented another distraction. His face. His eyes. He watched me so intently it was unnerving. I looked away and surveyed the room, noticing there were a few bikers sitting at a booth in the corner. It reminded me of the first night I'd met him.

"Gone to Maisie's lately?"

"Why? Want to go back?" He grinned.

I shook my head.

"I've been there once since then . . . it's a good way to mingle with prospective clients. If I open my own garage, it helps if I'm a familiar face among them."

I was right then. He went to Maisie's to further himself career wise. "So you want to open a bike shop?"

"Yeah. Custom bikes. My grandfather got me into them.

It's something we did together. I'm already doing all the bike work at the garage where I work now."

"I'd like to see some of your bikes." The words slipped out before I could stop them.

There was a pause before he said, "I'd like to show you."

I quickly looked down at my basket of food, concentrating on dipping another fry into ketchup. What was I doing making arrangements with him to see him again? I took another bite from my burger. The quicker I ate, the quicker this pseudo-date was over and I could get back to my room. Minus him.

"Pepper says you have a bunch of artwork in the studio on campus." My eyes snapped back to him. *Just how much had Pepper told him about me?* "I'd like to see more of your work."

I shook my head, struggling to swallow my food. My eyes teared up a bit as I swallowed a particularly spicy pepper in that bite. "I don't really show my stuff to anyone." Well, other than what I put up on my walls. Just the idea of him seeing the one I did of him made me shudder.

Of course my work would go on display at the winter showcase coming up. Not that I was mentioning that to him. The showcase was for a grade. I had to participate. But I didn't have to choose to display Shaw's picture.

"How can you be an artist if you never let anyone see your work?"

"I told you. I'm probably getting a real job after college." I used air quotes around "real." "There're a couple of design firms—"

"Lame." He took a drink, watching me over the rim.

My mouth sagged for a moment before I recovered my voice. "Excuse me?"

"I said that's lame." He set his glass down on the Formica tabletop with a click. "It's one thing to *try* to make it and not get anywhere, so you take a job behind some desk, out of necessity . . . but you haven't even given it a shot. You're not going to even give yourself a chance."

"You don't know anything about me," I bit out, his words seeping uncomfortably inside me.

"Well, tell me then. Explain how I'm wrong. Explain how not even giving your dream a shot is for the best?"

I stared at him, words strangling inside me. How could I tell him it was too hard? That putting myself out there like that, exposing myself in such a personal and intimate way . . . I just wasn't comfortable doing that. Not now. Not ever. I couldn't.

"I'm full." I tossed my napkin on the table. "Take me home now please." I dug around in my bag for my wallet.

"Put your wallet away. I got it."

"No. This isn't a date." I dropped a twenty-dollar bill on the table and scooted out from the booth. Without waiting, I strode out of the restaurant. He caught up with me quickly outside, his jaw clamped tight, so that I knew he was angry. He didn't touch me, just moved ahead of me to open my door. Again, like this was a date. I compressed my lips and uttered nothing. It was almost over. Next time I wouldn't let him persuade me to go out with him. It was sending the wrong message. Not just to him, but to my brain, too.

We sat in silence on the way back to my dorm. I slid him a glance. His jaw was still locked tightly. He was mad. Good. So was I. Arms crossed, I stared straight ahead again. "You were the one who twisted my arm into going out to dinner."

Why I felt compelled to remind him of this, I didn't know. Maybe I felt a little guilty for tossing that money down and storming from the diner. If this had been a date, it was ending badly. My chest felt hollow inside and I sucked in a deep breath as though I could fill every little empty corner. I was such a liar. The idea of never seeing him again made me feel like crap. Why was this happening to me? I slid another glance his way, wondering if I shouldn't just give in, surrender, and see where this could go. Just scratch the itch.

"That's right." He nodded as he turned on the street that cut in front of my dorm. "I'm such an asshole for trying to buy you dinner."

"I didn't say that," I whispered, my eyes suddenly burning.

"I wanted to take you out. You didn't really want to go. I get it. You made that clear from the start. You didn't do anything wrong."

Then why did I feel like I had?

He pulled into my dorm parking lot and parked in an empty space. Killing the engine, he climbed out of the vehicle. I watched him through the windshield as he stalked around to my door and pulled it open for me.

He walked me to the front of my building, keeping pace beside me. At the front door, he stopped and waited for me to open the door. I faced him. "Thanks—"

"Nu-uh." He shook his head. "I'm taking you to your door."

A quick glance at his face told me that this wasn't open for discussion. Almost meekly, I led him inside. Tension swirled between us as we rode the elevator to my floor.

Thankfully, my hall was empty as he walked me to my

door. I didn't need anyone glancing at his brooding expression and wondering if I wasn't being escorted by a serial killer.

I stopped at my door. "Good night." And I might as well have said good-bye because that's what this felt like. I'd done what I set out to do and pushed him away. I should be patting myself on the back.

He didn't move away. Just stared. Looked down at me with an unreadable expression. His eyes roamed over me. He wasn't touching me but it felt like he was. All over I felt him. My breath slipped in shallow spurts from my mouth.

"You know what the most frustrating thing about you is?"

I moistened my lips, and even though I told myself to say nothing, to not ask, I did. "What?"

"You don't know what you want."

That wasn't true. I knew what I wanted. *I wanted him.* I could admit that much to myself. I just wasn't going to let myself have him.

He continued. "I could walk away if I really believed there wasn't anything between us." It was like he was saying this more to himself than me. He lifted a hand to touch my face, but he stopped, his hand in midair, inches from my cheek. He lowered his head until our foreheads touched. "If you didn't look at me the way you're looking at me now, I could just go." His breath brushed over my lips and I couldn't help myself. I came up on my tiptoes and pressed my mouth to his, a betrayal to myself, but I couldn't help it.

It was like a wire snapped. His hands slid around my back and hauled me close. My head rolled back against the door, my throat arching beneath the onslaught of his lips on mine. Hot and devouring. His tongue parried with mine, stroked and tasted. My hands flattened against his chest, fingers digging into the solidness of his flesh, hating the fabric separating my skin from his.

So much for convincing him that I didn't want him.

In that moment, I didn't care. I couldn't care. There was only craving. Only need. If I could crawl my way inside him, I would.

"Fuck, Emerson," he mumbled against my mouth. "You taste so good." His hand slid down my back to cup my butt and lift me against him. Instantly I felt him. His hardness prodded against my belly and my stomach clenched with need.

A loud throat clearing penetrated dimly. Shaw lifted his head and I had to stop myself from diving back for his mouth. It took me a moment to focus my gaze on Georgia, standing there looking amused.

She waved, her eyes going back and forth between me and Shaw. "Hi."

"Oh, hey, Georgia."

Shaw stepped back from me, putting much needed space between us. I tucked my hair behind my ear, my hand shaking.

"Hey," she echoed.

I motioned with a still shaking hand toward Shaw. "This is Shaw. Shaw, my roommate, Georgia."

They shook hands. "Pleasure to meet you, Shaw." Georgia's smile was blinding, and I knew she was enjoying my discomfort a bit too much.

She motioned to the door. "Sorry to interrupt. I just needed to get something from my room, so if you two—"

"No worries," I said quickly. "Shaw was just dropping me off."

"Oh. Great." Her voice didn't sound like she thought it was great though. In fact, she looked a little disappointed. Like she regretted interrupting us if it meant our making out was coming to an end.

Shaw looked at me steadily, and I knew if Georgia wasn't here he would definitely be saying something more. Or, actually, maybe nothing at all. We'd probably still be lip locked.

I forced myself to meet his too perceptive brown eyes. "Thanks again."

He nodded. "Good night." His gaze skipped to Georgia. "Nice meeting you."

"You, too." Georgia's bright smile was back in place. We stood rooted to the floor in front of our room as he headed down the hall and stepped onto the elevator.

"Wow," Georgia murmured. "I thought I was going to have to get a fire extinguisher for you two."

My cheeks burned as I turned and unlocked our door. Stepping inside I tossed my bag on my bed and fell down beside it.

"That's Shaw? Forgot to mention just how beautiful he is."

"Pepper and I said he was hot."

"There's hot and then there's that." She waved toward the door.

"Don't you have a boyfriend?" I reminded her.

She shrugged. "That doesn't mean I'm blind. But more important, you don't have a boyfriend, so—"

"And I don't want one."

She sank down on her bed across from me. "So you and he are just—"

"Nothing," I cut her off. "We're nothing." I rubbed the center of my forehead where a headache was forming.

"That looked like *something* to me. It looked kind of intense."

I bit back the unkind reply that anything would look intense to her given that Harris was her barometer for passionate kisses. The guy seemed more inclined to kiss his image in the mirror than Georgia. I kept my opinion to myself. It wasn't my place to judge. What did I know about relationships anyway?

Deciding to change the subject, I asked, "Are you heading to Harris's tonight?"

"No. He's studying."

I frowned. "You said you just needed to get something from the room—"

"Well, yeah, I wanted to give you your space. I would have just grabbed some books and headed to the library or something. You were clearly in the middle of something, and I didn't want to ruin it. Thought I'd give you two privacy."

I smiled. "Thanks, but unnecessary. Remember? I don't have guys stay over the night."

"There's always a first time, Em."

I shook my head. "Nope." Those were my rules, and I wouldn't bend them.

Georgia rose and started to change. She kicked off her jeans and slipped a pair of comfy-looking pajama bottoms over her shapely runner's legs. "So, you going to see Shaw again?" she asked as she slid a knit T-shirt over her head.

I shook my head. I didn't plan on it, but then something

told me I hadn't seen the last of him. And that fired both excitement and panic through me. I really needed to get a grip.

Tugging off my boots, I rose and shrugged out of my jeans.

"You dropped some money." Georgia pointed to the carpet.

Bending, I picked up a crumpled twenty, deducing that it had fallen from my pocket. *Where I had not put it.*

"Damn him," I muttered.

"What?"

Just then my phone buzzed. I dug through my bag and read the screen.

Shaw: It was a date

With a growl, I flung the phone on the bed. The guy didn't play fair. I was always in control.

Except around him.

"What?" Georgia repeated.

My eyes snapped to her as determination rushed through me. "No. No, I'm not going to see him again."

Whatever it took, I had to get him out of my life.

My phone buzzed again. I glanced down, fully expecting another message from Shaw, but no.

Annie: You're in

I frowned, confused. I typed back three question marks and waited, watching as she typed.

Annie: The kink club. I'm a member now. After tonight, honey . . . of course, I am ☺

Me: Congrats

Really. What else could I say?

Annie: You're my first guest, girl. You better bring your game

My fingers hovered over the keys, unsure how to respond. I didn't especially want to hang out with Annie anymore. And the idea of the kink club might have sounded fun at first. But now . . . I wasn't that intrigued.

"Who is it?" Georgia asked.

"Annie."

"Ugh. Her." Georgia whipped her long golden hair into a messy knot on her head. "Let me guess. She trying to get you to go out?"

I nodded. "Something like that. She got into that kink club."

Georgia's eyes widened. "Really?" Her lips quirked. "Not surprising, I guess."

I nodded slowly, thinking. "She invited me to go with her next time." I lifted one shoulder in a half shrug. "Whenever she goes again. She'll get back to me with all the details."

Georgia's amused smile slipped. "You can't."

I sat up straighter on the bed. "Why not?"

"Well . . . Shaw . . ."

I bristled. Clearly I was doing something wrong if my own

friend thought I was so involved with a guy that I couldn't carry on as normal and go to a kink club. She wasn't hearing me when I said there was nothing between us. Okay, and maybe going to a kink club wouldn't exactly be my normal. It would be a first for me, but I had always been the kind of girl who would have embraced an opportunity like that. At least before.

"I'm going," I declared with a shrug. "Why not?"

Georgia looked at me warily, disapproval lurking in her eyes. "I hope you know what you're doing, Em."

Of course I did. I was taking control of my life again.

Chapter 12

WHEN THE UNKNOWN NUMBER popped up, I was in the process of stuffing my laptop into my bag. Sometimes my hair salon called to confirm appointments and they didn't always use the main line I had plugged into my phone. Zipping up my bag, I answered. "Hello?"

My art history professor, a Frenchman about my height, glared at me as I was squeezing out between desks. I sent him a small, apologetic smile. Class was over, but he didn't seem to care.

"Emerson? It's me. Justin."

I stopped, my fingers clenching around my phone until my joints ached.

A girl bumped into me from behind at my sudden stop.

"Excuse me," she said sharply.

I looked dumbly over my shoulder and stepped aside so she could pass, too shocked to even muster up an apology.

"How did you get this number?" My lips felt numb as the words passed out of my mouth. I stepped out of the classroom and walked slowly down the hall. It was crowded, lots of students buried in their phones or talking to the person next to them. Except for my snail-crawling pace, I didn't look out of the ordinary. Even if I felt it. Even if I felt like I'd just gotten hit by a semi.

"Your mom."

Of course. My thumb started to stretch for the end button, ready to push it and put to death his voice in my ear.

"Wait! Don't hang up," he pleaded. Like he could read my mind, like he knew what I was about to do.

I hesitated. I wasn't sure why, but I stopped. I'd never heard his voice sound like that. There was a thread of desperation to it. He'd always been cocky and teasing, but he had never sounded quite so human.

Unable to keep walking with his voice in my ear, I stepped to the side of the hall and leaned against the wall, staring blindly into the ebb and flow of students.

Thumb poised, I waited for him to say something else, something more . . . to reveal that he was a different person. That what had happened between us was just a mistake of youth. That it had been the alcohol and poor judgment.

He sighed into the phone. "We want you to come to the wedding, Em."

By "we" I assumed he meant Mom and him. His father wouldn't care either way. The good thing about Don was his lack of opinion when it came to me.

"I want you there," he added, filling the silence.

"Why?"

"We're family. Don't you think it's time we move past—"

"Are you owning up to what you did?" I cut in. Because

that would go a long way. If he just admitted it to me, I could maybe move on. If he admitted his mistake to Mom, even better. She had never believed me. She thought it was me being a pain in the ass and trying to wreck what she had going with Don.

He sighed again. "Will that change anything, Emerson? I want us to move on and not rehash old history."

A pause fell between us as I processed this. Just the fact that he was even calling meant he had changed.

But I was different, too. I wasn't as trusting.

"I just don't think I can go." Show up and pretend like we were the perfect family? No. I couldn't play that game. I waited, expecting him to turn nasty on me, but that didn't happen.

Suzanne walked into the building right then and spotted me. She was bundled up like she was going on an Arctic expedition. The usual for her. She was cold when it hit sixty degrees. She claimed that was her winter back home in Texas. She waved energetically and headed in my direction.

Justin sighed again. "All right. I had to try. Maybe you'll feel differently in the future."

I flexed my fingers around the phone. "I have to go." Suzanne was almost to me now, and the last thing I wanted was for her to hear any part of my conversation with Justin.

"Sure. Take care, Em."

The line went dead. I pulled back my cell and stared at it for a moment, not sure how I felt about the conversation. I'd made Justin out to be a monster for so long now. It was easier than accepting him as something real. As my stepbrother. And yet even though I'd turned him into this villain from the shadowy past, a part of me always knew the real villain was someone much closer to me.

Mom's betrayal wounded me the most. She was the one I couldn't expel from my life. Justin was nothing. No one. My mom . . .

She would always be my mother. And the hurt she'd inflicted went deep. It was like a wound that could never fully heal. The moment it would start to close up, she would come along and tear it back open.

I tucked my phone into the deep front pockets of my coat and smiled at Suzanne. Maybe overly bright, but she didn't seem to notice.

"Hey, you," she greeted me, her cheeks chapped from the outdoors.

"Hey, Suz."

"Finished with class?"

"Yeah."

"Want to go see that new Bourne movie this week?"

I hesitated for a moment, thinking about whether I should spend more time in the studio preparing for the upcoming showcase or not. No matter how much time I labored over my work, I never felt ready to reveal it to the world.

Apparently she misread my hesitation because she lifted her eyebrows. "Unless you're all booked up with . . . special plans with someone?"

I stared at her blankly.

"You know." She nudged me with her elbow.

I shook my head. "No."

"Hottie Shaw?" She lowered her voice and looked around. Like we were in high school or something and she didn't want anyone to overhear us talking about a boy. She was conservative like that. Discreet. A little like Georgia with her small-town roots. For her, hooking up with a guy overnight was a big deal and not something she would just talk about in front of other people. In other words—the polar opposite of Annie.

"Why would you think I had plans with Shaw?"

She shrugged one shoulder. "I don't know. I saw ya'll together, Em." Her voice dropped to a hush again. "And you brought him to your room." Her big brown eyes widened meaningfully. "You never do that, Em. Thought he might be . . . different for you." She looked almost hopeful as she said this.

I resisted agreeing with her. Yeah. Shaw was different. But that didn't mean he was suddenly in my life to stay.

"I don't have plans with Shaw. Let's go to a movie. Not before three though. My dad's in town and I have to see him."

She nodded, her smile subdued. Almost like she wished I did have plans with Shaw.

"Hey, you're not hoping I get all settled down and bor-ing like Georgia and Pepper?" I nudged her with my elbow. "Who'll be your wing-girl then?"

She shrugged and smiled easily. "Hey, I don't want to be single forever. I wouldn't begrudge you finding someone. I want that for both of us."

I groaned. "Not you, too."

"What?" She arched her dark eyebrows.

I started walking toward the door. "You. Pepper. Georgia. You're all leaving me for your happily-ever-afters."

"I'm an optimist, what can I say?" Then she shook her head, almost sadly. "But I'm not abandoning you. Haven't met anyone yet. Still looking."

She walked backward from me, inching toward her classroom door.

I shook my head at her. She wouldn't be for long. Sweet, attractive girls like her found boyfriends. Got married. Had kids.

I pointed. "You better start looking now because you're about to run into someone."

She whirled around seconds before colliding with a guy who was walking with his nose buried in his phone. She warded him off with a hand, narrowly missing him. He looked up from his phone and said something. Suzanne laughed, tossing her rich mane of brown hair. Her laughter was a tinkling sound I only ever heard from her when she was getting her flirt on. Yeah. The girl was looking all right.

Smiling, I turned and stepped out of the building. I had walked only a few feet before the smile slipped from my face and my mind drifted back to my phone call with Justin. I hated that he'd called. That all of it came flooding back. That I would be thinking about it and him and Mom and everything I had worked so hard to bury.

I needed a distraction.

My phone vibrated from my pocket. I dug it out and read the screen.

Shaw: Hey

My heart did a stupid little flip. *God.* I so wasn't that girl. The type who waited for the boy to admit he really really really liked her. That he wanted to *be* with her. I wasn't that sad. I knew he wanted me. This was the same guy who had declared I was going to ask him for sex. It was my job to make sure that didn't happen.

Me: Hey back
Shaw: Let's go out

Well, that was to the point. Not such a surprise though. I was coming to expect it from him.

Me: I don't date
Shaw: Except we did
Me: That wasn't a date, remember?
Shaw: Yes, it was. Remember?

I swallowed back a sound that was part laughter and part snort. Cocky jerk. I could almost imagine his too-good-looking face—calm and devoid of expression. Just matter of fact.

Me: No offense. I just don't date
Shaw: Is this some kind of rule of yours? You know what they say about rules

I smiled. I couldn't help it. I knew what he was implying. *Rules were meant to be broken.* And yeah, usually I would agree, except my no-dating policy was of my own making. I only had a few self-imposed rules, and those I didn't break.

Shaw: You seem like a rule-breaker type
Me: Not about this

And not with him.

Shaw: I can't stop thinking about you. The sound of your laugh. And the little sounds you make when I touch you . . .

Heat flamed my face. I gulped and glanced around like someone could *hear* the seductive whisper of his words. Thankfully, no one was looking at me. I wanted to see him again, too. It was an ache in my chest. And in other parts. He made me feel special. Like maybe I was unique to him. Dangerous thinking. I shoved the phone back in my pocket, determined to ignore him, determined not to look again even when I felt it vibrate against my hip. I wanted a distraction, true, but he wasn't it.

Facing forward, I resumed my trek across campus, tilting my face into the cold, welcoming the bite of wind, letting it chase away the lingering heat from a simple text conversation with Shaw. *Simple?* Nothing about him and how he made me feel was simple. And that was the problem.

In time he'd forget about me.

Even if I didn't forget him.

I could live with that. I'd learned to live with a lot. This would just be one more thing.

THE GRAPEVINE WAS A French-style country bistro just a few blocks from campus. I didn't need to drive there. I walked swiftly, determined to be on time. I jogged lightly over the crosswalk, my boot heels clicking sharply on the gravel street. Dad hated it when I was late.

It was the type of place you went to on a nice date—if the guy really wanted to impress you. It was a little pricey. At least that's what I'd heard. Some guy took Suzanne there once. She thought maybe he was "the one." At least she'd said that then. She'd said that a few times. Clearly he hadn't turned out to be the one.

It was also the type of place where parents liked to eat because it wasn't overrun by college kids. Parents like my dad. A Dartford alum and member of the board of trustees. He came to campus at least twice a year for meetings, and we always had breakfast or lunch on those occasions. Never dinner. He never stuck around long enough for that. He attended his meeting, checked in with me, and was gone by three. In and out and back to his life.

As I pushed through the heavy wood door, the hostess greeted me with a warm smile. "Hello, welcome to the Grapevine."

My gaze skimmed the tall brunette, immediately recognizing her. "Beth?"

She blinked, angling her head to study me. I was dressed

more conservatively than the last time she'd seen me, wearing a long wool skirt, my hair tamed smoothly around my face. I couldn't hide the magenta streaks in my dark hair but I could style it less dramatically. My turtleneck sweater peeked out of my coat. "Uh . . ."

"Hi. I'm Emerson, remember? Reece and Pepper's friend. I was at your engagement party."

Recognition lit her eyes. "Ah, yes." Her smile returned. "That was such a crazy night. I'm sorry I didn't recognize you right away."

I nodded. "That's okay. There were a lot of people there." *Including your cousin*, I was tempted to add. I could see a little bit of Shaw in her—in the width of her high cheekbones.

"Yes." She stepped closer, dropping her voice. "And I might have had a few too many margaritas."

"You had cause to celebrate."

Her eyes softened. "Yeah. I did." She was obviously thinking about her fiancé. Cynic that I was, I was happy for her. This girl who had lost so much—a brother—deserved some happiness. *And so did Shaw*. I couldn't stop my thoughts from going to him.

I knew I didn't know the whole story, but it just didn't seem right. "I'm friends with Shaw, too," I added without thinking.

And maybe I shouldn't have because the softness faded from her eyes and she just looked flinty-eyed and uncomfortable then. "You are." It wasn't a question. Only a statement. Turning sideways, she reached for the menus beside the podium. "Table for one or . . ."

"I'm meeting my father."

"Oh, he's here." She set the menus back down with a nod and smiled. It was the fake hostess smile again. The other friendly smile she had given me when I reminded her of who I was had vanished. "Right this way."

I followed her to the table where my father was sitting, talking on the phone with someone. He gave me a small wave.

Beth motioned to the chair and started to turn, clearly eager to escape.

"Thanks, Beth."

She looked back slightly, her hostess smile still firmly in place on her lips. "My pleasure."

I was still staring after her when Dad hung up.

"Emerson, how are you?"

I snapped my gaze to my father. "Good. How are you, Daddy? Did your meeting go well?"

He made a face. "Oh, they're interested in opening a new building for the Theater and Dance Department. Can you imagine? Why would they possibly need an entire building?"

I stared at him as he perused the menu, marveling that he could think so little of the arts when his own daughter was a studio arts major.

"Imagine that," I murmured.

The waiter appeared then and we placed our orders.

His gaze settled on me then, and even though he had seen me over the holidays he winced at the dyed streaks in my hair. Fortunately, he refrained from commenting. He'd already voiced his disapproval. I was spared from hearing it again.

"So. How's school?"

"Good." I sipped from my glass of water. "I've been busy on several pieces for the upcoming showcase—"

"Oh, that reminds me. I was talking to Bill Wetherford."

At my blank look, he added, "Of Wetherford Enterprises?"

I nodded like that rang a bell. He was looking at me like I should know the company.

Apparently he could see I didn't. "It's one of the largest toilet paper manufacturers in the United States. Anyway. Turns out Wetherford is interested in creating an in-house design team. And I told him all about you."

A design team for a toilet paper company? "That sounds . . . interesting."

Thankfully, our food arrived right then and he became more interested in his prime rib. Conversation was intermittent after that and he took two more calls. I found myself watching Beth as she came in and out of the room, seating other diners. It seemed like she made a great effort not to look my way, and I knew it was because I'd brought up Shaw.

I don't know why I had mentioned him. We weren't really friends. Sure, I hadn't kissed any other guy since I met him, but that was about to change. At least I assumed it would. I doubted a night at a kink club would result in anything less. Annie had texted me and we were on for tonight.

"So. Emerson," Dad said, clicking his phone shut. "Are you seeing anyone?"

I shook my head and reached for my glass, shoving the image of Shaw from my mind. "No. No one."

"Good. You're still young. Best to focus on your studies and get your career off the ground."

I nodded like that was it. Like that was the reason I wasn't seeing anyone. The reason I couldn't let myself have more than empty hookups. The reason I was going to a kink club. It had nothing to do with trying to get a guy out of my system.

Chapter 13

I DROVE MY OWN car, my fingers flexing on the leather steering wheel as if finding the right grip would some-how strengthen my shaky resolve. Annie offered to drive, but that was one mistake I wasn't repeating. My stomach was full of knots as I followed her across town, and I wasn't sure why. Deciding to go to the kink club was a lot easier in theory. Right now, when it was about to become a reality . . . it was a lot harder than I had expected.

I parked behind Annie on a residential street. The houses were nice, middle-class homes. Two-storied with driveways scraped fresh of snow.

Shaw had texted me off and on through the week . . . even called twice. I ignored him until he finally stopped. Either he had given up or he was just super busy. Pepper had mentioned that Reece went to visit him at work to check out the custom bike he was working on for some rich client, so there was merit in that theory.

Still, as I stepped from my car and locked it, I couldn't help wondering what he was doing tonight. I couldn't imagine him spending a Friday night alone, but Pepper hadn't mentioned that she or Reece had plans with him. Was he at Maisie's?

"C'mon!" Annie waved at me anxiously. As I hurried to catch up with her, she added, "This isn't the kind of thing you want to be late to. All the most interesting people are paired up by then."

Annie turned up the walkway of a two-story home that looked very . . . Well, not the location one would expect to host a kink club.

"This is it?"

"Tonight it is. It changes location every time."

I sent her a look. "Why?"

She laughed. "I never thought I'd say this, but oh, Emerson. You're so naïve." At my continued blank look, she sighed. "So we don't get raided."

"Raided? What? Are we walking into a meth house?" I looked around as if I expected the DEA to jump out of the bushes.

She laughed again. "Do me a favor. Don't sound like such a Girl Scout in there. Or maybe you should. Some of them might like that."

Misgivings trickled through me as we neared the front door. Music floated from behind it. She stepped up onto the porch ahead of me. When she realized I wasn't at her side, she started to turn back, but then the front door opened.

A girl dressed from head to toe in black leather stepped out followed by a guy. A guy I knew. And so did Annie.

"Logan," I breathed. "What are you doing here?"

He looked down at me in surprise from the porch. "Emerson. What are *you* doing here?"

"Logan," Annie greeted in a purring voice, sidling close. She stroked a hand along his arm. "I didn't know you were a member."

He gave her a distracted look, as if he didn't remember hooking up with her all that well. "Amber, hey. How are you?"

"Annie," she snapped. "It's Annie." She shot me a look. "I'll be inside." That said, she flounced in.

Logan and his friend descended the steps to stop in front of me. He repeated himself. "Em, what are you doing here?"

I looked from the friend back to him. "Same thing you are."

He shook his head and rubbed at the back of his neck, looking older than his eighteen years as he stared at me in concern. "Look, maybe you should go home."

His friend dug in her bag, pulled out a cigarette, and lit up. She watched us with mild interest, inhaling deeply.

"Why would I want to do that?"

He leaned a little closer, lowering his voice. "I'm not sure this is the place for you. You don't want to go in there."

I laughed, but the sound was forced. "Clearly you don't know me as well as you think."

He shared a look with his companion. She watched me in silence, her black fingernails a severe contrast to her milk-white skin as she brought the cigarette to her lips again. She worked her lips, puffing smoke in my direction. Her lips were painted so red they looked almost as dark as her fingernails. Her throaty voice scratched the air. "It's not for everyone, sweetheart. Maybe you should listen to him."

I squared my shoulders, affronted that Logan and this stranger thought I was somehow incapable of handling whatever was on the other side of this door. They didn't know me. I was strong. I wasn't afraid.

And I was fed up. I was tired of being pushed and pulled by others. Justin. My mother. And now, even though he was nothing like either one of them, to an extent . . . by Shaw.

I was in control. Meeting Logan's gaze straight on, I said, "I can handle it." I moved forward and they parted for me. Marching up the steps, I didn't bother knocking. Turning the doorknob, I walked inside the house.

IT TOOK PRECISELY FIVE minutes for me to realize I'd made a mistake.

It was dark inside the house. Candles big and small decorated several surfaces. Tables. Shelves. I was offered a blindfold, which I declined with a shake of my head. This only got me a frown from the woman dressed in a costume that resembled those cigarette girl outfits from the forties. She moved on with her tray of blindfolds. I didn't see Annie anywhere.

Sounds mingled with music as I carefully navigated the room. It didn't take an expert to identify the noises. Moans and wails and sharp, keening cries drifted from upstairs.

I told myself not to let it bother me. It's not as though I hadn't been to parties before. I'm sure people made use of rooms at all those other parties I attended. I just never had to hear quite so *well* what was going on inside them. Logan's voice echoed through my mind: *You don't want to go in there.*

Shaking off that echo, I moved on, searching for Annie.

Several people sat on a couch, all blindfolded. Three

women and one man. They were touching, kissing, slowly removing each other's clothing piece by piece.

As I skirted the couch, a woman approached me and offered me a drink. I smiled shakily as I declined. Something told me I shouldn't drink. Not only did I need a clear head, but who knew what could be in the contents of those glasses?

A hand stroked down my arm and laced with my fingers. I yanked my hand away and looked down. A guy sat in a sofa chair, a girl already snuggled up in his lap. He smiled at me and held out his hand as if I would just naturally accept it. He patted the seat next to him and then with that same hand he cupped the girl's breast, watching me as he fondled it.

My stomach dipped. I backed away and bumped into someone. I turned with an apology on my lips and came face-to-face with a life-size squirrel. Given his height I would guess it was a man.

A man inside a squirrel costume.

He bumped me again and I glanced down to see that he was anatomically correct. Well, disproportionately so. Peering at him in the dim lighting, that part of him jutted out bigger than the average man. Bigger than the above average man.

"E-excuse me," I stammered, jerking my gaze back up. The squirrel's big dark eyes stared down at me, wide as saucers.

With an awkward hip thrust, he bumped me again and I snapped, "Stop that!"

I shuffled backward to avoid his enormous . . . what even was it? A strap-on? Was it sewn into the costume? I shook my head and told myself this was one mystery I didn't want to unravel. I might have laughed, but my overriding emotion was annoyance.

"There you are, Chippy." A woman appeared at the squirrel's side. "Oh, did you meet a friend?" She gave me a flirty smile.

I mumbled something and backed away, still shaking my head. I didn't bother searching for Annie anymore. My overriding thought was: *Leave. Get out of here, Emerson.*

A guy reached for my arm, but I side-stepped him as I hurried toward the front door. I plunged out into the night and sucked a breath of bitter-cold air into my lungs, unaware until that moment that I had hardly been breathing since I stepped inside that house. Which totally mystified me.

I had wanted to check out this kink club ever since I heard of its existence. I figured it would be the perfect place where I could hook up with guys who didn't mind dominant girls who called all the shots. Only it hadn't been like that at all, and somehow I knew. Shaw was to blame.

He had ruined me. I couldn't even think about being with another guy. He filled my head. I wrapped my fingers around the porch post and stared out at the silent street, my fingers digging into the rough, cold wood. I needed to get him out of my system. And to do that . . . maybe I should just get my fill of him, satisfy my curiosity, my urges. Then I could walk away from him for good.

I took several more bracing breaths and released the post. Stepping down, I let that idea take root, testing it out, trying to decide if it was as crazy as it sounded.

I heard him before I saw him. Like the mere idea of him had conjured him up here.

Footsteps thudded against the sidewalk. His large shape

appeared, skidding to a stop at the end of the walkway, his chest lifting with breaths.

"Shaw . . . what are you doing here?"

Crazy, stupid delight coursed through me. I drank in the sight of him, standing tall before me, legs braced apart like nothing could take him down. The guy was built like a tank, and my belly fluttered, the very core of me reacting to him in the most fundamental way. A week without a glimpse of him and my heart reacted, pounding with longing. Such a treacherous thing. The heart really does have a mind of its own.

"I got a text from Reece."

Anger flared to life inside me. I approached him with hard steps, delight at seeing him withering away. "Why did Reece text you?"

"Logan told him you were here." His gaze flicked to the house. "He was worried about you."

Damn Logan. My life was none of his business. "And you raced over here? For what? To rescue me? I told you I didn't need rescuing."

His gaze slid from the house back to me again. I had no doubt that he knew what this place was. Reece hadn't left that tidbit out when he called him. And why had Reece called him anyway? Did he think Shaw and I were involved? Because that would be incorrect on his part.

"What are you doing here, Emerson?"

I compressed my lips, not about to tell him that I had been wondering the same thing. "I don't need Logan or Reece or *you* looking out for me like I can't take care of myself." This was the part where I could tell him that I had made a mistake and had decided to leave, that the kink club wasn't for me—that I was in fact leaving when he showed up, but I refused to give him that satisfaction.

"C'mon." He reached for my hand, but I yanked my arm back before he could claim it.

"I drove myself here. I can get myself home." I circled around him and started walking in hard steps away from him and toward my car.

He followed fast on my heels. "What were you doing here?"

He wasn't going to let it drop. "That's none of your business."

"This isn't you."

That only made me even angrier—if possible. My boots dug into the concrete with every step. I hit an icy patch and would have gone down. My arms flailed for balance, but he was there, grabbing me to stop me from falling. I struggled free from his hands and kept going until I reached my car. I whirled around at the door and jabbed a finger at him. "You don't know me." Emotion shook my voice, betraying me. I swallowed and inhaled a deep breath.

"I know you've tried really hard to keep me out, but it didn't work. I'm in your blood. And you're in mine. I know that." He stared hard at me, letting the words sink in. "And I know you. I see you."

I shook my head like a stubborn child, panic crawling up my throat.

He motioned back toward the house. "If you don't know why you're here, then I do. You're running from me."

I laughed and the sound rang brittle even to my own ears. "Oh, you've got ego."

He didn't care. Just kept talking. "I know that you're not half as wild or experienced as you pretend to be."

My laughter faded. I stared at him for a long moment, something that felt dangerously close to fear bubbling up in my chest. He couldn't know that. He couldn't see me. "I'm not pretending to *be* anything."

His eyes glinted knowingly as his well-carved lips flattened into a grim line. He didn't say the word but I heard it between us just the same. *Liar.*

"How?" I demanded. "How do you know anything about me?" I wasn't admitting he was right, but I had to know. I had to know what I'd said or done that gave me away.

Why was he here? Lately every time I turned he was there. He wasn't like any other hookup. If he was, he'd already be gone. Every guy I ever messed around with was happy to take what I gave and then move on. Why did he want more? *Why did he have to be different?*

He moved in then. Just three steps and he had me backed against the cold metal of my car.

"You know what they called me in the Marines?" I shook my head and he answered, his voice low and deep and raising goose bumps on my skin, "Hawk. And it was because I could read people, assess situations in an instant. Call it whatever you want. Street sense. Situational awareness. I have it."

Hawk. It fit him. I swallowed back the golf-ball-size lump in my throat. His deep voice, his closeness . . . My skin shivered uncontrollably. I hated that I trembled but at least I could blame it on the cold. He didn't know it was him and what he did to me.

Of course, he just claimed to be able to read a person. I gulped, worried even as I told myself he wasn't a mind reader. He couldn't be *that* perceptive. Even if he was a former Marine with a nickname like Hawk. He couldn't see my secrets.

My gaze darted from his eyes to his mouth, both so close. Even in the near dark, with only the glow from the streetlamp halfway down the block, I could make out the tiny flecks of gold in his brown eyes. My hands fluttered between us as though looking for a place to land. His chest felt so warm and inviting, a solid wall pressing intimately against me, against breasts that felt achy and swollen.

"Well, *Hawk*, you're wrong." I lifted my chin. I went for a mocking tone, but I missed the mark. My voice sounded breathless and affected in a way I was trying to pretend not to be. "I just did like four guys back in that house."

His mouth curved almost cruelly at my lie. "Such a liar."

Okay. Maybe I should have gone for a more believable number. Especially since Logan couldn't have called him more than thirty minutes ago. He reached between us and plucked the keys from my hand.

"What are you doing?"

He reached around me, his arm brushing my hip as he lifted the door handle. "I'll drive. Get in." He motioned for me to circle around my car.

I watched in astonishment as he pulled open the door and settled himself behind the wheel of my car, adjusting the seat for his long legs. I glanced at him and looked around. "Where's your truck?"

"I got dropped off."

That explained how he got here so quickly. He must have been nearby. I cocked my head. "Who dropped you off?"

"I was with a friend when Reece texted."

A friend.

I knew without him saying that it was a girl. Apparently he wasn't so into me that he excluded other girls from his life. The pain that flared to life inside my chest was so unexpected that it infuriated me. I shouldn't be feeling this way. *I had no right to feel this way.*

The familiar urge to storm off came over me. Unfortunately I had nowhere to storm. He was sitting inside my car.

I stalked around the car and dropped down into the passenger seat, sealing us in the cozy interior. There was some leftover heat from earlier. He started the engine and let it idle, the motor warming.

When I thought about the fact that I had just toyed with the idea of giving in to my urges, of just playing this thing out—whatever it was—between us, I didn't know whether to laugh or cry.

"You didn't need to end your date for me."

He leaned his head back against the headrest and gave me a lazy look. "Jealous?"

"Why should I be jealous? I do what I like, with who I like. You're entitled to the same."

He smiled slowly and that grin made my stomach flip over. There was such knowledge and experience behind that smile. Of the world. Of life. Death. And, as unlikely as it seemed, me.

"You like me," he announced. "You don't want to, but you do." He said this so easily, so matter-of-factly that I wanted to stomp my feet and yell *no*. I faced forward instead, looking out the windshield. "Let's go. Drive."

Chuckling, he put the car into drive. We traveled for several moments before he said, "I wasn't on a date."

"I don't care." Of course I snapped this off so fast that I sounded like I did care.

"Cara is a friend. We went to boot camp together. She was in town on leave for her nephew's christening."

A Marine like him. She must be strong. Tough. Probably sexy like Alice from *Resident Evil*. "How nice. You must have a lot in common."

"We do."

"Sounds perfect. Why aren't you still with her then?"

"Because you needed me."

"I didn't need you. I was leaving." My voice faded, full of regret over admitting that to him   that I had been in over my head at the kink club.

"Why? Doing four guys wear you out?"

I scowled and crossed my arms over my chest.

"C'mon. I know that didn't happen. You were leaving because it wasn't for you, right?"

I hated that he was right.

"Because," he continued, "you'd rather be with me."

I snorted. "I'm surprised you even fit in this car with that inflated ego of yours."

"Keep telling yourself that. Maybe you'll convince yourself that there isn't anything between us."

I sniffed and bit back the reply that there wasn't anything between us.

He chuckled and the deep sound sent shivers through me. I stared through the windshield, frowning. "Where are we going? This isn't the way to my dorm."

"My place."

The two words sent a jolt through me. "Why?"

"I'm without a vehicle."

"So I can drive myself home from your place, is that it?"

He nodded once, but there was something unconvincing in the motion that only seemed to heighten my own unease. Like maybe he was hoping I would stay. *You're just dropping him off, Emerson. You're not going inside.*

I had my own car. I was in control. As we turned onto the narrow road that wound around the edge of the lake, I reminded myself of this.

We bumped along the uneven gravel drive beside his house. The night seemed full of light out here. Moonlight bounced off the vastness of snow and ice. The lake stretched out into forever like a white sheet of glass. He killed the engine. "I'll get your door. It's slippery."

I watched, my pulse pounding, as he walked around for my door.

Stepping out, I held my hand up for the keys. "You didn't need to turn the car off."

"I thought you might like to see something I'm working on."

I frowned, certain that suspicion stared out from my eyes. He looked down at me so soberly. There was nothing sly in his gaze. It was just him, but he'd always been like that. From the very beginning. So direct and straightforward. He didn't say a lot, but when he did it meant something. It was truth.

He motioned to the work shed beside the house. "I've seen your art . . . at least what was in your room." He shrugged and rubbed the back of his neck. He actually looked a little self-conscious. A definite first for him. He always seemed so confident. Something fluttered loose inside me at this new side of him. "Well, this is mine, I guess." His art. That's what he was saying even if he was having trouble admitting it. Something loosened inside me, and I knew that I couldn't turn away from this part of himself he was offering to show me.

I glanced at the shed. I wasn't even going inside his house. I didn't have to step foot inside the cozy warm space that reminded me of a Norman Rockwell painting. I didn't have to see that big bed again to remember how comfortable it was.

It was just a shed. What could it hurt? I nodded jerkily and followed him to the shed. It was a little warmer inside, but not by much. He flipped on a switch and I blinked at the sudden flood of light.

Engine parts and pieces of bike littered the small space everywhere. There were at least three motorcycles that looked finished. I didn't know anything about bikes, but one was definitely a chopper. It was cherry red with shiny chrome. Beside that one sat another one that looked partially assembled. It wasn't painted yet. I stepped between the two.

"You built these?"

"Yeah." He stroked one of his bikes, and I couldn't help watching his hand. The long, blunt-tipped fingers. I remembered the unbelievable way they felt on me . . . in me. My face burned and I took a bracing breath.

Fortunately he was still looking at his bikes. "I'm making this one to sell. I have a client who's interested."

"If it looks anything like this one, you won't have any trouble selling it." I touched the red one, admiring it. All that fiery red was cold and smooth under my hand.

"I'm thinking about putting a mural on the tank and fender . . . maybe something patriotic."

"Like your tattoo?" I asked.

"A bit. It's a starting point at least, but I would like it to be something fresh."

"You could do an eagle's face up close . . . have the eagle's eye in actuality be the globe." I bit my bottom lip, contemplating. I moved my hand in front of me, fingers flexing like I could see it. Touch it. And in that moment, I could. It was like I was working the shapes and colors with my hands right then. "That could be cool . . . symbolic. Maybe clouds that look faintly like flags." I dropped my hand and shrugged. Glancing at him, I froze at the intent way he was looking at me. Like I had said something profound.

"Could you do that?"

"M-me?" My voice squeaked a bit. "I've never done anything like that. I work on paper or canvas."

"But you could do it." He uttered this so absolutely. Like he had no doubt. "It's just airbrushing."

"I could mess it up."

"Then we'd start over."

We. When did that happen? We weren't *we* in any way, shape, or form.

"How do you know you can't do it? You gotta try, right?"

He searched my face, his eyes peering into mine like he was looking into my soul, and suddenly I didn't feel like we were talking about airbrushing his bike anymore.

I shivered and chafed my arms, pretending it was the cold and not him. Not the way he watched me or talked to me. Not the memory of what his hands and mouth felt like on me.

He looked down at the bike again. "Have you ever been on one?"

I shook my head quickly, relieved at the change of subject. "No."

His mouth twisted into a half smile. "Afraid?"

"No. I've just never been with—" I caught myself and corrected. "I've never met anyone who had a bike before."

Something flashed in his eyes and I knew he caught my slip. Thinking that way was dangerous. You're not *with* him. *Never forget that.*

He patted the seat. "Hop on."

"What? Ride it? Now?"

"No. It's too cold, but try it on for size." His eyes roamed my face in that way of his that made my stomach flutter. Like he was really looking at me. Memorizing me.

I looked down at the seat and shrugged. Why not? I lifted one jeans-clad leg and straddled the bike. It wasn't like hopping on my beach cruiser back home. It was bigger. I had to spread my thighs wider. My hand stroked the seat cushion.

It was a little intimidating to think about flying sixty miles an hour down the highway on this thing.

His voice sounded close to my ear. "How's it feel?"

I grasped the handlebars in front of me. "It feels . . . dangerous."

"Here. Like this." His bigger hands closed over mine, adjusting my grip. My heart raced faster at the texture of his callused palms on the backs of my fingers, at the solid press of his chest against my back. I trembled, longing to twist on the seat and wrap my arms around him, pull him close and taste him again.

Only I knew where that would lead.

"And sit back a little farther." His hands skimmed along my arms. Even through my sleeves goose bumps broke out all over my flesh. His hands settled on my hips. He pulled me back on the seat in one easy drag. Like I weighed nothing at all. It heightened my awareness of his strength, his size. I was used to being smaller than average, but even I couldn't be called skinny. I had my curves. But Shaw made me feel almost delicate. "You don't want to be so far up front."

I nodded dumbly.

"Feel better?" he asked, his voice a deep purr near my ear. The question was innocent enough, but his hands lingered on me. The weight and pressure of them made me think of where else those hands had been. The delicious things he had done to me.

And how much I craved his doing them again.

As though he could read my mind, his hands drifted, skimming my hips, moving up to my waist. My breath hitched. I sat a little straighter. He hesitated for just a heartbeat. And then continued over my stomach, stopping just below my breasts. His thumbs pushed against the bottom swells, lifting them higher. My nipples hardened. The satin of my bra felt abrasive against the tips and I wiggled a little on the seat of the bike.

Suddenly the bike dipped a little with his weight. He sank down behind me, his thighs aligning with mine. Instantly, I felt warmer with his body behind me. He fit himself snugly against me. His lips grazed my ear, a teasing brush. I just had to turn my face and my lips could reach his.

I didn't move. My chest lifted high with deep breaths, thrusting my breasts out higher. His thumbs continued to drag back and forth against the undersides. I bit my lip to stop a moan from escaping, a small plea for him to stop tormenting me and just take me in his hands.

He pressed closer against my back and that's when I felt him against my bottom. The hard bulge of him prodded me and I clenched my teeth to stop myself from grinding against him. That was begging for trouble and I was already knocking at its door.

I released the handlebars and quickly climbed off the bike. I slid my sweaty palms down my front and then brought shaky hands up to tuck my hair behind my ears. "I don't think I'll be riding one anytime soon." At least I didn't stammer the words. The way I shook on the inside, it was surprising.

He sat there looking up at me, his eyes dark and heavy. "You don't have to. Maybe you can just take a drive with me sometime. In the spring when it warms up a little."

Riding with him? As in sixty miles an hour with the wind blowing all around us and my arms wrapped around him. Just the idea left me feeling exhilarated. He made the offer so casually as he climbed off the bike and stood with one hand tucked halfway in his front pocket. Even crazier than that was the idea that he would still be hanging around me come spring.

"Maybe." I shuffled my feet toward the shed door. "I really need to get back now."

He followed me from the shed without trying to stop me. Not a touch or a kiss. I almost expected him to. What was all that on the bike if he wasn't even going to try for more? Again, just more evidence that he wasn't like any other guy I'd encountered. And even more confusing was that I didn't know which emotion humming through me was stronger. Relief or disappointment.

He watched me back out of the drive, still looking relaxed. When I pulled out onto the street and left his house behind, in my mind I could still see him standing there.

I didn't think I would ever close my eyes again without seeing him.

Chapter 14

I WAS WAITING FOR Pepper the following morning. It was close to nine when I heard her enter next door. I bumped the partially open adjoining door with my hip. She and Reece sat near her desk, sorting through a bag of bagels.

She looked up. "Hey. Em!" Reece gave me a wave.

She must have read something in my expression. Pepper approached me, holding half a bagel in her hand, her eyes bright with worry. "Are you okay?"

"Yeah. Why wouldn't I be?"

She slid an uncertain look to Reece. "Well, last night Logan saw you and was a little worried that maybe you were in over your head—"

"Logan? Reece's man-whore brother? *He* was worried I was in over my head?" I pressed a hand to my chest.

"Yes!" Pepper's eyes flashed. "If Logan thought the situation was bad, then the situation was bad."

"Uh, hello?" Reece waved his bagel, his expression grim. "I'm right here. Can you not call my brother a whore anymore?"

"Sorry, baby." Pepper smoothed a hand over his shoulder.

"I just would like to know why you thought it was a good idea to text Shaw?" I tossed my arms out wide on either side of me. "Why? Is there something I should know?"

Pepper glanced at me and then looked at Reece searchingly.

Reece looked at me, his stare unflinching. "Is it that hard to figure out? The guy is into you."

"So that is supposed to mean—"

"He gives a shit about you, Em," he said, clearly having no trouble being direct with me. "Maybe that *should* mean something. He's a helluva lot better for you than those other losers you waste your time—"

"Emerson." Pepper's voice cut in, which was a good thing. I was about to go off on her boyfriend for lecturing me about what kind of guy I chose to spend time with. Pepper continued. "I know you like Shaw. I've seen you with him. He's . . . different. You're different when you're around him."

I wrenched my gaze off Reece's hard-eyed stare. He looked at me like I was the bad one here. Like I was screwing his friend over. What did they want from me? I couldn't be like Pepper. I couldn't just have a boyfriend and fall in love.

I stared levelly at Pepper. "I love you, girl, but you gotta stop this matchmaking business. Both of you." I glanced at Reece and then back at her. "It's not going to work."

She gave a single nod, but she still had that worried look. "Okay."

Okay. Good. I nodded, but the sense of relief I wanted didn't come. No relief or satisfaction or whatever. The hollow feeling inside me only yawned deeper. "Thanks." I waved at them both. "I'll leave you alone now. Carry on."

Pepper glanced at her clock. "I thought we were going to walk to class together."

"No, I'm going in early to work on my stuff for the showcase."

Pepper's eyes brightened. "That's right. That's coming up. When is it?"

"Next Friday."

Pepper glanced at Reece. "It's a big university art show that Em's in." She looked back at me. "Are you ready for it?"

"I think so." My mind drifted to the painting of Shaw and I fidgeted. Professor Martinelli made it clear she expected to see it in the exhibit. It was hard enough putting anything I created on display, but that painting? It would feel like I was baring myself up there on that wall. Like *I* was on display. But Martinelli had made it clear my grade would suffer if I left it out.

"What time?" Pepper asked. "Georgia and I want to go."

"Yeah. I'd like to see your work." Reece nodded. "Maybe I can take the night off."

"Um." I bit my lip. "It's not a big deal. You guys don't have to come."

They exchanged glances before looking back at me. "Why not? Georgia and I went last year—"

"I know," I cut in. "It's just not a big deal. You saw that last year."

"I thought it was awesome. I loved that painting you did of the dog waiting outside the Java Hut."

I smiled in memory. That was one of my favorites, too. I'd snapped the picture on my phone of a dog wearing a jaunty little neck scarf outside the coffeehouse.

"Why don't we meet outside afterward?" I suggested. The last thing I wanted was for them to see the painting of Shaw. Even though it was just his eyes, they would probably recognize him and that was just too mortifying to contemplate. "Really," I insisted. "It's no big deal. You went last year. It's just more of the same."

"I want to go. I would like to see what you've been working on. And don't you want someone there?" The instant the words were out there I could see the apprehension in Pepper's eyes. Fear that she had somehow hurt me with the reminder that I had no one to attend on my behalf. No family that cared enough to come out and support me. Last year family members had crowded the exhibit, all there to support their loved one.

"No. I'm fine. Really." I was accustomed to the lack of family in my life.

"If you're sure," Pepper said, but she still sounded unconvinced. "I really would like to go though."

"Pepper," I chided. "I'm sure you can think of a lot more entertaining things to do. Like tie this hot boyfriend of yours up to a bed or something."

Reece laughed.

"Em!" Pepper looked shocked even though I knew there wasn't much that could shock her these days. Not since she and Reece had hooked up. They couldn't keep their hands off each other. I was surprised they ever left the bedroom.

"Just let us know if you change your mind," Reece said, rubbing Pepper's back. "We want to be there for you."

I nodded, but I knew I wouldn't change my mind. There was no way anyone could see that painting.

ON MONDAY NIGHT, SHAW came to my room. It was a little after eight. I had just gotten home from study group. On top of Friday's showcase, I had a test coming up in my Medieval Art class. To make matters worse, Mom was calling again. I answered her calls, worried that if I didn't talk to her she would just show up in my dorm again. So I endured her recriminations. She went back and forth from accusations to pleas. She even tried bribing me with a trip to Europe.

I had enough on my plate without Shaw showing up. I stared at him through the peephole as he knocked. Three steady knocks. He waited, glancing left and right down the hall, one arm braced along the wall near the door. Holding my breath, I appreciated the square cut of his jaw, the strong line of his nose. The well-carved lips that haunted me still. Everything inside me lurched and responded to the sight of him. *Sexy as hell*. I bit my lip.

"Emerson, you in there?"

I held silent. Compressing my lips, I watched him until he turned away. The sound of his tread faded. In the distance, I heard the ding of the elevator. Releasing the breath I'd been holding, I collapsed against the door, sliding down its length until I was sitting on the floor. At least Georgia wasn't here. I didn't need her witnessing me coming apart over a guy. Especially Shaw. Shaw with his eyes always on me, watching and intent, devouring. Shaw with his shirt off, his body hard, muscles rippling under his tanned skin. He was beautiful. The most beautiful guy I'd ever seen, and it wasn't just his looks. He'd be beautiful twenty years from now. It was a quality he had. A confidence. It was in his voice when he talked about Adam.

When he showed me his bikes. When he told me I needed to pursue my art and screw a desk job. And it was in his eyes when he looked at me. In his hands when they touched me.

I swallowed. I'd clearly let it go too far if I was feeling this way.

Lying in bed that night, I was almost asleep when my phone buzzed beside me. I reached for it on the shelf that edged the bed and stared at the lit screen in the dark.

Shaw: Hey. I stopped by to see you

I bit my lip and stroked the screen with my thumb, almost like I was touching him.

I stared at his words, debating replying or just letting his text go unanswered.

It was as if I could hear the deep purr of his voice. I clutched the phone in both hands and held it close to my chest, at war with myself. I wanted to reply. I wanted to pick up the phone and tell him to come over. But I resisted. After a few minutes, the phone vibrated in my hands. I glanced down anxiously, feeling like a thirteen-year-old girl with her first call from a boy.

Shaw: Good-night, Emerson

BY WEDNESDAY SHAW QUIT texting me altogether, and something in me died a little because I knew he wouldn't anymore. He'd given up. And why shouldn't he? I'd put up all my walls so that he would do just that.

I went to class, spent every free moment I had at the studio. Ate. Slept. Staying busy helped. Until my mind strayed to him. At night it was impossible not to think of him. Alone in my bed, staring into the dark, I should have dropped into a dead sleep. Instead I thought about him. I thought about how I couldn't stop thinking about him and how that had never happened to me before.

Jeff from the Java Hut texted me. At eleven thirty on Thursday night. It didn't take a rocket scientist to figure out what he wanted. I read between his simple words and knew he was looking for a hookup.

It would have been easy. Undemanding and straightforward. He was attractive. We'd hooked up before, but now all I could see was Shaw in my mind. Was this how other girls felt when they got themselves all worked up and desperate over a boy? When they let themselves get used and trampled on? No thanks.

On Friday morning, I was walking to the campus bookstore, which happened to be located across the street from the Grapevine. I stared at the restaurant for a moment before moving to the crosswalk. Before I could even consider what I was doing, I was hurrying across the street and diving inside. The delicious aroma of fresh-baked bread greeted me, but I wasn't interested in food.

To my relief, Beth's was the first face I spotted, standing behind the hostess's podium.

"Emerson," she greeted, her manner as stilted as the last time . . . once I had made it known I was friends with Shaw. "Good to see you again. How many in your party—"

I held up a hand, cutting her off. "I came here to talk to you."

She blinked, and then glanced around uneasily as if she might call for backup.

"Just hear me out." I inhaled, determined to do this. I had to do this. For Shaw. "I know you don't know me, but I—Shaw and I—" Hell, what was I supposed to say? "Shaw's my friend." Forget the fact that he had stopped texting and calling me. Shaw was special. He deserved . . . hell, he deserved everything. He deserved better than me. He deserved to have his family in his life.

I could see it all stretching ahead. Beth inviting him to her wedding. Embracing him back into the fold. Maybe he'd fall in love with one of her bridesmaids. A girl named Amy who liked to fish. She'd bait her own hook and they would fish off the dock at his lake. A year from now, he wouldn't even remember the color of my eyes.

God, I hated Amy.

I swallowed and shoved this imaginary girl from my mind. Moistening my lips, I said in a firm voice, "I care about Shaw."

It was like a shutter fell over her eyes. "Did he send you—"

"No. No, he would never do that, and if you really knew him, then you would know that." Something flickered in her eyes. I stepped closer, softening my voice. "I think you do know that. In fact, he'd probably be pissed if he knew I was talking to you."

She ducked her head and sighed. When she looked back up, moisture glimmered in her eyes. "What do you want from me?"

I'd come this far. I couldn't stop now. "I can't even begin to know what you've gone through. What you and your family have gone through, but Shaw . . . Shaw's your family, too.

You're not the only one who lost Adam. Shaw lost him, too. And he blames himself. He feels responsible for Adam being there. You not talking to him, cutting him out of your life . . . he thinks he deserves that. He thinks he deserves to be alone. And you know he doesn't."

Beth stared at me, saying nothing.

I stepped back, wiping my damp palm against my thigh. "And that's all I needed to say."

I turned and headed for the door.

"Emerson."

I stopped and looked over my shoulder. Beth took one step after me, her gaze sharp and penetrating. "He's not alone anymore. Is he? He has you."

I stared at her for a moment, waiting for the denial to come hard and swift. But I couldn't say it. I couldn't deny her words.

"You care about him," she added.

Emotion rose up in my throat, making speech impossible. Even if I wanted to respond. Even if I could.

Turning, I pushed through the door and stepped out into the cold.

BY THE TIME FRIDAY night arrived, I was a wreck. I couldn't stop thinking about Shaw. Seeing Beth had only made it worse. I ached when I remembered his mouth on mine. The way his eyes looked at me. I thought about when he showed me the bike he was building. Because he thought I would appreciate it. Because he cared about my opinion. Every once in a while I pulled out my phone and read the last text from him.

It didn't help that I spent all my free time putting the finishing touches on his painting, concentrating on the memory of his face. I named it *A Winter's Morning*.

The showcase was held in the Student Memorial Center the same as last year. Lots of wall space and room for easels. It was probably more crowded than the year before, which only made sense. We had more students in the art program this year.

I smiled and made nice as Gretchen introduced me to her parents and grandparents. They'd traveled all the way from Colorado to be here. I mingled, but stayed near my work. Professor Martinelli stressed the importance of being available for discussion.

A Winter's Morning elicited a great deal of attention. This was both gratifying and troubling. It felt like me hanging up there. It wasn't me, I knew. No, it was worse than that. It was Shaw. How I saw him. How he affected me.

"I'm very proud of you, Emerson." My face warmed as Professor Martinelli stopped to stand beside me. "Outstanding work. If you don't mind . . . I have a friend who owns a gallery in Boston. I'd like to show her some of your work." She pointed at my canvas. "Especially this one."

"Really?"

She nodded, studying the canvas thoughtfully. "If you keep this up, I think you have quite the career ahead of you." Winking, she moved away, her bangle bracelets clinking.

I was floating, elated from her praise until I realized she wanted me to produce more work like *A Winter's Morning*. Work that ripped me open and came from someplace inside that I really didn't want to keep visiting. I didn't know if I could

keep this up. If I could do it again. I'd shut myself off from emotions for so long, from anything that felt too raw.

My smile felt pained and brittle after that. I maintained my
composure, smiling and talking. I accepted compliments and
answered questions.

And then I saw him across the crowded room.

Not twenty yards away. He was leaning against the wall,
wearing his leather biker jacket, a thin dusting of snow on his
shoulders. He was so much darkness against the white wall.
A black T-shirt peeped out from his dark jacket. His dark hair.
And those eyes.

He gaze was intent. But not on me. On the painting. The
painting of him.

Bile surged in my throat and I felt like I was going to be
sick. When his gaze jumped from the painting to me I was *posi-
tive* I was going to be sick. Those eyes blazed right through me.

"E-excuse me," I mumbled to the people I'd been talking
to. Wrenching my gaze off Shaw, I commanded my feet to
move. I just couldn't stand facing him with *A Winter's Morning*
hovering over us. The idea of making small talk with him as
he stared at the shadow of his face on canvas made my stomach
turn inside out. I couldn't do it.

It was too much to bear . . . knowing he saw that painting.
I might as well have been standing naked in front of him with
a sign around my neck that said: I LOVE SHAW.

I pushed through the crowd, my heels clacking furiously
over the marble floor. I hoped he wouldn't follow, but somehow knew he would. He didn't come here to stare at me from
afar. And now. Now he had seen the painting.

It was a challenge navigating the room. There were so many people mingling throughout the long gallerylike space. Not to mention waiters walking around with trays.

I probably looked like a madwoman pushing through people as if a guy in a ski mask was after me. I was almost to the front door. From there I could run for my dorm—take the shortcut behind the engineering building. He wasn't a student here. He wouldn't know it. As I came up on the coat-check desk, I didn't even worry about collecting mine. I just kept going.

I was two steps from the double glass doors, ready to push them open, almost free, when a hand clamped down on my wrist.

"Hey, Emerson. I thought that was you. What are you doing here?"

I blinked. It took me a moment to process the barrista from the Java Hut, the very guy who'd texted me the other night.

"H-hello, Jeff. How are you," I said as he pulled me into a close hug, his hands stroking up and down my back.

"Great. My roommate's girlfriend has an exhibit here and I told her I'd come. What about you?" Before I could answer, he draped an arm around me and talked close, into my ear. "I texted you the other night. Thought maybe we can get—"

Before he could even finish his suggestion, Shaw was there, eyes still blazing. He trained his gaze on me. It was like Jeff wasn't even there—or was beneath his notice.

"Emerson," he said tightly, his hand claiming mine. "Let's go."

Jeff's arms tightened around my shoulders. "Hey, buddy—"

Shaw's gaze swung to him, finally giving him his attention. "I'm not your fucking buddy. Now get your arm off her."

Jeff made no move, but I felt his uncertainty in the slight tremble of his body against me.

I opened my mouth to speak but no words arrived.

A muscle ticked in Shaw's jaw. He inhaled and the motion only drew attention to his broad chest. His eyes were hard and dark as they stared at Jeff. In that moment, maybe more than ever, I saw the Marine in him. "You can take your arm off her or I will."

The words had their desired effect. Jeff immediately dropped his arm, holding his hands up in front of him. "Jeez, man, okay. I didn't know she was with you."

Shaw didn't respond. He was finished with him. Unfortunately he was just beginning with me though.

I barely managed a squeak before he hauled me past the coat counter, past a wide-eyed coed. His long legs covered the ground quickly, leading us past the bathroom and around the corner. We passed a few numbered doors. Offices, I guessed. I'd never been in this part of the Student Memorial Center before. The voices of the party were faint and faraway. He spun me around and pressed me against the wall, presumably satisfied we were alone.

He stared down at me, fury glittering in his eyes, his chest a rock-solid wall against me. I didn't know what I expected to see in his face, but it wasn't anger. What did he have to be angry about? Did I need his permission to paint him? I'm the one who should be angry for him showing up uninvited. I suppose feeling anger was better though than what I had felt moments ago—when I'd seen him standing there, his gaze glued to my painting of him. Fear, I hated. Fear, I couldn't allow. Anger, I would gladly take.

"That was totally unnecessary," I hissed. "You embarrassed me."

"I'm done watching other guys paw you, Emerson."

I moistened my lips, thinking that I was done with that, too. I had been. Ever since I met him. His were the only hands I wanted on me, but I wasn't about to admit that. I'd endured enough mortification for one day, thank you very much.

"I almost didn't come to this tonight, you know. You don't answer your door or respond to my texts. You made it pretty clear that you don't want to see me anymore."

I closed my eyes in a long, pained blink. "Why did you come then?" I whispered. "How did you even know about this?"

"Pepper mentioned it."

"Of course she did," I snapped, not having very kind thoughts of my roommate just then. She was supposed to be on my side.

"You almost had me convinced, you know."

A small shiver ran through me as I searched his face, so unbearably close I could see the tiny flecks of gold in his eyes. Our breaths panted, mingling between us. Even though a whisper inside me warned that I should just let the subject drop, I demanded, "Convinced of what?"

"That I should quit. That I should give up on you. That's what you wanted me to do." He paused, letting the words sink in the thick air between us. "But now I've seen your painting and I know better."

I shook my head, a protest forming on my lips, but the words never made it out.

His mouth crushed mine, slanting over my lips and robbing me of any coherent thought.

My world spun. He was everything then. His lips hot and consuming. His tongue tangled with mine. My arms looped around his neck. He leaned into me, pressing the hard length of himself against my body. His hands were everywhere. My face, my neck. They skimmed down my body to my hips, clutching the black fabric of my dress in his fists and holding me there.

He dragged his mouth down my throat and, honest to God, I saw spots. My head dropped back and lolled against the wall. I felt as limp as a rag doll, my blood molten, my muscles like Jell-O. His hands cupped my bottom, pulling me harder against him, grinding his erection into me and I moaned.

He lifted his head and looked down at me with eyes that were as deep and dark as a bottomless well. "Let's get out of here."

I nodded dumbly.

Grabbing my hand, he led me back the way we had come and straight out the front doors. My adrenaline pumped hard and fast through me as we hurried the few blocks to my building. I trembled as the cold bit into me.

"Fuck, you're cold," he said, stopping. He shrugged off his jacket and put it around me. I slid my arms through the too big sleeves, immediately enveloped in his heat, in the clean, musky scent of him.

He grabbed my hand again and we continued. I was waiting for the voice. The one in my head that had always stopped me from going too far before. It never came. There was just this blood-pounding need, this hunger—and him, pulling me along like we were racing for our lives.

He caught the outside door as someone was leaving and held it open for me. The twenty-second wait for the elevator was excruciating. The simple contact of his hand, his strong fingers laced with my fingers, the throb of his pulse bleeding into me was enough to keep the blood roaring in my ears and my feet shifting in place.

The fire still burned in his eyes. It scalded me. The elevator doors opened with a swoosh and we stepped inside. The doors had barely shut before he hauled me in his arms again, lifting me off my feet and kissing me until my lips felt numb. I kissed him back. Kissing and gasping, mouth parting for the invasion of his tongue.

I didn't even register the ding of the elevator telling us we'd reached our floor. He tore his lips from mine and pulled me after him to my room. I fished my key out of the small purse dangling from my wrist and unlocked the door.

I stepped inside my room alongside Shaw and froze, my chest heaving as though I had just run a marathon and wasn't the most turned on I'd ever been in my life.

"Hey, Em, how'd it go?" Georgia's greeting served as a slap in the face.

"H-hi, Georgia. Good. It was good." Did that breathy, throaty voice belong to me? "I-uh, bumped into Shaw." I motioned to him with a weak wave of my hand. He still held my hand and did not appear inclined to let go. In fact, his jaw was locked and he looked rather incapable of speech.

"Hi," he managed to get out. Twin brackets edged his tight-looking mouth. "How's it going?" His voice actually sounded like it was in pain. I shot him a helpless look. Maybe this was a sign? Maybe we just needed to take a minute and—

He shook his head swiftly at me as though he could read the direction of my thoughts, his eyes searing and intent.

"Well. I-uh, was just on my way out."

At this statement my attention whipped back to Georgia. "You're leaving?" My heart picked up speed again.

"Yeah. I'm uh, going to study at Harris's place. You two can hang out here." Bending over in her chair, she quickly stuffed her feet into her tennis shoes. Rising, she crammed her books and a notebook into her backpack. Shaw and I stood awkwardly, tension swimming in the air around us. I'm sure Georgia could feel it, too.

It was clear she was leaving so we could be alone. I knew it. Shaw knew it. She knew we knew it. Considering that, it felt silly to pretend otherwise, but we did.

At the door, she grabbed her coat off its hook. "Well, night. Good seeing you again, Shaw."

He gave her a distracted smile. "You, too."

"Bye, Em."

With that parting farewell, the door clicked shut after her. And we were all alone.

Chapter 15

ISLIPPED MY HAND from his and stepped back, all nerves again. We'd been alone before, but everything felt stripped away right now. Exposed. He'd seen the painting. I couldn't pretend anymore that he didn't affect me. He knew he did, and he wasn't going away this time. I couldn't make him leave.

I didn't want to.

I slipped the strap of my small handbag from my wrist and dropped it onto my cluttered desktop. His feet moved in a slow half circle as his eyes followed me.

"How long have you been working on that painting?"

Oh. He was going right for the jugular then and cornering me about the painting. I angled my head as I slid off his jacket and draped it on the back of my chair. Shrugging lamely, I slipped off my earrings. Dropping them on my desk, I said simply, "I don't want to talk about the painting."

"Say nothing. Reveal nothing. That's your MO." He approached me with slow steps and I felt stalked. I moved aimlessly, staying just out of his reach, wishing the room was bigger right then as he closed in on me. "But silence reveals, too, you know."

"Yeah? And what have I revealed?"

"You're scared of me."

I shook my head fiercely.

"Yes," he announced, smiling grimly. "Because you feel something for me."

My heart beat faster. "Arrogant, aren't we?"

"That's my face up on the wall at your fancy art show. Not any other guy's. Admit it. You like me."

I snorted. "Maybe I just think you're hot . . . a good subject to paint."

"You like me," he repeated, pausing to reach behind his neck and pull his shirt over his head. My chest ached, actually hurt as I took in his masculine beauty. At the hard abs that could probably break a fist.

"Maybe I just want to fuck you," I flung out, waving at him with a shaky hand. "You said I'd beg you to. And I mean, look at you. You look like someone who would be good at it."

His eyes almost appeared dilated they were so dark. His smile deepened with satisfaction, and there was such wicked promise in the curve of his lips that I knew I was in good hands.

His gaze dropped, skimming my body. "Nice dress."

"Thanks."

His hand toyed with the thin blue belt that wrapped around my waist. It took me only a second to realize he wasn't merely toying with it. As though he knew exactly how it functioned, he undid the tiny silver bow that clasped at the front. It fell to the floor with a soft thud.

"I bet it would look even better on the floor." He bent slightly, watching my face as he clutched the hem of my dress and pulled it up over my head in one swift move.

A cool draft swept over me. It was just me in my bra and panties. Black satin and lace. His breath caught. Just a few inches separated us, but he didn't touch me. I could feel the warmth radiating from his body to mine but he didn't lift a finger to touch me. He only stared at me, his gaze hot and devouring.

I moved to kick off my heels but his voice stopped me. "Leave them on."

I froze under his perusal, resisting the urge to cover myself with my hands. I had never been the shy type, but with him I was. With him everything was different. Everything was new.

He wrapped his arms around me. I reveled at his maleness, at the flex of his biceps. Our foreheads touched as he spoke, the words fanning my lips, "I'll take what you're willing to give me, Emerson." His hands gripped my bottom. "For now." In one move, he lifted me off my feet and guided my legs around his waist. "We can start here."

Then he was kissing me again. Hot, drugging kisses as he carried me slowly to the bed, his big hands clenching on my bottom, singeing me through my panties as his mouth slanted one way and then the next.

I wrapped my arms around him, relishing the sensation of his back under my fingers, the quiver of his smooth flesh as he carried me.

He sat down on the bed with me straddling his lap. His hands moved to my face, broad palms cupping my cheeks, fingers burrowing into my hair as we kissed, our heads angling as if we couldn't taste enough of each other.

There was no such thing as too close. My breasts smashed against his chest. I was desperate, hungry for more of him, loving the hard strength of him surrounding me. The pressure of his mouth increased. He nipped me with his teeth before dragging his open mouth down my throat. When he got to where my shoulder and neck met, he bit down, not hard enough to hurt but enough for me to release a shuddery moan.

He slipped the thin straps of my bra down my shoulders until the cups sagged loose. He closed both hands over my aching breasts. I arched into his palms. His dark head descended and his mouth closed over one nipple, drawing it deep into the warm heat of his mouth.

"Oh, God," I cried, burying my hands in his hair and holding him to me. "Don't stop."

He moved his mouth to my other breast, his words fanning over my moist nipple. "We're just getting started. This is going to take all night."

A shudder ran through me at his words, at what his mouth was doing to me. I felt his hands at my back, unhooking the clasp of my bra. It fell down between us. The only thing barring me from complete nudity was the slight scrap of my underwear. His hands gripped my waist and ground me down harder against his erection. Moaning, I widened my thighs and rocked against him, searching for relief. He felt delicious, hard and insistent against the heat of me, and I throbbed. My belly clenched with need and I writhed, wiggling desperately against him, losing whatever rhythm I'd found in my rocking movements. My panties grew wet. I couldn't take another minute of this. My fingers dug into his back, urging him on.

My dazed gaze focused on his face. "Please."

"What? What do you want?"

My hands went for his belt, fingers fumbling, hating that he still wore his jeans. That I wore my panties. That there was any barrier at all between us. "This. I want you. Inside me."

There. I'd said it. I didn't even regret it. I just wanted it to happen. *Now.*

In one swift move, he lifted me off him and set me down on the bed. I watched, every part of me trembling as he stood and made quick work of removing his boots and jeans.

He stood before me in tight black briefs that did nothing to hide the hard outline of him. My eyes widened at the sight of his bulge. I squeezed my thighs together in an attempt to assuage the pulsing ache at my core, but it didn't work. There was only one cure for that and I was staring right at him.

I slid off the bed and stood before him. I touched his face lightly, loving the bristly scrape of his cheek under my fingers.

His eyes ate me up. "Emerson," he breathed. He pressed an open-mouthed kiss to my palm. Wrapping his arms around me, he lifted me off my feet, his forearm coming under my bottom, bringing me to eye level.

He came down over me on the bed. I felt small and delicate as he kissed his way down my body. He was so much bigger than me, hard and muscled, and I felt fragile. Cherished. *Loved.*

His hands hooked around my panties and slid them down my thighs and past my ankles. I couldn't summon the slightest will to resist. No protest jumped to my lips. Shockingly enough, I felt like everything in my life had been leading to this moment where I finally released control. When I finally trusted someone else. When I let Shaw in.

His fingers touched me, feather light, skimming up the inside of my thighs, I arched, clawing my duvet cover as his fingers found me, parted me, and delved into my heat.

"Shaw," I choked out, bewildered as his thumb found that tiny, hidden nub and pressed down on it, and then rolled it between his fingers. He'd done this to me before, but the memory paled in comparison to this moment. To now. "Shaw, please."

"Not yet." He slid down my body and put his mouth there. I screeched and came up off the bed. He flattened a hand against my belly, holding me down as his fingers pushed and pulled back the tiny hood of my clit, drawing it between his lips, his tongue playing against me as he sucked.

I gasped and shuddered, sensation eddying out from the spot where his mouth worked on me to every single nerve in my body. I seized his head, fisting his hair. His hands slid under my ass, lifting me higher and holding me in place for him like I was some kind of feast.

"Shaw, please!"

"Tell me, baby." His lips moved against me and this only made me wilder. I tugged on his hair, trying to bring him back up on top of me. He continued to work my oversensitized flesh with his lips, tongue, and teeth, toying with me. I released a long, keening moan as he eased one finger deep inside me, adding to my torment.

"Tell me," he demanded, adding a second finger inside

me, pushing deeper, hitting a spot that sent me spiraling. His mouth sucked me harder then, only adding to the intensity of my orgasm, making it go on forever.

I was still shaking, pleasure rushing through me when he disappeared from my body.

"Shaw," I moaned his name, squirming where he left me on the bed, watching him in a daze as he shed his briefs and fumbled with his discarded jeans. I heard a slight crinkle of paper and he was back, settling between my thighs. There was a rip of paper and I knew he had a condom—that he was putting it on.

Still no panic. No urge to jump off the bed and run away. I wanted this. I wanted him. Unbelievable as it all seemed.

Then his mouth was on mine again and I arched up, my tongue parrying with his. The hard length of him slid along my wetness, not penetrating, just teasing against my opening. The friction tantalized me, and I lifted my hips, my breath in shallow pants. "Please. Please," I begged.

"What, Emerson? What?" His dark eyes glinted down at me. "I won't. I'm not moving a muscle until you say it. What do you want from me?"

"I want you." My nails dug into the skin of his back.

"What do you want me to do? Say it."

"Take me . . . fuck me." I moistened my lips, something else running through my mind.

And like he knew that, like he could read my mind, his hand cupped my face. His mouth brushed my ear. "I'm going to do that, baby. But what else?" Goose bumps broke out across my skin at the hot fan of his breath against the whorls of my ear. "Say what else I'm going to do to you. You know."

I knew what he wanted to hear. I remembered what he had promised to do to me.

"Make love to me." Was that my voice? I didn't even recognize the low purr. "I want you to make love to me . . .

He pulled back to smile, slow and wicked, at me, and a shiver rushed through me. "All right then."

I felt him then. The head of him right there, his hardness easing inside me. It was surreal. My fingers clenched his biceps like I was clinging to a lifeline. My wide eyes flitted everywhere, seeing nothing, feeling everything, excited and alarmed at what was happening.

At what was *finally* happening.

"God, Emerson," he groaned, dropping his head in the crook of my shoulder, his mouth moving against my sensitive flesh as he added, "You feel so good."

His hands slid under my back, his fingers curling over my shoulders, anchoring me between his body and the bed, pulling me even closer, if possible.

And then he plunged, pushing deep inside me, tearing through the thin barrier of my virginity, seating himself to the hilt, his fingers tight on my shoulders.

"Oh!" I gasped at the sudden invasion, at the sharp pain. I felt stretched, full in a way I had never imagined possible. My muscles stretched to accommodate him, burning and throbbing around his hard length.

He stiffened over me, his head lifting off my shoulder. "Look at me." I fixed my gaze on him. He smoothed a lock of hair from my forehead. His dark eyes gleamed with emotion . . . something that looked suspiciously like regret. "Why didn't you tell me?"

I shook my head, unable to form words, too busy adjusting to him, processing everything. Like how he actually seemed to grow inside me. How my muscles clenched around him and that shot sensation to every nerve in my body. How could I explain *anything* at a time like this? Certainly not that I was a fake. *A virgin.* It was my secret. At least it had been. Now it was neither a secret nor true and I just wanted to move on to the obvious benefits of not being a virgin any longer.

I wiggled, testing out the feel of him in me.

"Oh, God," he groaned. "Baby, don't. When you do that, I just . . . *don't.*" He started to withdraw and that slight movement made me moan. My hands flew to his ass, dragging him back inside me. That slight thrust made me gasp and arch under his body. "Don't leave me."

"Oh, Emerson, I couldn't if I wanted to." His bracketed arms trembled on either side of me. "But you probably shouldn't move right now," he hissed.

"I can't." I had to move. It was like something propelled me. It certainly wasn't experience that had me lifting my hips up and down, seeking a repeat of the friction that I'd just experienced. With him over me, pinning me to the bed, I couldn't move enough and I let out a sound of frustration, my nails clawing him.

His hips lifted then, pulling out almost completely. I whimpered at the drag of him against my aching flesh, clenching his firm ass, hoping this was it. He would finally move, finally satisfy my desperate hunger.

His cock hovered at my entrance. I felt the top of him there, and it killed me. Small, animal-like sounds I didn't even recognize escaped me. Finally, he thrust deep once again, his hands anchoring on my hips. There was no pain this time, just pleasure. "God, Emerson. You're so perfect, so tight."

He kept a steady pace then, slow and even, cautious, almost like he was worried that he would hurt me if he let go, if he went faster. The friction drove me wild. A pressure built at my center, coiling in my belly. My body demanded more, needed it harder.

I angled my hips, taking more of him inside me, following my instincts, searching for a way to bring him closer, deeper, to assuage that ache that only seemed to pulse and grow. "More," I pleaded.

"Emerson," he choked. "You don't know. You're so small—"

"I won't break," I growled. Lifting my head, I bit him, my teeth clamping down on his shoulder and it was like I flipped some invisible switch in him.

"Fuck!" He moved then, his big hands sliding under my bottom and lifting me higher, holding me off the bed, angling me in a way that changed everything. Stars blinded me as he slammed into me, hitting that magic spot buried inside me. I screamed his name, my spine arching, head dropping back on the bed as he did precisely what I asked. He took me. He fucked me. He loved me. And I knew with a sense of shock that this was more than sex. He'd stamped himself not just on a canvas for me. He'd etched himself on *me*. Indelibly. He was under my skin. In my blood. A part of my soul.

I shuddered, coming apart. His arms wrapped around me, pulling me close as he joined me, pumping several more times until he shuddered and then stilled. I clutched him close, one hand buried in his hair, the other at his back.

The sound of our ragged breaths filled the air. I didn't want to let go, didn't want to face the questions I would see in his eyes.

His head turned to press an open-mouthed kiss to the side of my neck. "Emerson."

A question hung in the sound of my name. I sighed, relaxing my arms around him. He pulled back and studied me for a moment before rising up from the bed. I watched him, a twisting ache in my chest. I'd done it. Given up control. And I was terrified. I pasted a smile on my face and hoped it didn't look too thin. I sat up and reached for his shirt, pulling it over my head. I curled my knees together, wincing a little at the soreness between my legs.

He watched me carefully as he disposed of the condom. My face burned. He pulled several tissues from my Kleenex box and then sat back down on the bed. "Let me."

I shook my head fiercely, mortified. "I can do it." I snatched the tissues from his hand and turned halfway on the bed, cleaning myself off. The sight of the blood on the white tissue only drove home what I had just done. I wadded up the evidence in my hand and rose to dispose of it in the trash can. While I was up, I grabbed a fresh pair of panties from my drawer.

"Emerson." The sound of his deep voice pulled my gaze back to him. So unbelievably hot and still naked. Not a flicker of embarrassment crossed his features. "Why?" He shook his head like he didn't even know where to begin.

I decided to make it easy for him and get to the point. "I never said I wasn't a virgin."

"But you let everyone—me—assume—"

"I can't help what people think." Lame, I know, but if I was honest with him, I would be giving him too much of myself and I'd already given him enough for tonight.

"C'mon." His mouth quirked into that sexy half grin. "What about Pepper and Georgia? Do they even know?"

I looked away at that, unable to hold his gaze. I let Pepper and Georgia assume I was experienced—maybe even implied it on more than one occasion.

"Wow. Your own best friends."

"Why should it matter?" I snapped, looking back at him.

"It doesn't. I still would have wanted you. I still do." His eyes gleamed fiercely. "But I might have liked to know before this happened." He motioned between us. "I could have made it better—"

"You were fine." I dropped on the bed beside him, splaying a hand on his chest, directly over the tattoo. *Fine?* Try amazing. "Better than fine. It was . . ." I paused, suddenly self-conscious under his intent gaze. "It was beautiful."

He dipped his head swiftly and kissed me then, long and tender. I would never have suspected when I first spotted this guy at Maisie's that he was capable of such tenderness. That Hot Biker Boy would be the one to change everything. Change me.

He broke the kiss and whispered against my mouth, "No more secrets. I want to know the real Emerson."

The real Emerson. The idea of that sent a bolt of panic through me. Could I do that? Could I be real with him? I nodded, determined to try. I'd come this far.

"Good." He sat up and reached for the lamp, his muscled bicep flexing as he stretched his arm and flipped it off.

He came back down, pulling me against his hard body. Smooth, warm, male skin surrounded me. I found my voice. "W-what are you—"

"Staying the night."

I swallowed, thinking about my rules. Spending the night with a guy was a big no-no. One of my cardinal rules. But then so was sex and that had just kind of gone out the window. I sighed and nestled my head against his chest.

I guess it was a night for breaking rules.

Chapter 16

A N INSISTENT KNOCKING WOKE me. Blinking, I sat up, clutching the sheets to my bare chest. Shaw was already up and buttoning his jeans. I paused, gawking at him. There was no other word for it. With sunlight streaming through the blinds, there was no hiding the brilliance of his body. Seriously. He was criminally hot. Everything about him shouted strength and power. Heat washed over my face as I recalled that body joined with mine—as I remembered how easily he had lifted me up in his arms. His body wasn't created from hours at the gym. It was the result of his life. Playing sports. Years in the Marines. Hours of labor. He was real. He wasn't a boy. He was a man. A man who made me feel like a woman for the first time in my life.

The knocking started up again and jarred me to action. I scrambled to my feet, yanked his shirt off me and tossed it at him. He grinned, his eyes devouring me as I darted to my closet in my panties.

I slipped on a pair of yoga pants and a University of Dartford sweatshirt as he pulled his shirt back on. A glance at the clock revealed it was eight forty-five A.M. I didn't know who it could be, but the RA was rather free with her master key. If it was Heather, I didn't want to risk her walking in on us partially dressed.

Shaking my hair back on my shoulders, I pulled the door open and faced a girl I had never seen.

She clutched the strap of her messenger bag, her wide eyes sweeping over me. "Emerson?"

"Uh, yes."

She held out her hand. "I'm Melanie, Justin's fiancée."

Heat flashed through me, followed by a sudden rush of cold. Justin's fiancée. What was she doing here? I glanced over my shoulder at Shaw. He watched curiously.

She followed my gaze, noticing him. Pink brightened her cheeks. *Wholesome.* That's the word that popped into my mind. This girl was sweet and wholesome. And she was marrying Justin. Ugh. That made about as much sense as bananas going into a peanut butter sandwich.

"Oh. Hello." She waved once at him.

Shaw stepped forward and offered his hand. "Hello, I'm Shaw."

She visibly relaxed at the courtesy, shaking his hand in turn. I certainly hadn't shown her any such courtesy. I was too bewildered at her appearance. "Melanie."

"Emerson's boyfriend," he added.

My gaze whipped to him and I forgot that Justin's fiancée was standing in my doorway. He looked at me mildly, as if he hadn't uttered the most shocking thing. *Boyfriend?* I'd never had a boyfriend before. There had been boys, sure, but I'd never had a *boyfriend*. To hear him call himself that both thrilled and terrified me.

"Oh," Melanie practically gushed now, drawing my attention back to her. "It's so nice to meet you, Shaw."

Feeling annoyed, I asked as gently as possible, but there was really no way to take the bite from my words, "Melanie . . . why are you here?"

Her cheeks colored again. "I know this is unexpected . . ." She shook her head and smiled weakly. "This is more awkward than I thought it would be."

Suddenly she riffled through her bag and pulled out two envelopes. "I know you probably got these already. We mailed them, but here are the invitations to the wedding and the rehearsal dinner. It's next weekend."

"I know," I said through numb lips. "I got them."

"Yes, well. I'd love for you to be there. Justin and your mother . . . well, they've told me all about you."

They did?

"Did my mom send you? Or Justin?"

Her pretty blue eyes widened. "Neither one actually sent me. But they know I'm here. Your mother is heartbroken that you won't come."

I swallowed back a snort. In order for her to be heartbroken she would have to possess a heart. "What did she tell you?"

"Er, just that you two had a fight a while back."

Try five years ago.

"I know it's none of my business. I'm not trying to pry. It would just mean so much to her and Justin if you came. And, well, me. I'm an only child . . . I kind of thought it would be nice to have a sister-in-law." She smiled that smile again, her hands fluttering self-consciously in front of her. Genuine and self-effacing, and the insane urge to tell this girl to run as far as she could from my stepbrother and mother seized me. I wanted to warn her that she was marrying into one ginormous hot mess of a family. Mom. Justin. Even my blah of a stepfather. All three of them equated the family from hell. A crazy impulse, of course. If I did that I would have to explain why, and I wasn't having that conversation. Especially not in front of Shaw.

Not for the first time I entertained the thought that my stepbrother had changed. The possibility—the *hope*—had been there ever since that phone call. Melanie seemed like a smart girl. I doubted she was diving into marriage without knowing the man she was marrying. She at least knew him better than I did. These days anyway. I couldn't claim to know Justin at all anymore. Could I still hold him to the same judgment of five years ago?

"Here, just take them . . . . in case you lost the others." She thrust the invitations into my hand. "Feel free to bring Shaw." She flashed a sparkling smile at him. "It should be a lot of fun. The menu is amazing. Daddy pulled some strings and got last year's James Beard winner to cater the wedding."

"Sounds fabulous," I murmured.

"Friday night's rehearsal dinner is at the Four Seasons, overlooking the Public Garden. Your mother would have nothing less. It might even outdo the wedding." Melanie started to edge out the door, but she hesitated before turning back around and folding me in a hug. "I hope we can be friends, Emerson." Her lips brushed my hair as she spoke.

I patted her back awkwardly. *Damnit*. Why did she have to be so nice?

Releasing me, she stepped back, her cheeks pink again. She really was a Girl Scout. "Well. I hope to see you soon. At the wedding or . . . maybe Easter."

Easter? Did she think I regularly spent holidays with my mother? I nodded rather than explain how that wasn't going to happen. "Bye." With a flutter of her fingers, she turned and disappeared down the hall. I closed the door behind her.

Shaw arched an eyebrow. "What was that about?"

I shrugged. "Family."

"Yeah. Apparently yours wants you to attend a wedding."

"I'm not going." I moved for my closet and grabbed my shower caddy, still bewildered by Melanie's visit and needing something to do with myself.

He reached for my hand, stopping me. "Why does it sound like there's a story there and you're trying to avoid sharing it?"

I shrugged. "I'm not tight with my mom. Even less so with my stepbrother." I lifted my robe off the hook.

"Why?"

Why?

Such a simple question, but loaded with so much pain. I lifted my gaze to Shaw, my chest tight and aching. For the first time there was a longing to unload, to unleash everything that I'd kept bottled up inside me all these years. Maybe because of last night. Maybe because he knew almost everything about me already. He was closer to knowing the real me than anyone else. Could I tell him the rest?

He must have seen something in my face because he

squared himself before me, both of his hands on me now, gently chafing my arms. "Hey, it's okay. You can tell me, Em. I want to know. You can tell me anything."

I nodded jerkily, the scald of tears rising up in my throat. He tugged me toward the bed and forced me down on his lap.

"I'm a mess," I choked, warm tears dashing down my cheeks.

"Hey. Ssh." His fingers ran over my cheeks, the callused pads wiping the tears away. "I didn't mean to make you cry."

I sniffed noisily. And I couldn't believe I was crying. I wasn't the type of girl to cry in some guy's arms. I wasn't weak like that.

"It's not you." I sniffed again, wiping at my nose. "She just . . ." I motioned to the door where Melanie had just stood. "She seemed so nice, right?"

"Yeah." He nodded, his expression worried as he watched my face.

I sucked in a wet breath. "I can't believe she's marrying Justin. He's such a douche." I stopped and exhaled, shaking my head. "No. I always blame my stepbrother, but he's not really the one who's turned me into this." I waved at myself.

"And what is 'this'?" he asked. His fingers stilled on my cheek. His touch was feather soft, and my heart squeezed a little. "I happen to like *this*."

I snorted. "*This* is a girl who flirts and parties and acts a big game but is really just a big phony. I've used guys for years. Played them." *Until you*.

He was quiet a long moment, staring at me. I laughed humorlessly. "No denial there."

He nodded once. "I kind of figured out that you had less experience than you pretended to have. Even before last night, I knew. The real question is—why? Why have you been doing this?"

I sucked in a breath. He was going there, poking around all those raw and tender places. I'd started this though. No backing down now. "I did it because it made me feel in control . . . and I guess I got off on calling the shots and manipulating boys." There was so little I controlled. I had parents who didn't really want me around. My mother put everything else before me. She always had. When I was fifteen I'd learned how little she valued me. It was a harsh lesson. I was still a kid then. I thought mothers protected their daughters. Not mine. My world flew off its axis then. It had been off course ever since.

With another deep breath, I met his stare head-on, part of me stunned to be confessing this to him, but the other part? There was only relief. Like I was releasing a pent-up breath. "But I couldn't do that with you."

"Emerson," he said gently, his fingers flexing on my arms. "What happened to you?"

"When my mother started dating Don, I was living with her. I moved in with Dad afterward. After she chose Don over me." I sniffed again, bitterness filling me as I remembered the morning I approached my mother and told her that Justin had crept into my room the night before. He had just come home from a night out with his friends. His breath reeked of alcohol. I guess I should be grateful that he was so drunk. It made him clumsy.

"After what? What happened?"

"At first I thought Justin was nice. He always paid me attention. He was twenty and drove a cool car. All my friends thought he was cute. I was fifteen, an only child. Suddenly having a cool older brother was . . . well, cool."

Shaw's face hardened and I knew he'd already guessed where this was headed, but he said nothing, just nodded for me to continue.

"It was just little things at first. He would always touch me, brush my hair back from my face. Then he started walking in on me in the bathroom, my bedroom . . . he acted like it was an accident . . ."

"Bastard."

"I told my mom he was making me uncomfortable and she told me I was being silly. Then New Year's Eve happened. It was really late. I'd stayed up to watch the ball drop and went to bed afterward. He came in my room drunk. Good thing, I guess. He wasn't that coordinated, so I could shove him off before he did anything. He passed out on the floor next to my bed. I actually left him there and slept in the guest room. With the door locked. Mom and Don were out."

Shaw's gaze glittered brightly with a light I'd never seen before in his eyes. "He deserves to be in jail. What did your mom do when she got home?"

I shrugged. "Nothing. She told me that even if it happened, I was exaggerating the event. And that's when she let me know she was marrying Don and I needed to learn to get along with Justin."

"Oh, Emerson." His hand cupped my face, his thumb grazing my cheek back and forth.

"That hurt the most, you know. It's not so much what my stepbrother did. He was nothing to me. But Mom? Her betrayal was the worst thing. She's my mother. She's supposed to protect me. What did I do for her—"

"No. It's not you." His hands tightened slightly on me. "Baby, there's something broken in her. A mother would die protecting her kid."

I nodded, looking away, blinking burning eyes.

"I would, Emerson. I would die protecting you."

My gaze jerked back to his face, my heart clenching at his words. They were words I hadn't realized I needed to hear, but I guess I did. I needed to believe that someone cared enough to fight for me. That someone could love—

I killed the thought before it fully formed. No one had said the L word. Certainly not him. I wasn't going to allow myself to even think it. Shaw was a Marine. He was conditioned to serve and protect. I didn't need to read more into it than that.

He kissed me. His warm lips moved over mine. I slid my tongue along his, pouring all my feelings into it, all the turmoil that Melanie's visit had stirred in me, all the emotions that this conversation with Shaw had created.

His hand cupped the back of my head. I deepened the kiss, pressing against him, delighting in the way my breasts mashed against his chest. I looped my arms around his neck. We fell back on the bed, me splayed over him, our mouths fused, slanting one way and then another, growing hotter, more feverish.

He stopped abruptly, holding the hair back from my face with both hands as he looked up at me. "No way can you go to that wedding." His eyes scanned my face, intent and determined.

"I wasn't going to."

Concern etched the lines of his face like he wasn't fully convinced, but he nodded. "Good. I don't want you anywhere near your stepbrother." Some of my hair fell forward, dangling between us, and he smoothed it back with his palm, wincing a little as he added, "Maybe I don't have any right to get all caveman and tell you that . . ."

I pulled back slightly. No one ever told me what to do. I'd been on my own too long to let a guy start controlling me now. It was one thing to sleep with him, but he couldn't start dictating my actions. If that happened, then I had given up all control entirely.

He exhaled a great breath, evidently reading my reaction accurately. "I know I sound like a controlling prick."

Suddenly I remembered him at the club, informing me that I had had enough to drink right before he yanked me out of there. I shook my head, unwilling to consider any of this right now and ruin whatever tenuous bond that was forming between us. "But it's a nonissue anyway because I wasn't planning to go."

His thumb gently stroked my cheek. "It's not only your stepbrother, you know. It's your mother, too. She doesn't deserve a daughter like you, Em. And I don't trust her not to hurt you again."

Okay, so he was bossy and high-handed and sent my feminist hackles sputtering, but he was sweet, too. He gave a damn. He cared. I let him in and he reacted with concern. With more than concern. There was a hint of . . . I don't know . . . possession in those words. In his expression. Like a part of me belonged to him now. Like we belonged to each other. *God.* And I guess I wanted that. He tempted me on every level. It was beyond appealing to just lose myself in him and let him protect me.

Only it wasn't that simple. I shook my head slightly as if to jog some sense into myself. She was my mother. Nothing could change that. He couldn't save me from what I was. He couldn't save me from everything wrong in my life. But a part of me melted to realize that he wanted to. My hand crept up between us to cup his face. My palm flattened against his cheek, fingers curling inward ever so slightly. I reveled in the scratchy hint of beard coming in.

Suddenly the door to the room opened and Georgia stepped inside. "Oh, sorry," she mumbled. "I should have texted to make sure you didn't have company." She turned away, but not before I glimpsed her ravaged face—and ravaged was putting it mildly. It was splotchy pink and her eyes were puffy and bloodshot.

"Georgia!" I hopped off Shaw and rushed to her side. "What's wrong? What happened?"

She shook her head, trying to turn away. I took hold of her arms and turned her around gently. She buried her face in her hands and spoke between her fingers. "I don't want to interrupt—"

"Georgia, tell me what happened," I insisted.

"It's Harris."

"What happened? Is he okay?"

"Oh, he's great." She laughed brokenly, the sound wretched and lacking all levity. "It's over. He ended it. Five years . . . and it's done. Gone."

I inhaled sharply. "What? Why?"

"Apparently I'm boring. He said he wants someone more . . . adventurous. Can you believe that? And guess what? He already has her picked out. He's been seeing a girl in his econ class behind my back."

"That asshole!" I exploded.

Shaw lightly touched my arm. "I'm going to go." He pressed a quick kiss to my lips, flicking a sympathetic look at Georgia. "I'll text you later, Em."

I nodded, watching him as he slipped from the room. With a snap of my head, I refocused on Georgia.

She sniffed back a wet sob as the door clicked shut. "You and Shaw . . . I guess things are going well."

"Let's not talk about me right now, honey." I smoothed a hand over her back in soothing circles.

"No. Let's talk about you. I'm so happy that you've finally found someone." She smiled, clearly miserable but determined to shift the focus from her to me. "Guess it's my turn to be single now."

I hauled her closer, hugging her taller frame. "Maybe he's just stressed. Maybe you guys can work it out—"

"He's seeing someone else, Em."

I winced. "Yeah. Well. You two have been together for a long time. He's going to be miserable without you. He'll come to his senses. Maybe he'll—"

"Emerson. I appreciate what you're doing, but it's done. You didn't see his face. It's over."

I nodded, a lump rising up in my throat. For Georgia. For the quiver of pain I heard in her voice. I hated that she hurt. She didn't deserve this, but it was happening anyway.

I nodded resolutely. "I know this is the last thing you want to hear . . . but I always knew you were too good for him." I looked at her anxiously, biting my bottom lip. "Too soon?"

She laughed weakly. "Now you tell me."

"You'll see. It's hard to believe now, but—"

"I'll be glad it happened? This is all for the best?"

I shook my head. "I'd suck if I said that." Even if I thought it. Even if I had thought she would be better off without Harris all along, I wouldn't be that insensitive. "I wasn't going to say that at all." I tucked her hair behind her ear. "I was going to say, how do you feel about going out for some pancakes?"

A shaky smile curved her lips. "Chocolate chip pancakes?"

"Are there any other kind?"

Chapter 17

A SQUIRREL? ARE YOU kidding me?" Georgia rocked on the bed, clutching her bag of Twizzlers to her chest as she laughed. As far as she was concerned Twizzlers went with Chinese food like milk went with cookies, and since she was the girl mourning the loss of a five-year relationship, who was I to argue?

Pepper cuddled with Georgia on her bed while I stretched out on mine, several white cartons from the Golden Palace between us. *Law and Order* played on the television. A safer choice than the romantic comedies that seemed to be on every other channel.

"I kid you not. He was a giant squirrel . . . man." I waved my hands all around me for emphasis. "And he kept bumping me with his squirrel penis!" I sat up on my knees on my bed and jerked my hips for illustration. "It was more like a body check really."

Pepper's eyes bulged. "A squirrel penis? What did that even look like? I mean was it . . . squirrel size?"

I settled back on the bed, shaking my head. "I'm not an

authority on squirrel penises, but this one—" I gestured with my hands. "About so big, so I'm gonna go with no."

Georgia's laughter turned into gasps. She fell sideways on the bed.

"Are you serious?" Pepper paused, her fingers clutching popcorn midway to her mouth. "All the girl squirrels must have run away screaming when they saw him coming."

"It took everything in *me* not to run away screaming."

"Oh, oh! Stop! I can't breathe," Georgia wheezed, her laughter slowing to pants.

"And you didn't want to stay after that?" Pepper teased. "The infamous kink club didn't live up to your expectations?"

I shrugged. "Not all of it was that absurd. There were some"—I searched for the right word, remembering the sounds drifting from rooms upstairs—"interesting things going on for the more adventurous in spirit."

Georgia's grin slipped away. *Damn.* Poor word choice. She'd gone over in more detail all the reasons Harris had given her for breaking up. The fact that she was predictable, unexciting, and all-around boring being his chief points. *Asshat.* He actually told Georgia that their sex life sucked.

Pepper mouthed at me: *Nice going.*

I shrugged helplessly, feeling wretched.

"Maybe I need to go then," Georgia said glumly, rolling onto her back and flinging her arm over her forehead. "Maybe I could learn how to not be so boring."

"You? At a kink club?" Pepper wrinkled her nose.

"See!" Georgia stabbed a finger in her direction. "You think I'm boring, too."

"No, I don't," Pepper denied.

"Georgia," I said gently. "Why would you want to go? You don't have anything to prove."

"Yeah," Pepper agreed. "Are you actually hoping to get Harris back? You're better off."

I nodded. Pepper and I had been doing our best over the weekend to cheer Georgia up. We pulled out all the stops. It was a true girls' fest replete with takeout, movies, and late-night milkshake runs. Suzanne joined us for some of it, but she had a group project to prepare for, so it was mostly just us three.

"Ugh, I'm going to have to run every day this week." Georgia tossed her chopsticks into a box.

My phone buzzed on the shelf beside my bed. I reached for it, my heart speeding up, already suspecting who it might be. Okay, hoping.

I hadn't heard from Shaw since he left, which could mean two things. He got what he wanted and was done with me. Or he wanted to give me time to be with Georgia. Somehow I knew he wasn't capable of the first. He wasn't a user. And he sure as hell wasn't anything less than honest. If he'd been looking for a fling, he would have been up front about it. My gaze landed on the screen.

And I was right. I smiled like an idiot.

Shaw: I miss you

I was still grinning over his words when he texted again, before I even had a chance to reply and tell him I missed him, too.

Shaw: How's Georgia?

Me: Good

Shaw: Good enough to be left alone yet? I have this bed that's too big. It needs you in it. *I need you in it.*

"Oh my God, you're blushing. I think that's a first. What's lover boy saying?" Pepper teased in a singsong voice.

My face flamed. "Shut it."

"I never thought it would happen. You're in love." Georgia smiled almost sadly. I knew she was happy for me, but it must be a bitter thing to watch something grow between me and Shaw while her love life crumbled. I couldn't help feeling a little guilty even though I knew she wouldn't want me feeling that way.

My thumbs moved over the keys.

Me: Can't tonight.

Shaw: Understand. You're a good friend

I smiled, my chest swelling. He understood. He didn't try to guilt me. He really was unselfish that way. Or he wasn't nearly as anxious to see me again. Not as anxious as I was anyway. My smile slipped. Ugh. This relationship business really messed with your head.

Shaw: Let's go out this week

Me: Are u asking me out

Shaw: Assbackwards, but yeah. I am. We're overdue a real date

Me: Ok. But I have big test Thur that I need to study for

Considering I hadn't studied all weekend, I was really going to have to cram over the next few days.

Shaw: You're killing me, but I guess I can wait that long. As long as I get to see you. Thur night then?

Me: Ok

Shaw: Bring an overnight bag minus pjs. You won't need those

I set my phone back down on the shelf and curled my legs up to my chest, hugging my knees. Pepper and Georgia both stared at me with funny expressions on their faces.

"What?"

Pepper grinned. "Guess you don't mind my interference now, do you?"

I rolled my eyes. "Whatever. Don't sound so smug. It's not like he's my boyfriend." I didn't know what he was.

"Not yet." Pepper arched her brows. "Give it one more week and you'll be saying 'I love you.'"

I snorted and reached for another crab rangoon. "That's a reach."

"We'll see."

I settled back on the bed and turned my attention to the cop chasing down a bad guy on the screen. I bit into my crab rangoon and resisted the idea that her suggestion could possibly be true. That it wasn't crazy. Not feeling the way I did.

WE MADE ARRANGEMENTS TO meet at seven at Mulvaney's. Reece owned the place, but they also had great burgers. From there, who knew what we would do. Or where we would go. Okay. I had a few ideas of what we would do. I'd packed an overnight bag like he'd suggested, so I knew where the night was going to end. Leading up to that point I wasn't sure.

Friday night felt like a long time ago. All I could think about was being alone with him again. Just the idea sent all my girl parts dancing. I might not know what we were, exactly, to each other. More than friends? More than a passing hookup? But I was glad it was him. I was glad I'd waited all these years. I couldn't imagine my first time being with anyone else.

I cleaned up my station around four P.M. I wanted to shower before heading to Mulvaney's. I'd started a new project this week. I wasn't sure where I was going with it yet. Right now it was just a lot of blue on the canvas.

"Emerson." Professor Martinelli came up behind me. "I wanted to talk to you about the showcase."

I cringed, hoping she wasn't going to fuss at me for leaving so early last Friday.

"Your work received much praise."

"Oh." I flushed, delighted and embarrassed at the same time.

"My friend, the gallery owner from Boston, was very interested in your work. Especially *A Winter's Morning*. In fact, she would like to display it in her gallery."

"Are you serious?" I hopped anxiously in place, feeling like a kid at Christmas.

Professor Martinelli reached inside her pocket and

pulled out a small business card. "She would like you to contact her."

I took the card with shaking fingers. "Thank you. I will."

She smiled and squeezed my shoulder. "I'm proud of you, Emerson."

Her words warmed me all over. From the inside out. I wasn't accustomed to praise. Maybe I was even starved for it. It wasn't something I ever got from my parents, after all.

"Thank you."

"Keep it up. You'll go far, Emerson." Nodding, she turned away.

I took a step after her. "Professor Martinelli." She stopped and looked back at me. I moistened my lips. "Would you know anything about airbrushing?" I didn't even know I was going to ask the question until the words came out.

"Airbrushing?"

"Yes. I was interested in trying a new medium."

She cocked her head, considering it. "Interesting. Tell you what, you get me a list of the materials you'll need, and I'll order everything for you, okay? I'm fascinated to see where you go with this, Emerson." She scanned me. "You never cease to intrigue me."

My heart swelled. "Oh, thank you, thank you!"

After she left, I hurriedly finished cleaning my station and left. My boots crunched across the snow-coated sidewalk. The suite was empty and I shot Georgia a text to check on her before jumping into the shower, where I shampooed, lathered, exfoliated, and shaved.

Georgia's reply was waiting for me when I got back to the

room. She'd gone to see a movie with Suzanne. I sighed with relief, glad she wasn't alone. She seemed to be doing okay, but I knew she wasn't sleeping well. Even if I didn't hear her tossing and turning at night, the shadowy smudges under her eyes served as evidence.

I was dressed and ready by four forty-five. I sank down on the edge of my bed, smoothing my hands over the thighs of my skinny jeans. I glanced at the clock. Only one minute had passed since the last time I looked at it. Seven seemed a long way off.

An idea hit me. Grabbing my keys, I decided to get this night started.

I PULLED IN FRONT of Shaw's house at half past five, the heavenly aroma of meat, cheese, and fried goodness wafting to me from the passenger-side floorboard. At five, there was no line at Mulvaney's. I only had to wait ten minutes for them to prepare my order. I assumed a guy like Shaw could eat his weight in food so I'd ordered two large sides of Tijuana fries and fried pickles to go along with our burgers.

I eyed Shaw's truck, relieved he was here. Only after picking up dinner from Mulvaney's had it occurred to me that he might not be coming from home before meeting me.

Hefting the warm bag from the floorboard, I exited the car. My boots thudded up the front porch steps. I knocked on the front door and hit my heels into the porch, shaking loose some of the snow so that I didn't track it into his house. A full minute passed before I knocked again, not wanting to appear overly impatient. Maybe he hadn't heard my first knock.

Another minute passed and I was starting to feel foolish for coming here unannounced and debating whether to knock for a third time or just skulk away. I could toss the food and show up at seven like we had originally planned.

God, when did I turn into one of *those* girls? The kind who was always second-guessing herself when it came to a guy.

Not that he was *any* guy. Clearly. From the first moment I met him he had been different. *I* had been different.

I'd started to turn away when the door was suddenly pulled open.

"Emerson."

I turned, my hand shifting slightly to the bottom of the bag and the heat practically singed my fingers, but I didn't care. It was nothing compared to the heat that swept through me at seeing him standing there damp from the shower, a towel wrapped loosely at his waist.

"Hi." My voice was strained and breathless. I lifted the bag in my hands. "Change of plans."

His dark eyes scanned me and the bag, his mouth quirked in that sexy half grin I was coming to love. "We're eating in?"

"Hope you don't mind."

"Are you kidding? A beautiful woman just showed up on my doorstep with food. I might be in love."

My smile froze on my face. Heat swarmed my body and I knew I must be every shade of red from the neck up.

It was just an expression. A joke. Of course it was a joke,

but everything inside me seized with a mixture of fear and hope.

And that's when I knew I wanted the words to be true.

"C'mon inside." He waved me in, either unaware of or prepared to ignore how his words had just shattered me. He couldn't know what they did to me. How badly I wanted them to be real.

I carried the food to the table and began removing cartons with trembling hands. It was embarrassing. We'd already had sex. The ultimate intimacy. Why did I still feel so vulnerable and exposed around him?

Because you just realized you were in love with him and that gives him the ultimate power over you. Even if he doesn't realize it.

I felt him before he spoke. His body radiated heat as he stopped beside me, his chest aligned with my arm. "Hey." His voice whispered across my cheek. "Why are you shaking?"

I didn't look at him. If I looked at him he would know. He would see everything I was feeling shining in my eyes. Too bad running away at this point wasn't an option. I'd come here. I had to stand my ground and hope that I didn't make a fool of myself.

With slow movements, I removed my scarf, then my coat. Drawing a deep breath, I faced him.

"Hey," I whispered back.

"I missed you." His thumb dragged down my cheek.

Stretching up on my tiptoes, I kissed him, slowly, tenderly, savoring the smooth firmness of his lips. I savored him and the moment. Our first kiss with my full knowledge that I loved him. Whatever else happened, I could have this.

His hands came up to hold my face. I deepened the kiss, licking his tongue, nipping his bottom lip as my hand went for his towel. It was too easy. Just a tug and it was gone. His naked body pressed against mine and it was achingly clear that I had too many clothes on.

He lifted me in one smooth move. My legs wrapped around his waist. Lips locked, he walked me to the bed. That great big bed where I had woken alone so many nights ago. I wasn't going to be alone in it this time.

He stopped at the edge of the bed and we feverishly removed my clothes, our hands flying, bumping clumsily in our haste. Until I was equally naked. The room was more well-lit than my suite last weekend and heat scored my cheeks as he surveyed me from the top of my head to my bare feet.

"You should never wear clothes." His eyes gleamed, dark with appreciation.

I released a nervous laugh.

"At least around me," he amended, his hands coming to rest on my hips. "No one else should get to see you like this. There would be riots."

I laughed harder. "Stop." My gaze flicked over him. I couldn't help myself. He was all lean muscle and sinew. I placed my hand directly over his heart, feeling its steady thump as I covered his warm, inked skin with my palm. "You would cause your own share of riots."

He inched me back on the bed, his big body covering mine. His arms braced on either side of me, keeping his weight from crushing me completely.

I gasped at the sensation of him. At his erection prodding

the inside of my thigh. I parted my thighs instinctively, already yearning for him, needing him there, desperate for him to assuage the clenching ache. I squirmed and wiggled under him, but he just shook his head at me, smiling wickedly. "Not yet."

I sighed as he lowered his head to my neck and started kissing his way down my throat, over the slope of my shoulder. Slow, long kisses where he used his teeth and tongue.

I stared straight ahead, seeing nothing. Seeing everything. My fingers sliced through the thick strands of his hair, tugging the silken locks.

I was already gasping by the time he reached my breasts. I could have wept as he sucked my nipple into his warm mouth, pulling it deep, his tongue laving the hard tip.

I moaned his name, surging restlessly under him. His hands spanned my hips as his mouth descended, kissing down my belly and arriving between my legs. His mouth landed unerringly at my core. He blew on my moist heat, driving me wild. He tongued me, lapped at me, circling that tiny hidden nub before finally taking it and sucking it firmly between his lips.

I came in under five seconds, shuddering against his mouth, at the deep pulling drags of his lips around me.

My arms dropped above my head. Panting, I stared up at him as he rose back up to grin down at me. "Hang on one second."

He moved to the small nightstand by the bed and grabbed a condom. I scrambled to my knees, pushing my hair back off my face as he came back to me. "Can I put it on you?"

He handed me the small packet. I pushed him back on the

bed with one hand on his chest. He tucked his arms behind his head, a relaxed pose that belied the dark need in his eyes.

My gaze drifted down his body, stopping on his erection. A smile curved my lips as I settled between his thighs. I closed my hand around the hard length of him, slowly gliding my thumb over his silken head. His breath caught and my eyes flew to his face. His jaw was clenched, a muscle ticking in his cheek.

I stroked him again with my thumb, loving the feel of him, silk on steel. His breathing turned ragged. Watching him, I dipped my head and licked the head of him. I waited, almost expecting him to stop me like the last time I'd tried this. When he made no move, my smile widened and I licked him again, my tongue circling the tip of him. I closed my lips over him, just about an inch. I sucked, running my tongue over him, tracing the shape of him, the silken underside of his cock, the slit at the very tip. I reveled in this, in holding him at my mercy with just my mouth.

I dragged my fingers down his shaft to cup his balls, and in that same motion I slid my mouth all the way down the long stretch of his erection. He groaned, thrusting himself into my mouth, almost hitting the back of my throat. I held him deep, sucking hard as I tongued the length of him.

"Please," he begged, his fingers diving into my hair. "I need to be inside you."

I smiled around him, loving the taste of him and the way he groaned.

"God, Emerson." His fingers flexed in my hair. He didn't jerk on my head. He didn't try to pull or direct me. He just massaged my scalp, thrusting his hips against my mouth, trying to get me to take more of him in.

His groan rippled through me. Desire tightened my belly. I pulled back, sucking just the head of him, my cheeks caving as I drew him in, my hand closed firmly around the base of his shaft, holding him captive to my ministrations.

"Fuck, Emerson, don't toy with me." He reached for my arms to pull me up, but I wasn't having it. I dipped my head, taking him in deep again, my fingers gently flexing around him.

He groaned and gave up his hold on my arms, both hands fisting in my hair. Satisfied, I released him, popping him from my mouth like a lollipop. I snatched up the condom from where I'd dropped it on the bed and fumbled with the wrapper, my hands shaking.

He plucked it from my hands and brought it to his mouth, tearing it with his teeth in one jerk. We were both panting. I scrambled to my back, my hands propping me up as I hungrily watched him slide the condom down his hard cock.

His big hands closed around my hips. In one yank, he hauled me toward him on the bed.

"Wait," I panted, pushing him onto his back on the bed.

"Emerson," he growled, his voice thick with a need that matched my own. His expression actually looked pained.

"I want to do this." I wanted to feel him under me, his big body subject to my whim.

"Then you better be quick. I can't wait any longer."

Neither could I. Straddling him, I reached between us, circling him in my palm and guiding him inside me. I sank down slowly, seating myself on him. I gasped at the fullness of him, stretching me to capacity. His hands flexed on my hips.

This position brought him deeper. I had never felt so full. My muscles surrounded him like a glove. The pleasure of him buried inside me bordered on pain.

He breathed my name, his eyes closing. "Emerson, God, you feel so good." His hips surged, pushing himself deeper. "So. Tight." My breath fell harsh and fast as my body adjusted to him. His hardness pulsed in me, sending sensation shooting to every nerve in my body.

I settled a hand on his flat stomach. Muscle and sinew rippled under my palm as I lifted my hips and brought myself back down on him, gasping at the delicious friction.

His hands slid down my back to grip my bottom, guiding me, showing me how to set the pace. I balanced my hands on his rock-hard chest, working my hips over him. His eyes glowed darkly, feasting on me, above him. "That's it." He squeezed my ass, and the pressure of his hands on me coupled with his hoarse, "Faster," nearly sent me over the edge.

I angled my body forward, grabbing hold of the headboard as I curled over him, finding what I liked, coming apart with a cry each time he hit that hidden spot. I ground against him, our bodies coming together with loud smacks, whimpers spilling faster and faster from my lips.

"That's it, baby," he encouraged. "Make yourself come." He sat up, his hands sliding up my back, rough, broad palms gliding over each tiny bump of my spine. I shivered as his mouth settled on my throat, his teeth scraping my flesh and dragging my pounding pulse point into his mouth.

I wrapped my arms around his shoulders, hugging him close to me as my hips undulated, pumping over him. I reveled in the feel of his body, the smooth skin stretched over firm muscles. I rained kisses over his shoulder, taking tiny bites, nips at his salty flesh.

"God, Em, I can't take it anymore." He wrapped one arm around my waist and flipped me in one smooth move, staying fully lodged inside me, never once breaking contact. I yelped at the sudden impact of the bed at my back and him over me, driving deep. He thrust hard and fast. "I'm sorry. I need—I can't—"

I lifted my head off the mattress and planted my mouth on his lips, letting that kill any worry he might have that he was being too rough with me.

He gripped my thigh, hooking a thumb behind my knee and pushing my leg up toward my head. The angle brought him in even deeper and I cried out into his mouth, shuddering beneath him as his strokes came hard and swift. Words tripped from my lips, spilling into his open mouth. *More. Faster. Harder.* The pressure building inside me finally snapped.

He thrust several more times. Each stroke felt deeper than the one before and had me arching beneath him, my fingers clutching his biceps, nails scoring his flesh. I closed my eyes and saw actual spots, bright flashes of color behind my eyelids as I came apart, every nerve exploding with sensation as I flew into pieces in his arms. White-hot pleasure eddied through me. I melted. My muscles turned to hot liquid.

He slammed into me one final time, groaning into the crook of my neck. I held him tightly, folding my arms around him, my hands smoothing over his slick skin.

He moved to pull out of me, but I squeezed my legs around him. "I don't want you to go," I whispered.

"I'm too heavy."

"It's a good weight."

He braced his arms on either side of me and looked down, framing my face in his hands. His fingers played with my hair, brushing my cheeks.

I smiled, sated, replete, wondering how the hell I could have stayed away from him even this long. From the moment I met him that night at Maisie's we could have been doing this. "It was even better than before and I didn't think that was possible." I practically purred the words.

"You know what they say? Practice makes perfect."

"Then we should practice. A lot," I teased, deliberately not thinking about how very permanent that sounded. I wasn't going to let myself think about where this was going—if anywhere. That would only make panic creep in.

I didn't do relationships. I was sure to fuck this up. I killed the thought. *You just said you weren't going to think about the future.*

He rolled to his side, slipping from me. Immediately I felt bereft, hollow inside. I tugged the comforter over me, watching as he rose from the bed, admiring his taut backside as he removed the condom and disposed of it in the trash can. Turning, he strode back to the bed and slid in beside me, his warm flesh surrounding me and affecting me all over again. My softness melted into his hardness. His arms felt like muscled bands around me.

My fingers skimmed his muscled shoulders and biceps. He really was too beautiful. I would love to paint his body, all the shadowed dips and muscled swells.

"So this is afterglow?" I grinned against his chest, turning my face into the curve of his shoulder. "Now I get it."

He chuckled. "You had doubts of its existence before? Like it was all some urban legend?"

"Something like that. I mean I've heard . . ." My voice faded and I bit my lip, embarrassed. What was I supposed to do? Share the stories I'd heard from my friends over the years?

His fingers trailed through my hair. "What have you heard?"

"Um, nothing that prepared me for this."

"Careful. You're inflating my ego."

"As if it's not inflated already."

His fingers slid down to tickle my side and I jumped. "Hey, you're making me sound like I'm some arrogant man-whore." He lifted up on one elbow to watch me, still tickling me so that I writhed and squealed under him.

"No, stop, stop!" I laughed breathlessly, tears streaming down my face.

His touch eased up on me then, his fingers just grazing my ribs tenderly with the rough pads of his fingers. "Yeah, and that just wouldn't be true 'cause the only girl I've even wanted to be with since I got back here is you."

I stilled, my smile evaporating as he gazed down at me intently, his expression as serious as a heart attack.

He continued. "When I came back here, I just went

through the motions. My mom was gone. My grandfather, too. I worked. I ate. Went out. I didn't have anything or anyone. I was even thinking about reenlisting."

My chest grew tight, felt constricted as I looked up at him, thinking about that. That one night's chance encounter had put us in each other's paths. We could have never met. He could have shipped back out and I could still be that same girl going through the motions, moving from one hookup to the next. Just the idea made my heart hurt.

"What about your cousin? Beth?" I asked, searching for something normal to say when I was totally freaking out inside over a hypothetical.

The slight smile that curved his well-carved lips faded. He eased back down on the bed. I propped myself up on one elbow to look down at him now, concerned I'd said something wrong. "Shaw?"

He dropped an arm over his forehead, staring up at the ceiling. "Beth doesn't want anything to do with me. She and my aunt. They're not even inviting me to Beth's wedding."

"What?" Outrage coursed through me. "Why—"

"I remind them of Adam."

My mouth worked, hunting for the right words, but there were none. "That's not fair."

He exhaled. "I can't blame them. They lost their brother. Their son."

"He was your cousin, too. Your friend. You lost him, too."

"Yeah. I know. But I was supposed to look out for him. He joined because of me."

"That can't be your—"

"He joined because of me . . . so he died because of me."

I shook my head. "That logic is just . . ." I lifted a hand and brought it down on his chest, pressing firmly, as if I could somehow convey the utter *wrong* of this. "It's just screwed up."

"Beth tried." He shrugged on the bed like it was nothing. Like he wasn't talking about his family rejecting him. Like it didn't hurt. But I knew. I knew just how painful, how devastating it could be. "She's always been Little Miss Fix-it. Whenever Adam and I got into fights as kids, she would force us to make up. One summer in high school we were all drinking out at the lake and Adam's girlfriend tried to kiss me. He took a swing at me, but Beth set him straight. She wouldn't let anything get between us. We were family then."

"You're still family," I whispered even as I realized how ridiculous those words were coming from me. What did I know about family?

"Beth came over here shortly after I got back." His hand slightly tightened in my hair. "She wanted to know about Adam. About what went down over there. How it happened. The family isn't given many details, but she sat at my kitchen table and told me she had to know everything. She had to know how her little brother died."

"And then what?"

His chest lifted on a breath. "So I did what she asked. I told her. Everything. And now she can't look at me. Now she sees that . . . the image I gave her of Adam. Dying. I am that memory for her."

"That's not fair," I repeated, my eyes burning with unshed tears. "You did what she asked. You told her—"

"Yeah. I did. I thought it was the right thing. She deserved the truth. Closure, I guess. I would still do it again even knowing now that I would lose her." He looked at me then. He brought his hand to my cheek. "Look at you. You try to act so tough, but you're just a big softie, Emerson."

I smiled wanly. "Yeah. Now you know my secret." I was soft. Weak. Shaw gave his cousin what she wanted no matter what it cost him. She was the last of his family here. His mom had moved on and started a new life without him. Beth should have been here for him. Like he had been there for her when she asked for the details behind Adam's death. He needed her. For some reason this made me angry. It was as if Beth represented my parents. The rejection they had dealt me all my life. After their marriage ended, they really didn't have room for me in their lives.

But Shaw told Beth the truth and tried to give her the closure she needed. That was him. He stuck to his principles and did what he thought was right in any situation whether it was easy for him or not. He pursued me even when I shoved him away. When any other girl out there would have been happy to fall into his arms, he kept coming after me.

I wanted to be more like that. Bold and courageous.

I wanted to live without fear.

I was scared. All the time. I realized that now. I've always been scared. My desperate quest for control, only picking guys I could twist around my finger and manipulate, never letting one in even if they wanted more from me. It was just me running. Hiding. And I didn't want to run or hide anymore. I couldn't do it. Not if I was going to ever become whole. Not if Shaw and I ever stood a chance.

I brushed my hand along his strong jaw, reveling in the scratchy end-of-day bristle. I thought about all he'd seen. All he had overcome. The dark things he had lived through and he was still here, unbroken. Still ready to embrace life.

Suddenly I wasn't scared anymore. He gave me courage.

I knew what I had to do.

Chapter 18

I WAS A LITTLE late to the rehearsal dinner. Parking on a Friday night was a bitch. I hovered in the threshold of the ballroom, eyeing the crowd. There were at least two hundred people in attendance. If this was just the rehearsal dinner, I couldn't imagine how many guests would be at the wedding tomorrow. I guess if your dad was a senator, you could expect half of Congress.

I scanned the crowd, spotting Mom looking half her age in a canary blue cocktail dress. She wove through the tables, laughing and smiling, shaking hands and kissing cheeks. She was in her element.

Her face lit up when she spotted me. She rushed over to greet me, taking both my hands in her own. "My sweet girl! You're here!" She made a great show of kissing each cheek, her gaze flitting around to see who was watching us. "You couldn't have worn something with a little bit of color?"

I glanced down at my black dress rather helplessly. It was classy. V-necked with tiny straps gathered loosely at the shoulders. My two-toned black and camel half boots looked good with it. Pepper and Georgia at least had expressed admiration. I'd tried on a number of outfits for their approval before landing on this ensemble.

"Don!" Mom called my stepfather over.

He extricated himself from the small circle of men he'd been deep in conversation with and approached me.

"Emerson." He hugged me. I endured the stiff embrace. It never felt natural or genuine. It was weird to consider that we were related. I was on friendlier terms with my dentist.

"Don," I returned.

"Glad you could make it."

"Of course she made it," Mom inserted, her gaze flicking around again, clearly desperate that no one overhear and get the idea that we were anything less than the perfect family.

"Come." Mom linked arms with me. "Let's mingle."

The next thirty minutes was a whirlwind of introductions. I pasted a smile on my face, but I felt like I was holding my breath. Waiting for the moment when I would come face-to-face with Justin and Melanie.

It was as if Mom was distracting me. I could see the wariness in her eyes every time she looked at me. Like I might spit pea soup or something when I finally saw Justin. I guess she hadn't thought this far ahead when she begged me to attend.

The inevitable happened when Melanie spotted me. She went from glowing to radiant as she hurried across the room to hug me. "Emerson! You came! I wish I'd known. I would have seated you at the head table—"

I laughed weakly. "That's okay. Besides." I looked around at everyone milling in the room. "Is anyone even sitting?"

Her fingers clung to my arms. "True." She glanced around. "Everyone seems like they're having a good time."

"Of course they are," Mom gushed. "The food is delish." As if to prove her point, she plucked a lobster canapé from a passing tray and bit into it with a groan. "The champagne is superb. The orchestra is lovely." She gestured widely with her hand. "It's the Four Seasons."

I resisted rolling my eyes. Nothing like Mom patting herself on the back. I'm surprised she wasn't wearing a flashing button that read WORLD'S BEST HOSTESS.

"Have you seen Justin yet? He'll be so thrilled you made it." She stood on her tiptoes and searched the crush. "Oh! There he is! Justin!" She waved him over.

I followed her gaze. My stepbrother looked up. Grinning, he made his way over to us. My stomach churned as I assessed him. He'd changed in five years. He was a little bit thicker. No longer a lanky twenty-year-old. His jaw was less defined, his face somewhat bloated looking.

His small blue eyes leveled on me. "Emerson." He folded me into his arms and it felt . . . okay. Brotherly and natural. "So glad you're here. Thank you." He patted my back, his voice softer, for my ears alone, "Thank you so much for coming."

"Thanks. I'm glad I came." I looked from him to Mom to Melanie, and I meant it. It was a good thing. I'd conquered my fears.

Mom beamed and squeezed my hand. "I knew you would."

"C'mon. I want to introduce you to my parents." Melanie pulled me after her. Justin followed, a dutiful fiancé, still smiling and shaking his head indulgently.

Over the next hour I was plied with drink and food and introduced to almost all two hundred people in attendance. At least it felt that way. Melanie kept me close to her side. "I'm just really mad at you, you know." She pouted at me.

I blinked. "Why?"

"Because you didn't come around sooner. You should be in my wedding, only now it's too late."

"Oh." I smiled, flattered even as I was relieved that I wasn't. Coming here tonight was one thing. Actually being in the wedding party? No thanks. "That's okay, really."

"No, you should be one of my bridesmaids. Seriously, my cousin, Pauline, who I can't stand, is a bridesmaid. And you're not. How does that make any sense?"

I stifled my cringe at the idea of me in Justin's wedding. He might appear to have changed and I might really like his bride-to-be, but that would just be . . . weird.

I was saved from lying and agreeing that I wished I could be in her wedding when someone bumped me from behind and caused me to collide with Melanie. Her cocktail splashed down the front of my dress.

"Oh!" She patted at me with a napkin. "I'm sorry."

"It's okay," I assured her. "It's black. I'll just go pat it dry."

She clasped my hand and gave it a warm squeeze. "I'll go with you."

"You don't need to do that."

At that moment, Melanie's mother appeared at her side. "Dear, you've hardly said more than a hello to Mrs. Rothman."

Melanie looked at me uncertainly. "Ugh. I used to babysit for her."

"You go. I'll be fine," I assured her.

Melanie's mother nodded. "See? She'll be fine, Melanie. Let her mingle. She's a pretty girl. Some nice young man will latch on to her." Melanie's mother beamed at me and nodded, her well-coiffed hair not even moving with the action.

"Okay. I'll find you in a little while."

I nodded and worked my way through the crowd outside the ballroom. There was a line outside the ladies' room, so I crossed the hotel lobby to use the restroom on the other side.

As I suspected, it was empty. I took my time, breathing in the silence and decompressing after the noise and deluge of people. As I washed my hands, I stared at my reflection for a long moment. The girl who stared back at me wasn't the same girl from a couple of months ago. That girl would never have come tonight. She would never have faced her past or been open to the fact that maybe things could be different. That she could possibly have a relationship with her mother. That her stepbrother maybe wasn't Satan after all—or at least not anymore.

Maybe. Maybe she could fall in love and have a normal relationship.

An image of Shaw filled my mind. Okay, above normal. Maybe I could have an amazing relationship with an amazing guy.

My reflection smiled slowly back at me, tentative and hopeful. With a lightness to my step, I exited the bathroom, my boot heels clicking on the tiled floor. I pushed through the door, stepped into the corridor, and stopped.

Justin was waiting there, leaning against the wall, one hand tucked casually into the front pocket of his slacks.

"Justin," I said rather dumbly.

"Hey, Em."

"Hello," I replied, feeling my forehead crease. What was he doing here? "Did you follow me?"

"I just wanted a moment alone to thank you for coming. It was the last thing I expected after I called you."

"Well." I nodded. "You were right."

He arched an eyebrow. "I was. About what?"

"Maybe it is time to move on and try to be a family."

He smiled. "I'm so happy to hear you say that." He pushed off the wall and advanced on me. "I've only ever wanted us to be friends. We were once, remember?"

I nodded, backing up until I couldn't go any farther. "Yeah. Before that night."

He flattened a hand against the wall, near my head. "About that night. I was wrong." He shook his head. "It was so stupid of me."

I exhaled. It was the closest he'd ever come to admitting what he did—the closest he'd ever come to an apology. "Thank you for saying that," I murmured.

"I was drunk. You were young. I should have waited. You weren't ready." He dipped his head and smothered my lips with his, ramming his tongue inside my mouth.

Stunned, I pushed at his chest, shoving him back. He blinked down at me, startled. I slapped him, my palm connecting with a crack to his face.

He flattened a hand to his cheek. "What the hell—"

"What are you doing?" I shook my head. "I thought you had changed! I thought you were different, but here you are.

The same prick you always were. Only now I'm not a little girl. So stay the fuck away from me." I stabbed a finger in his chest.

He snatched hold of my finger. Unsmiling. Eyes hard. "I get it now. You came here for a little payback. Right?" He sneered. "You spread all those lies about me all those years ago and now you—"

"They weren't lies," I reminded him, tugging my finger free. "You know it happened."

His upper lip curled over his teeth. "What happened was that you couldn't leave me alone."

"*Me?*"

Everything inside me burned to lash out. To remind him that I had been fifteen years old. If he hadn't been so drunk, if I hadn't run out of the room, if—

I blinked hard. Then that night would have ended very differently.

"Yeah. You kept throwing yourself at me from the moment our parents got together."

Is that how he saw it? I had looked up to him like a brother. And he wrecked that, sneaking into my room in the middle of the night. I shook my head, unwilling to argue with him about what had really happened all those years ago. "Whatever. I didn't come here to stir up the past." No. I came here because I thought I was burying it. *Stupid*. I saw that now. "You're still an asshole." I tried to step around him, but he grabbed my shoulder and slammed me back against the wall. I bit my lip, muffling my cry.

"And you're still just a cocktease." He looked me up and down, his gaze lingering on my cleavage. I had thought the dress tasteful before. Classy. But the way he looked at me made me feel dirty.

He traced the neckline, his finger dipping inside to brush the top of my breasts. "Or maybe not such a cocktease anymore. I bet you spread your thighs plenty these days." He shook his head and made a tsking sound with his tongue. "I fantasized about popping your cherry."

"Go to hell." I slapped his hand away from me.

He chuckled, looking me over. "No little girl anymore."

"That's right. I'm not a little girl anymore. You don't scare me. And you can't do this to me." Not again. "Maybe I'll march in there and tell Melanie—"

His creepy smile vanished. "You stay away from Melanie." He jabbed a finger close to my face again. "One word and you'll see just how big of an asshole I can really be."

His fingers tightened on my shoulder and I winced, certain he was bruising me, but determined not to show he was succeeding in hurting me. "What's the matter? Afraid she'll believe me?"

Beneath his mask of fury, I read the anxiety there. Yeah. He was worried. Maybe something had happened before. Maybe she already had doubts where he was concerned, but he had persuaded her to his side.

"You little cunt," he bit out. "Don't fuck with me—"

"Justin?"

I sucked in a breath and looked around him for the source of that soft voice, even though I knew gut deep who I would see.

Melanie hovered there in her beautiful yellow dress. The

pink flush that had brightened her cheeks all evening had vanished. She looked pale as bone as she clutched her hands together in front of her.

"Justin, what are you doing?" Her keen blue eyes flitted back and forth between us.

"Nothing, pumpkin." He advanced on her quickly, taking her clutched hands into his. "Emerson and I were just talking—"

"You called her a . . . you called her a horrible name." It didn't surprise me that she couldn't say the word. She probably never had, and she clearly couldn't fathom why he would.

Melanie swung her gaze on me, pinning me to the spot. "Emerson?" My name hung there, heavy with question as she tugged her hands from his.

I shrugged helplessly. What could I say? Should I actually open my mouth and warn her about the kind of man she was marrying? "I'm sorry, Melanie."

She gazed at me with those large blue eyes and it was like she was peering into my soul, searching for the truth.

"Emerson," Justin growled, the sound low and deep. Threatening. Melanie glanced at him sharply. She hadn't missed his tone either.

Screw it. She'd heard enough already. I could see it in her face, in the stiff way she held herself. She wasn't stupid. "He doesn't deserve you," I declared.

She could take what she wanted from that. I didn't need to say anything else. I unglued my feet from the floor. Shaking, I moved past her down the corridor.

I was back in the ballroom before it occurred to me to wonder what I was even doing here anymore. There was no reason for me to stay. Except maybe Mom. My gaze drifted toward her. She had been almost human tonight. Like a real mother. I moved toward her, compelled to say good-bye at least.

"Emerson." Her face brightened when she saw me.

"Hey, Mom . . . I have to go."

She frowned. "What? They haven't even served dessert."

I glanced over my shoulder, almost expecting Justin to appear at any moment and continue tearing me down. Thankfully, I didn't see him. He was probably still sweet-talking Melanie. I turned back to face Mom. "I'm sorry. I have this thing early tomorrow."

"But the wedding—"

"I'll be there," I lied. It was easier to just assure her of that. I'd come up with some excuse over my absence later.

Her frown softened, making her look somewhat mollified.

"And, Mom." I shifted on my feet. "Maybe we can go to lunch next week."

She stared at me and I wasn't sure what she was thinking—and I wasn't going to find out because the voice behind me chased every other thought in my head away.

"Emerson."

I whirled around, my gaze sweeping over Shaw's tall form. Heart hammering, I stepped up to him. "What are you doing here? How did you—" I stopped and shook my head, not bothering to finish the question.

"You weren't answering my texts." Had he been texting me? I hadn't even glanced at my phone since I'd parked the car and tucked it into my clutch. Now I wished I had. I wished

I had fed him some excuse. A lie. Anything to have stopped him from coming here. "And I remembered that tonight was the rehearsal dinner . . ." He glanced around, waving a hand to encompass the room before settling his gaze back on me, searching. "I got the feeling you might be here."

I inhaled thinly. Of course. Melanie had announced the rehearsal dinner was at the Four Seasons. He knew where to find me.

He stepped closer, his chest brushing mine and everything inside me quivered. At his nearness. At the husky pitch of his voice. "What are *you* doing here?" He lifted his hand, touching my hair, rubbing several strands between his fingertips. "I thought we agreed—"

"I agreed to nothing." I tried to sound casual, but defensiveness crept into my voice. "I didn't think I was coming, but I changed my mind. I can do that, you know."

His jaw ticked, signaling his displeasure.

"Emerson?" Mom was there, at my side, her voice full of question as she looked Shaw up and down. He was dressed more formally than I had ever seen him, in slacks and a button-down shirt, and I knew he had tried. For me. And yet he still looked apart from everyone here. More virile. Strong. Rough edged. A man who made his living with his hands and not a spreadsheet. Something melted a little inside me. I think I might have kissed him right then if we weren't standing in the middle of my stepbrother's rehearsal dinner with Mom's face set to full-on glare.

I turned to her with a bright smile. "Mom, this is—" My voice stalled. Did I really want to introduce Shaw as my boyfriend and endure an inquisition from her on the subject? Was he even that? Aside from introducing himself to Melanie that way, we hadn't discussed what we were. He hadn't asked me.

"Shaw," he supplied, sticking his hand out for her. Only I knew him well enough by now to know that the smile was strained. He didn't like her. Not knowing all he did. He couldn't like her.

She stared at his hand for a moment as if not sure whether she should touch it or not. She looked from his extended hand to his person again and her lip seemed to curl back over her teeth.

"Nice to meet you." Her fingers settled lightly on his hand as though afraid to touch him any more than that.

"A pleasure, ma'am."

"I didn't realize Emerson had checked plus one." Accusation hummed beneath the comment.

I bit back a snort. I hadn't even sent the RSVP card in. I had only decided I was coming last night. Less than twenty-four hours ago when I was naked and in bed with the guy standing in front of me.

Oh, what I would have given to be back in bed with him now rather than standing here.

"Are you a student at Dartford?" Mom asked, plucking a glass of wine off a passing tray.

"No, ma'am."

"Oh?" She looked him over again. "Another school in the area? Or did you graduate already?" She smiled slightly, like that must be it. Like it had to be that because anything else would be unacceptable.

"I don't go to college."

Her perfectly smooth face looked doll-like in its utter lack of expression. Only in her eyes could I read her total lack of comprehension. Her overly plump, glossy lips finally managed to form words. "As in . . . ever?" She looked at me as if needing confirmation and then back to him. "What do you do?"

This is where if he announced he had a fat trust all would be right in her eyes.

"Since I got out of the Marines, I've been working as a mechanic."

"A mechanic?"

Oh. God. Her body actually shuddered as if he'd confessed himself to be a serial killer. Her eyes looked ready to bug out. She was so blatantly horrified I actually felt the crazy urge to laugh.

She looked at me, that impossibly immobile face of hers looking ready to crack. "Are you serious, Emerson?" Her gaze flitted wildly about the room, as if expecting someone to jump out with a hidden camera and declare all this a joke. Or maybe she was just worried someone would point at Shaw and identify him as the hardworking blue-collar middle-class guy he was.

I shook my head and reached for Shaw's hand. "C'mon, let's go." I was finished here. Justin's ugly words echoed in my ears. I didn't have to wonder anymore. He hadn't changed. Nothing had. I had no family here.

I didn't make it one foot, however. I stopped breathing when I heard the voice at my back.

"There you are, you little bitch."

Chapter 19

I FROZE, EVERYTHING INSIDE me wilting at the voice, too fresh in my mind.

I stared ahead, Mom's face in my line of vision, and if I hadn't recognized the voice already I would know who was behind me based on her body language. And her eyes—the only thing in her plastic face that revealed any emotion.

Her gaze flashed to shock and then dread. I glanced swiftly at Shaw, embarrassed; mortified that he was here for this. Even though I had shared my past with him, seeing it firsthand, witnessing it—*living* it with me—was an entirely different experience and I just wanted to shrink away until I was invisible. And anywhere but here.

I assessed his face. He looked confused. He'd heard the voice, too—the ugly words as clearly as anyone else near us—but he didn't yet realize they were directed at me. Several people around us had stopped talking. They stopped and stared.

Run. *Get away*. The urge pounded through me. I just wanted to escape before this twisted from bad to hellishly bad. I stepped to the side and tugged Shaw after me, hoping to avoid Justin altogether. Maybe it was crazy or delusional, but I thought I could leave the room without a confrontation. Without having to look at my stepbrother one more time.

"Did you hear me, Emerson?"

A shudder rolled through me. There was no mistaking who he was talking to now.

Shaw stiffened beside me—went rigid in like one nanosecond. His fingers tightened around mine, and I knew there was no breaking that contact. That he wasn't letting go of me.

Justin's voice kept coming, a barrage of knives I couldn't duck. "Where do you think you're going? I'm talking to you, bitch."

Yes, he was talking to me. Because I had come here. Because I'd thought that maybe things could be different. That I could be a normal girl who didn't have a totally messed-up family.

Shaw turned slowly, taking me with him. I looked somewhere above Justin's shoulder, staring blindly ahead, unwilling to even look at his loathsome face. "What did you call her?"

I'd never heard Shaw talk in a voice like this before. He'd lost his temper in front of me, but his voice had never been like this. Low and chilling, with an undercurrent of menace.

Justin didn't answer him. There wasn't a sound coming from anyone around us. All conversation had ceased. The orchestra played on, oblivious.

I brought my other hand to Shaw's arm. "Let's just go."

"Oh, now you want to leave?" Justin's face twisted. "After you trash-talked me to Melanie and convinced her to call off the wedding? Now you're happy to go."

"Oh, Emerson," Mom cried behind me. "You didn't!"

"Oh, she did." Justin nodded. "I should have known she would do this."

I tried to deny this. "I didn't come here to—"

"You came here to do just what you did." Justin closed the few feet of space between us. He didn't even look at Shaw. It was as if he could see nothing beyond me. His eyes, so full of rage, fixed solely on me. As he took another step, Shaw flattened a hand to his chest and pushed him back, keeping him from getting any closer.

Justin looked at him, finally seeing him. He blinked. "Who the hell are you?"

"I'm the guy who's going to kill you if you say another word or take another step toward her."

Justin held his gaze for one moment, still leaning forward, pushing his weight into Shaw's hand. They stared at each other, assessing, sizing the other one up. Finally, Justin stepped back. "Whatever. Take her and go."

I released a shaky breath, relieved. I tugged on Shaw's arm. "Come on."

Shaw moved slightly, walking in a semicircle around my stepbrother, obliging me. And then we were clear, finally past Justin. Our backs to him.

"Emerson." It was my mother's voice.

I shouldn't have hesitated. Shouldn't have turned. But I did. She was the whole reason I'd come. I had to see, had to know.

She would always be my mother.

Mom stood beside Justin, staring at me with dead eyes, and a pang punched me in the chest. She *still* stood with him.

"You're such a disappointment."

I inhaled through my nostrils. Slow and deep, marveling at how those words could still cause me such pain.

I turned away, finally ready to go, but Shaw didn't follow. I moved one step and realized that he still stood there facing Mom and Justin.

"*She* is a disappointment?" he demanded. His body went rigid and I could feel the anger radiating off him in waves.

Mom lifted her chin. "I don't know who you are, but this isn't any of your business. You weren't even invited to this party. Leave before I call security."

The threat didn't move him. He didn't budge. "You're the disappointment . . . the failure as a parent."

I hurried to Shaw's side and seized his arm with both my hands, looking around at the avid faces watching our little drama. It was an unpleasant sensation. I felt like a lamb surrounded by wolves. "Shaw, what are you doing?" I hissed, panic spreading through my chest.

He glanced at me with bright, furious eyes and then looked back at my mother. "You don't deserve a daughter like her."

"You're right. I don't," Mom flung back. She lifted her chin and raised her voice an octave so it could be heard clearly. "My daughter is a very troubled young woman. She's given me nothing but grief." She looked around the room, addressing the onlookers now as much as Shaw.

His arm clenched under my fingers. "First off, Emerson is amazing and smart and kind . . . but I could see why anyone would be 'troubled' with a mother like you. Oh, and that piece of shit standing next to you who—"

"Shaw!" I shifted my weight anxiously, fear scratching the back of my throat at what he was about to say.

He turned on me in a flash, his dark eyes relentless as his hands seized me by the shoulders. "No! I know what this guy did to you." His voice dropped to a hiss, for my ears alone. "*Everyone* should know exactly what he is."

I shook my head. *No, no, no!* No one could know. Mom and Shaw were the only two people I had ever told. Not even my best friends knew. Not my father. This room full of people couldn't know. The world couldn't know.

Suddenly Shaw was wrenched away. Justin gripped him by the shoulder, motioning to two uniformed hotel employees. "See this trash to the door."

Something snapped in me then. I saw red. Shaw was not *trash*. Shaw was good and noble. The exact opposite of Justin.

I came at Justin, tearing his hand from where he gripped Shaw's shoulder. "How dare you! Never touch him. Never! You're the . . ." Fury and indignation consumed me. "*You* tried to rape me." I whirled on my mother. "And you did *nothing* about it when I told you. Nothing!" My voice tore into a strangled choke at this last part.

Sometime in the last few minutes the band had ceased to play.

My stomach dropped as my words echoed throughout the room and I thought I was going to be sick. My words reverberated on the air. Jarring and awful. The sound of them seemed to run on forever, echoing through the room, bleeding into my soul.

I had never said them before either. Not *those* words. Not to my mother when I told her. Not to Shaw. Not even to myself. But that's what had happened. I'd used other words.

He had *bothered* me. Or *messed* with me. Gentle euphemisms.

He tried to rape me.

I felt everyone's eyes on me, exposing me, pulling me apart, revealing everything inside.

I staggered back several steps, suddenly feeling lighter. As if those five little words had been anchors on my soul and now they were gone.

Justin jabbed a finger in my direction. "You fucking little liar!"

I winced.

There were no more words after that. One moment Shaw was standing still and then he was a blur, going after Justin. His arm pulled back, fist connecting with Justin's face with a sickening smack of bone on bone.

"Shaw, no!"

He ignored me and struck him again, shaking off the hands of the hotel employees as they grabbed for him.

"Stop it! Stop it!" I clutched my face, covering my ears as if I could drown out the sound of Shaw's knuckles connecting with Justin's face.

Justin went down. Mom screamed. The crowd parted wide. Shaw stepped over him, his feet splayed wide on either side of his prostrate body. Shaw reached for Justin, pulling him back up to his feet for more, but I was done. Justin's ugly words, Mom's disgusted glare. I felt like I was fifteen all over again.

I'd had enough. Shaking and wrecked, I could feel only those stares. Everyone gawking at me like I was something dirty. No way was I sticking around to watch him beat my step-brother to a bloody pulp. That would be just the cherry on top of a craptastic night.

Turning, I fled the ballroom, barely stopping to grab my coat. My heels clicked on the outside sidewalk in a flurry as I hurried toward the parking lot. My shaking fingers fumbled over the front buttons of my coat.

"Emerson!"

A quick glance behind revealed Shaw running down the sidewalk.

Shaking my head, I turned and ran. I didn't care how undignified I looked.

"Emerson!"

The sound of his voice was close behind me, and I choked on the realization that I wasn't going to outrun him.

His hand fell on my arm. Emotion scalded my throat, bursting free as he spun me around.

"How dare you?" I whispered, wrenching my arm wide. "You shouldn't have come! I didn't want to announce to a roomful of strangers what they did to me!" Because it had always been what *they* did to me. Not just Justin. But Mom, too. Mom's betrayal had been maybe the worst of all. It still was. "And I didn't need you beating up Justin and causing a scene! What did that prove? You shouldn't even have come here. I could have handled this on my own. I didn't need you! I don't need you!"

"But *I* need you, damnit," he growled, his dark eyes searching, digging deep and threatening to take hold of me if I let him. I shook my head and slid a step back, as if distance would protect me. He followed. "And I want *you* to need me." He took my face in his hands, hauling me against him, dropping his forehead to mine, muttering against my lips, "I couldn't let him talk to you like that. You might be okay with them treating you that way, but I couldn't let them—"

"Don't! This wasn't about you!" I fought the urge to sneak my arms around his neck. "What are you even doing here?"

"You think once I figured out you were here that I would just wait at home . . . do nothing while you're in the same room with some guy who tried to rape you—"

"Stop saying that!" I wedged my arms between us and shoved him away with a grunt.

He angled his head, eyes softening as he gazed at me. "It's the truth, Em."

"You don't think I know that?" Tears sprang loose, streaking hotly down my face. "I just announced it to everyone! It's out!" I lifted my face and gulped in air, waving to the hotel. "Two hundred people know that now, thanks to you!"

"Me?"

"Yes, you! I wouldn't have blurted it out like that if you hadn't shown up. If I hadn't gotten so mad when Justin called you trash." I wouldn't even have come tonight at all if it wasn't for Shaw. If I hadn't gotten it into my head that I needed to stop running. That I needed to stop hiding. That I could confront my past and be brave like Shaw.

He stuffed a hand in his pocket, and I realized then that he was without a coat. He had to be freezing standing there, but he didn't so much as shiver. He just stared at me, his expression stoic. "Is that it? You're mad at me because I forced you to face the thing you've been running from forever?"

"Yes! N-no!" I looked up at the winter sky as if I would find something, some truth or answer, in the dark gray clouds scudding against the darker night. Nothing.

He was right. He'd shaken me loose from my self imposed cocoon. Since I met him, all the old hurts had returned. The fears. I shouldn't have come here tonight. Letting him in had been a mistake.

I lowered my gaze back down to him. He waited, staring silently, his eyes so full . . . so judging. That's what I felt at least. Exposed and raw. Like he could see me and what he saw was something broken. Something that needed fixing.

"You can't fix me. This wasn't your fight," I whispered.

"Your fight is my fight. What hurts my girlfriend hurts—"

"No. I took several sliding steps backward, shaking my head. "I'm not your girlfriend." I shrugged. "I'm not."

I watched him for several more moments, absorbing the sight of his face as my words sank in. His eyes seemed to dim. "You're scared," he said quietly.

"Scared?" I scoffed. "Of what?"

"Of anything real. And what we have is real. You love me and it terrifies you."

"I don't love you," I lied.

He grabbed my face then, dragging me closer with both hands. "You love me. I know you do. I know it because I can see it in your eyes . . . in the way you look at me." He inhaled. "It's the same way I look at you."

"No," I bit out. I couldn't be so transparent. Love was pain. It was being out of control. Like the hot mess of tonight.

He kissed me. Hard. I struggled for a moment before relenting and kissing him back. I couldn't resist. He had that effect on me. He turned my brain to mush and made all my girl parts tingle. His mouth softened then, turning coaxing and sweet. His tongue traced the seam of my lips and I gave myself a mental shake. Seizing control again, I pushed him away.

My chest heaved with gasping breaths that fogged the air in front of me. I stared at him for a long moment before tucking my shaking hands into my front pockets.

"I want you," he said starkly, the barest quiver in his hoarse voice. "Me and you. Together." He drew in a deep breath, his broad chest lifting. "But I can't chase you forever."

I nodded in understanding. It was an ultimatum. Fair, but an ultimatum nonetheless. After tonight, I couldn't even contemplate it. It was all too much right now.

Without a backward glance, I walked away.

Chapter 20

THE NEXT TWO DAYS passed in a blur. Georgia and Pepper watched me with worried eyes. I ignored their questions, sleeping through most of Saturday and then watching mindless television on Sunday. I checked my phone, but it didn't matter. He didn't call.

That night played itself out over and over in my mind and every time made me sink a little deeper into my bed, made my legs curl up a little tighter into my chest. I'd walked away from him. And he was done coming after me. I chose safety. And control.

So why did I feel so wrecked?

Pepper and Georgia marched into the room Sunday evening, flipping on the light, a bag of what smelled like nachos gripped in Georgia's hands. "You need to eat," she declared.

"And we need to know what's going on," Pepper added.

I sat up slowly. "What is this? An intervention?"

"Call it whatever you want." Georgia started pulling boxes from the bag. "I got your favorites. Fajitas nachos. Guacamole on the side."

"Wow," I murmured. "Carbs."

"For you, I'll splurge. Especially if it gets you talking."

I smiled and it actually didn't hurt too much. "Bribery. You guys didn't have to do this."

"Of course we did."

I stared at Georgia, humbled. She had just been dumped by her boyfriend of five years. Her first love. Her only love. I couldn't imagine how she must be feeling. "You're an incredible friend, Georgia. We should be taking care of you—"

"I've grieved enough," she said with a wave of her hand. "No more tears for me." We dispersed cartons of nachos and small cups of hot sauce, settling into our respective spots. Me on my bed. Georgia and Pepper on the other one. Mine was too littered with pillows and clothing.

Pepper wasted little time. "So. The rehearsal dinner. How'd it go?"

"Oh. About as bad as it could have gone. But the highlight might have been Shaw beating the crap out of my stepbrother."

"What?" Georgia tossed down a nacho and leaned forward over her carton. "Why?"

I stared at my friends and sighed. It was time. Maybe it had been time a long time ago, but the fact that I had already outed myself to a roomful of strangers made this moment easier somehow. They deserved to know. I loved them and they deserved the truth.

They watched me solemnly, as though they knew I was reaching some decision.

Opening my mouth, I told them. Everything poured out. They didn't say a word. They listened as I told them about my mother. And Justin. And Melanie. Everything leading up to Friday night. And then I told them about the rehearsal dinner. With wide eyes they listened as I described it. Including Shaw showing up.

"Wow," Georgia murmured, setting her carton down on her nightstand.

Pepper shook her head, her eyes wide. "Why didn't you ever tell us any of this? About your mom and stepbrother?"

"I just didn't want you to look at me differently."

"Differently how?" Georgia dropped down next to me on my bed, heedless of the pile of clothes I had yet to put away. "Like we wouldn't love you anymore?"

"No, of course not." I shook my head, tucking the hair behind my ear, feeling silly about this now. I couldn't explain why I'd kept it to myself. There was too much shame wrapped up in what happened to me. Not just what my stepbrother did, but because my mother rejected me. She hadn't protected me— that most basic thing a mother does for her child. Even Pepper's mother, a messed-up drug addict, had, in her own way, loved and done her best to protect Pepper. And Georgia came from two great, loving parents. Not me.

I exhaled. "I just didn't want you to think anything was wrong with me. I didn't want your pity."

"Em," Georgia said softly. "There isn't anything wrong with you. You got a crappy family. Not. Your. Fault."

"Yeah. That's not a reflection on you. Trust me. I know about crappy families." Pepper dipped a nacho in hot sauce, nodding vigorously. "I don't pity you. Right now, I want to shake you for keeping this bottled up forever."

I smiled wanly. "I told Shaw."

"Well, that's something," Pepper allowed.

"Yeah, and then he showed up, beat the crap out of Justin—"

"Hallelujah." Pepper nodded in approval.

"Because he loves you," Georgia cut in. "You know that, right?" Her eyes softened. "I know you've never felt like this about a guy before, that you're scared of your feelings . . . loving someone can be scary."

I looked at both of them, Georgia's words echoing through my mind. *Loving someone can be scary.* Something in me caved in and broke loose at the truth of that statement. I did love him. But could I do this with him? Be normal? Take love and love someone back?

Pepper nodded. "I think the guy has been in love with you ever since he hauled your ass out of that bar."

I set my food down beside me on the bed and curled my knees to my chest, rocking slightly for a moment. So far this conversation wasn't making me feel better.

"He made you happy," Georgia reminded me. "I haven't seen you like that with any guy. Like ever. He brought something out of you. You were . . . real. Not Emerson the t—"

I looked at her sharply. Her cheeks grew pink with embarrassment. "Emerson the tease?" I finished.

She nodded, looking contrite, but I didn't blame her. I had fostered that image. I kept everyone from seeing the real me. Because only the real me could get hurt. Not fake Emerson. Nothing touched her. No one.

No one but Shaw.

He'd gotten to the real me.

"The only thing standing in the way of you being happy is you," Pepper quietly added. "Take it from me. I almost lost Reece. Don't let Shaw go."

I unwrapped my arms from around my knees and reached for my phone on the shelf, rubbing my thumb idly over the screen, thinking about Shaw, wondering what he was doing, if he was thinking about me.

"Are you gonna text him?" Pepper asked, hope in her voice.

I nodded slowly. "I—yeah." Sucking in a deep breath, I typed, deleting and starting over several times before I settled on:

You don't have to chase me anymore

I set the phone back down and shrugged like it was no big deal. Like I didn't just pull my heart from my body and fling it down on the ground to see if he would pick it up.

The three of us sat there for several moments, waiting to see if he replied. After a few tense minutes, I grabbed the remote control and forced a smile. "Let's see what's on TV." I felt Pepper and Georgia watching me but feigned great interest in channel surfing. "Oh, look, *Teen Wolf* is on."

AFTER WE FINISHED EATING, Pepper left us to head over to Reece's place. I couldn't quite lose myself in *Teen Wolf* like usual. I had a Medieval Art quiz on Wednesday, but there was no concentrating on that. I'd read up on the buttresses of Notre Dame later.

"I'm going to the studio to get some work done," I

announced to Georgia as I tugged my Uggs up over my leggings.

"It's your favorite episode," Georgia said, pointing to the screen at the hot boy running through the woods at missile-launch speed.

"Eh." I shrugged, staring almost broodingly at the television for a moment. None of the yummy boy actors held a candle to Shaw. He was the real deal.

I pulled a thick Irish sweater over my boy's T-shirt. Standing, I leaned down and pressed a kiss to her head. "I won't be too late."

She laughed. "Right. You always say that and then you lose track of time. You never even hear your phone half the time when you're in there."

Exactly. I stood up, looping my wallet and keys around my wrist.

"I know what you're doing, Em. You're trying to distract yourself from the fact that Shaw hasn't texted you back yet."

I forced a smile. "You know me well."

"Em, wait. At least text him and tell him where you're going. In case he—"

"I don't think that's necessary."

"Humor me!"

"Bye." I fluttered my fingers at her. Slipping on my bulky coat, I left our room and walked toward the elevator. On the way down, I buttoned myself up. Stepping outside, I cringed against the blast of cold. I hadn't emerged from my dorm since Friday and I'd almost forgotten it was winter outside. I looped my scarf around my neck twice, tugging the soft fabric up to cover my chin.

I turned my phone over and over in my pocket, Georgia's voice buzzing in my head. Muttering, I pulled the phone out and texted Shaw.

I'm headed to the studio to work

Shoving the phone back in my pocket, I expelled a breath. "There. Satisfied, Georgia?"

I beat a familiar path to the studio, thumbing the keys that dangled from my wallet as my feet ate up the distance. I passed a few students heading back in the direction of the dorms. Others took the turn past the student center, doubtlessly heading for the library.

The studio loomed ahead in the darkness, its glass windows gleaming like the flat surface of a silent lake, unruffled by wind. I toyed with the key. Professor Martinelli only granted a few students after-hours access to the studio. It humbled me to be one of them.

I walked up to the door and inserted the key into the lock. Or tried anyway. I fumbled, turning it over until I got it right. Until it slid inside. The building was old and the thick wood door groaned as I swung it open. The key stuck in the old brass lock and I struggled to yank it free.

Suddenly I was shoved from behind. My shoulder banged against the edge of the door as I tumbled inside. I cried out, hitting the ground. There wasn't time to put out my hands. My entire body took the brunt of the fall. Even my face didn't escape. My cheek scraped the concrete floor.

I moaned, too stunned at first to move. I heard the door

slam and then I was hauled up to my feet. I wasn't quite ready to stand. The fingers digging into my arms held me up.

"Hey. *Sis.*" Hot, sour breath blew into my face.

I cringed, pressing a hand to my raw cheek. "What are you doing, Justin?" I squinted at his features in the dark. I could discern very little. Just the gleam of his eyes and the movement of his lips. The light switch was by the door, but I wasn't reaching it with his grip on my arm.

"Just paying you a visit. I wanted to catch you alone. You've been holed up in your dorm all weekend but I had only time on my hands. You know . . . since my wedding got canceled."

"You're drunk." It was an unpleasant reminder of another time. Him. Like this in the dark. Me stunned, caught off guard and shrinking away from him.

He laughed, slurring his words. "I've been drinking since Friday night. Since you ruined my life."

"You didn't need any help from me to do that."

"Melanie won't even talk to me."

"Good for her," I snapped. Maybe I shouldn't have, but I couldn't help myself.

His fingers squeezed tighter, hurting me. There'd be a mark tomorrow. "Yeah. You're glad about that, aren't you? You showed up with your friend and spouted a bunch of lies."

"They weren't lies."

"Oh yeah? I'm a rapist?"

I quit tugging on my arm and looked him in the face. "You tried to rape me." The moment the words left me I felt free. The fear—there had always been fear—evaporated. Faded like smoke into the air.

"Tried." He laughed. "Not much distinction, is there? Be--tween a would-be rapist and a rapist. I mean Melanie looks at me like I'm some kind of pervert now." He paused, the stink of his breath pungent in my face. "No distinction." His voice was low now. A growling whisper. "I might as well do it. Be what Melanie thinks I am."

I didn't have to be a genius to understand his meaning. All I could think in that split second before I moved, before adrenaline fired through my limbs, was that I was stuck in a familiar nightmare again.

I BROUGHT MY HEAD forward. Hard and fast. I'd seen it done in movies countless times. I only hoped it worked.

It worked. And it hurt. I staggered, stunned from the force of my head hitting his face. I was too short to reach his nose. My forehead smashed into his chin and mouth.

His hand dropped from my arm. I ran, his curses burning on the air. Where he stood, he blocked the door, and I was too worried about getting that close to him. If he grabbed me again, it was all over. He would overpower me. He was too big. Twice my weight. I couldn't let him catch me. I had to avoid him. Hide. Wait until he moved from the door and then make my escape.

I knew the room well. Even in the dark. I ran on silent feet and ducked behind a large canvas. Heart hammering, I took a gulping breath, listening.

Justin's laughter rang out. "Where'd you learn that move?" He bumped into the edge of a table, rattling the supplies sitting on it. "Well, I can't wait to see what other moves you have."

His voice was closer. He was walking down the center of the room. I crouched and started circling the room's perimeter, seeing the front door in my mind.

"If it wasn't for you, I'd be on a beach in Martinique right now, married to Melanie." I kept moving as he talked. "And that job I had lined up working on her father's campaign? That's gone, too. You owe me, Emerson."

I debated reasoning with him. Faking an apology, but then I dismissed it. He wasn't in a forgiving mood. He was drunk. And he had nothing to lose. He'd lost everything.

"Why don't you just come out so we can get this over with? C'mon."

I was almost to the door. A few more feet.

Suddenly my phone started ringing. The ring tone was loud and shrill in the vast space of the studio. I fumbled for it, desperate to reach it and make it stop.

His footsteps slapped on the concrete. My fumbling fingers dropped the phone and I bolted for the door, diving between two easels. Justin just tore through them, knocking them aside like they were toothpicks.

His hands grabbed me. Air rushed over me as he slammed me onto a table. I felt wetness at my back and knew I was on top of someone's freshly painted project.

It was a mad scramble. Rough hands yanked at my clothes. I fought. Clawing and punching. His fingers curled around the waistband of my leggings. My arms flailed on the table, knocking into supplies, and my hands brushed something familiar.

Not a week passed without one in my hand. I snatched it up without thinking, rotating it in my grip. Tip down, I jabbed the end of the paintbrush into his chest.

He screamed. I didn't know how hurt he was—how much damage I'd done—but he howled and fell off me. Gasping, I dropped down from the table. I moved backward in the dark, barely able to support my weight on shaking legs.

Then light flooded my world. I threw a hand up over my eyes to shield me from the sudden glare.

I heard my name. Arms surrounded me and I screamed, attacking them.

"Em! Emerson! It's me."

I shook the hair from my face and peered up at Shaw as if I didn't quite recognize him. "Shaw?" I started to ask him how he knew I was here, but stopped, remembering that I had texted him. With a choked cry, I flung myself against him and hugged him tightly.

He hugged me back, one hand at the back of my head, the other at the small of my back, warm and firm, fingers splayed widely. "Emerson!" He pulled back, his gaze scanning all of me, from head to toe, missing nothing. "Are you hurt?"

I winced as he brushed his fingers against a raw patch of skin on my cheek. "I'm fine."

He gaze drifted over my shoulder, narrowing as he caught sight of my stepbrother. "Did he—"

"No." I shook my head and the motion made me slightly sick.

Justin moaned behind us. Turning, I surveyed my handi-work. The paintbrush was embedded high in his chest, right above the V neck of his sweater, below his collarbone. No mortal wound, but it looked painful. "You stabbed me!"

"You're lucky to be alive," Shaw snarled, pulling out his phone and dialing. I inched from his side, only distantly hearing him speak to a 911 operator as I studied my stepbrother with an odd sense of curiosity.

Standing over him, I murmured, "You can't hurt me. Not anymore. Not ever again."

And I realized I had been letting him do that. Him and Mom. All these years. I'd been letting them keep me from living life and finding happiness.

Justin panted, his face sweaty and creased with pain as he stared up at me. "God, it fucking hurts, Emerson. Call an ambulance. Please! I'm sorry! Please!"

Shaw moved back to my side, wrapping an arm around me. He spoke gently, as if I was something fragile that might shatter. "An ambulance is coming. The police, too. I'm sure they're going to want to talk to you." His gaze skimmed my face. "And probably take you to the hospital."

I nodded.

"What about me?" Justin whined.

All softness fled from Shaw's voice. "Yeah, you, too, asshole. After they arrest you, of course."

Justin dropped his head back on the floor, whimpering now, his hand hovering over the paintbrush stuck in his chest. "No, please. I'm fucking dying here. Isn't that punishment enough?"

Shaw's eyes were hard and uncaring. "It's just a flesh wound, pussy." He moved to crouch over my stepbrother. He tapped the paintbrush and Justin yelped. "What I should do is bury it in deeper." Shaw glanced at me, his eyes softening as they lingered on me. "She's a better person than I am. Because that's what I would have done. If I'd caught you attacking her, I would have killed you."

Justin's eyes grew enormous and he shook his head wildly, whimpering all over again, but this time I doubted it was due to the pain. It was fear.

Shaw continued. "It's no less than you deserve, and I promise, if you ever come at her again, I'll kill you."

"I'm sorry, man." Justin's gaze flicked over to me. "I'm sorry, Emerson. I'll leave you alone. You'll never see me again. I promise."

Shaw stood again and reclaimed my hand, warm fingers lacing tightly with my fingers. "You all right?"

It was over. What began all those years ago. What turned me into a creature who went through every day in a state of quasi existence. I existed but didn't live, hiding inside myself, looking out at the world but never stepping into it.

Shaw knew that. He saw it in me.

I squeezed his hand back. "I just want to go home." I sagged against him, content to lean on him, to let him hold me. For however long he wanted. I was finally ready to step outside.

Chapter 21

IT WAS AFTER TWO in the morning when I was released from the hospital.

I had to be examined. Photographs taken and my minimal injuries catalogued. The same police officer who stayed with me through the night and took my initial statement led us to his car in the hospital lot.

I slid into the backseat of the cruiser. Shaw followed, settling beside me. His strong arms wrapped around me and held me. I released a pent-up breath I hadn't realized I'd been holding. We'd barely pulled out of the parking lot before my head dropped on Shaw's shoulder.

Shaw had remained at the hospital with me, holding my hand like he would never let go, leaving only during the doctor's exam when they forced him to step outside the room. He called Georgia and Pepper for me, backing me up when I insisted that I didn't need them to come to the hospital. I spoke to each of them briefly, assuring them I was fine. Pepper's voice had cracked when I talked to her and I knew she was on the verge of tears over what had happened. Fortunately she hadn't been in front of me right then or we would have both ended up blubbering like babies.

"Thanks," I murmured as I settled into the backseat. "For everything."

"Don't mention it. I . . ." His voice faded.

"What?" I prompted, keeping my voice low, aware of the police officer a few feet away in the front seat.

"I should have been there sooner. I was working in the shed. I left my phone in the house. I came as soon as I read your text."

I smiled tiredly, playing with his fingers where they rested on my thigh. Trust him to blame himself for not rescuing me.

"You were there when I needed you." I yawned and nestled against him.

"Not tonight," he murmured, his low voice deep and earnest. "You saved yourself."

I smiled as my eyelids sank shut. "I did, didn't I?"

I WOKE TO THE smell of coffee and frying eggs. My stomach grumbled. Blinking, I rubbed at my eyes. The nachos of yesterday were a long-ago memory. I was wearing one of Shaw's T-shirts. I didn't even remember changing. Last night must have really wiped me out.

Sitting up, I looked around Shaw's home. He moved about in his kitchen wearing only pajama bottoms that hung low on his narrow hips. I followed the lean, muscled lines of his body as they pulled and flexed with his actions. His dark hair was wild, sticking out in every direction on his head. Everything about him was strength and vitality. And mine. He was all mine. A slow smile curled my lips.

He moved back and forth, light on his feet, between the stove and the counter, sliding eggs and bacon onto plates. He turned a dial, shutting off the stove. Bread popped up from the toaster and he grabbed the hot slices, muttering a curse as he added those to the plates. Picking up the plates, he headed toward the bed.

His eyes lit up when he saw me sitting in bed. "You're awake."

"How could I sleep with the smell of bacon in the air?"

Grinning, he sank down on the bed, carefully balancing a plate in each hand. "Very true."

I took one plate from him. "So." I bit into a piece of bacon. "This is a little déjà vu." I plucked at the T-shirt for illustration. "I'm guessing you changed my clothes for me." This time, at least, the idea didn't overly embarrass me.

"You fell asleep in the car."

I swallowed my bite of toast. "I didn't realize we were coming back to your place."

"I wanted to keep you with me." His eyes were steady on me, watching me like I might bolt at his words. "Can you blame me? After last night?" Suddenly I had an image of him watching me while I slept. I tucked a tangled lock of hair behind my ear and winced at the grimy texture. I must look a mess. My cheek was still sore. I felt achy and gross all over.

"I need a shower," I mumbled, my hand reaching around to feel the dried paint crusting my hair while my other hand lifted another slice of bacon to my mouth. Chewing, I gestured to my overflowing plate. "Is it wrong that I want to finish this first? It's really good."

"No. Eat. Then you can shower." He waggled his eyebrows. "I'll help."

I smiled slightly at the wicked way he was looking at me. "You'll help me shower? That's awfully sweet of you. So selfless."

"I'm just a sweet guy like that. And I'm kind of into you. A lot." He ran his thumb down the curve of my cheek. The wicked glint faded from his eyes . . . leaving something that made my chest squeeze. "Get used to it."

My smile slipped and the air suddenly shifted, grew strained and uncomfortable. His hand dropped away. I wet my lips, knowing that things needed to be said. "I'm sorry I walked away from you at the rehearsal dinner—"

"No, I'm sorry. I had no right to show up like that. You didn't want me there. I should have respected that."

I studied my plate, my fork stabbing at a bit of egg. "Maybe. But you were right though, you know. Everything you ever said about me. I was scared. I've always been scared. Of getting close to anyone. Of letting anyone in. Especially you. Oh. God. *You* . . ." I lifted my gaze to his face and said hoarsely, "You terrified me."

An emotion like agony flickered across his face. He moved forward as though he would grab hold of me, but then he stopped, restraining himself. His hands opened and closed into tight white-knuckled fists at his sides.

"The reason you terrified me," I explained, forcing the words out, "is because I cared about you. I knew that I could love you and that scared me. Honestly, it still does." And I knew now that it always would.

Like Georgia said. Loving someone is scary. That was part of it. Always. Knowing that at any moment for any reason it could be lost. But I wanted that. I wanted love. Even if I couldn't control it. I wanted it. I wanted him.

Some of the agony faded from his face at my admission, but it wasn't gone entirely. He averted his gaze, staring down at his clenched hands. "I push too hard. I've always been guilty of that. I should have learned from Adam. I led the charge, convinced him that he should sign up with me. I just took over for both our lives, made all our choices. I don't want to do that with you."

I covered his fists with my hand and squeezed them. "You didn't force Adam into doing anything he didn't want to do. And trust me, no one makes choices for me either. I'm stubborn."

He sighed long and hard, his chest lifting and dipping. "I've pushed you and bossed you around simply because I thought I knew what was right for you." He dragged a hand through his hair, sending dark strands in every direction again. "And then I went after Justin right in the middle of that party because I wanted to tear him apart. It was about my anger in that moment. I didn't care what you wanted." He shook his head, looking so sorry that I wanted to grab him close and comfort him. "I just lost it. I didn't care if my actions made you uncomfortable—"

I kissed him hard, delving my fingers in that hair I had been dying to touch. I slanted my lips over his and opened my mouth, thrusting my tongue inside his. His hands came around my back and hauled me closer with a groan.

"Just love me," I breathed into him.

He froze against me, the air crashing from his mouth into mine. His broad chest rose and fell against me with each of those ragged breaths.

I pulled back, holding his face in my hands, letting my words hover between us. I waited with my heart rising to my throat, drowning in his brown eyes.

He stared at me, saying nothing. Doing nothing.

Time hung, suspended, and I began to wonder if he had even heard me.

"Say something," I whispered.

He spoke haltingly, his hands tightening on my back. "Again. Say that again. So I know it's real and not a dream."

"Love me. Please." I inhaled, then shook my head fiercely. I hadn't come this far, to this moment, to utter only half of it. "Like I love you, Shaw. Because I do." I kissed him. "I *do* love you." Another kiss. "I love you." I kissed him several more times, breaking up each kiss with a choked *I love you*.

He moved then. Heedless of our plates and the food he sent sliding across the bed and floor, he came over me, folding me into his arms. His lips smothered mine, kissing me until I couldn't breathe. I kissed him back, deciding that air was over-rated. Who needed it when there was this?

"I love you," I whispered brokenly against his lips. Tears leaked out at the corners of my eyes. He pushed the hair off my face, clearing me for his view. Our noses touched, we were so close. His fingers trailed over my face, drying the tears from my cheeks as quickly as they fell.

"Don't cry, baby. I love you. I love you, Emerson." He

pronounced the words slowly, like he was savoring them. Or maybe he just wanted me to absorb them. Maybe he wanted them to sink in so that I would feel them as clearly and completely as I felt his hands on my face, his lips against mine . . . his heartbeat vibrating from his chest into my body.

So that I would believe in them. Believe in him.

And I did. I felt them. I believed in them.

I believed in *us*.

Chapter 22

Three months later . . .

I SHIFTED ANXIOUSLY ON my high heels, standing in front of *A Winter's Morning* in the packed room. Voices congested the air, mingling with the clink of glasses and laughter. I'd been invited to show two pieces in the exhibit at the posh Boston gallery and had taken position in front of my favorite one—naturally the one that most reminded me of Shaw.

Smiling, I exchanged pleasantries with a pair of ladies who admired *A Winter's Morning,* and answered their questions.

When they moved on, my gaze strayed several feet away where my father chatted with the gallery owner. When I invited him, I hadn't expected him to attend. Even more shocking than his presence tonight was that he seemed impressed . . . even proud of me. While it loosened something inside my chest and made me feel lighter, I didn't need it. I was glad he was here, but I didn't need his approval. I'd found my own sense of self-worth without him. Without my mother.

"Hey, beautiful."

I started a little and then smiled as Shaw came up beside me, sliding an arm around my waist.

I leaned into him, relishing the hard press of his body against me. "Hey, you."

Gazing up at him, I knew my heart was in my eyes because I could feel it there. Since the night I woke up at his house after Justin's attack, I held nothing back. I loved him and made no effort to hide it. It was in my every word. My every action. We'd become as bad as Pepper and Reece. Inseparable other than when we had to part from each other's company for class and work. Correction: as *good*.

Granted, a lot of our time together was spent undressing each other. At his house or my dorm. Mostly at his house though. We couldn't get enough of each other—but we also spent a lot of time together in his shed. Working. Creating. I had started learning how to airbrush. Shaw kept bringing pieces of metal for me to practice my craft. It was gratifying to work side by side with him . . . moving toward a like goal. He was hoping to open his shop by the fall. He'd already found a space, and I was hoping to be ready by the time he moved in to tackle airbrushing his bikes. He claimed I was ready, that I was better than the professionals he'd worked with before, but I still wanted more practice. I wanted to be a real asset to his business. *Our* business. He insisted that we were in this together—or as much as I wanted to be. And I wanted to be.

He lowered his mouth to my ear, the movement of his lips on my skin sending goose bumps racing over my arms. "If you don't stop looking at me that way, I'll have to find a storage closet and hike up this little black dress of yours—"

"Hey, guys! Sorry we're late. Parking was a bear."

Face flaming and my breath tight in my chest, I looked up as Suzanne, Pepper, and Reece closed in. I hugged the girls as Reece and Shaw shook hands.

"Thanks so much for coming, guys."

Pepper and Suzanne stood back to admire my work.

"We wouldn't miss it. This is so thrilling." Pepper squeezed my hands excitedly.

Suzanne shook her head in awe as she stood directly in front of the painting. "Oh my goodness, it's gorgeous, Emerson. You are *so* good!"

"Thank you." I glanced around. "Where's Georgia?"

Pepper and Suzanne exchanged looks. "You haven't heard from her?"

I frowned. "No."

"We haven't seen her since this morning, and she's not answering our texts."

"Huh." I glanced at each of them. "Hope everything's okay."

Pepper shrugged. "I know she planned on coming tonight."

"Maybe she's with . . ." Suzanne's voice faded suggestively. She lifted her eyebrows meaningfully.

"Hey, she's a big girl. Don't worry about her," Reece cut in, waving over a waiter carrying a tray of champagne flutes. "Let's have a toast."

Everyone took a glass and lifted them up in the air.

"To Emerson," Shaw declared. "As talented and brilliant as she is beautiful. Inside and out."

My friends *ahhed* and heat crawled over my cheeks.

Shaw leaned down and pressed a lingering kiss to my mouth. "And I love her."

Glasses clinked as we all toasted. I looked from my friends to Shaw and exhaled a shaky breath, giddy butterflies fluttering through me. Life was good.

Shaw took my hand, his fingers lacing with mine. "Happy?" he asked.

I smiled, my chest swelling with emotion. "More than I ever thought possible."

He kissed me, murmuring against my lips, "Get used to it. This is only the beginning."

Want to know what happens to Georgia?

Find out in *Wild*, the final book in the Ivy Chronicles.

Available everywhere November 2014.

He took my arm and dragged me through the room. "I told you that you shouldn't come here," he said over his shoulder, his voice deep enough that he didn't even have to lift it over the thumping bass for me to hear.

His long strides moved swiftly, leading us through the press of bodies and out the front door. As if it was his right to touch me. As if his brother dating my best friend gave him the right to interfere in my life.

We stepped out onto the empty porch. Empty because why hang out here when there was privacy inside to do all kinds of wild and wicked things. The type of things one did at a kink club. Things I had yet to learn about. Thanks to him.

I pulled free and crossed my arms across my chest, chafing my hands up and down the sleeves of my cashmere sweater. "And I told *you* not to tell me what to do."

I tried to look down my nose at him the way I had seen my mother do countless times when squaring off with some mouthy delinquent. My sister and I called it her *principal look*. If she ever used it on us, we knew we were in trouble. But the effect was lost on him.

Yeah, he stood over six feet, but it wasn't that. Logan had an air about him. A confidence rare for anyone, much less an eighteen-year-old guy. He held himself like someone who knew who he was and his place in the world. And that annoyed me. Why was he so damned self-assured?

I was a mess, but here he stood looking all cool and collected . . . telling me where I didn't belong.

"You want to explain to me why it's any business of yours what I do? I mean . . . don't you have a curfew or something?" It was a deliberate dig. Instead of getting offended though, he grinned. And that grin was devastating. Seriously. No wonder he had such a reputation. Girls must throw themselves at him. His mouth was sexy as hell, too. His lips well-defined, wide, the bottom fuller beneath the top lip. *Oh, the things I bet he could do with those lips . . .*

I blinked at the totally wayward thought.

He laughed deeply. The sound sent goose bumps over my flesh and settled in the pit of my stomach. "I've never had a curfew."

Never? I shook my head, telling myself now was not the time to wonder at his parents' lack of supervision. My mom firmly believed no good could come of staying out past midnight. When I went home on break my parents still imposed a curfew on me. As if I wasn't in my second year of college. As if I hadn't been staying out all hours of the night doing all manner of naughty things. Yeah, okay, so I wasn't. But I *could* be.

This reminder of my sheltered existence just made me more determined to live my life on my own terms. To do tonight what I set out to do. To stop living such a boring existence. I was almost twenty and I'd been living the last four years like a married woman. School. Studying. Sex once a week. *Shit. Liar.* I couldn't even be honest with myself. The last year with Harris we maybe had sex every month.

Standing there looking at this incredibly hot guy who had

a hell of a lot more experience than I did *and* was younger, only flustered me. I flipped the hair back over my right shoulder, noting that his eyes followed the move, skimming over the long trail of hair before moving back to my face.

I started to walk past him, but he blocked me.

I edged back from the wall of his chest, careful not to touch him. I think Reece mentioned his brother played sports. It explained the breadth of his shoulders tapering down to a lean waist. The flat stomach. I'd glimpsed Reece without a shirt when he stayed the night with Pepper. It was criminal. Logan was in good shape, too. My gaze flicked over him. Okay. *Great* shape. He was probably ripped under the black thermal shirt he wore. Just like his brother. Ridiculous six pack, defined biceps and all. I swallowed against the sudden thickness of my throat. Shoot me. Was I actually drooling over a guy still in high school?

"That guy you were talking to?" He rubbed a hand over his scalp, dragging his hand over the close-cropped dark blond hair. "Georgia," he expelled my name on an exasperated breath. "You don't have a clue about the things he's into . . . the things he'll do to you."

I shivered a little beneath the weight of his blue eyes. "I can handle myself."

"Do Pepper and Em—"

"Pepper and Emerson aren't my parents," I snapped. "I'm a big girl, thank you very much. I don't need permission to be here."

He looked me up and down, his gaze lingering at my throat. "Sure you do, Pearls. You fit in here about as much as a bull in a china shop."

My hand flew to my necklace. The pearl necklace had been a graduation present. For some insane reason the hot sting of tears pricked the backs of my eyes. *I would not cry. He would not make me cry.*

"I'm tired of people telling me who I am." First Harris. *Always* my mother. I lived halfway across the country and she was still trying to tell me how to live my life. Even Pepper and Em, in their well-meaning way, did.

And now him. This guy who didn't even know me.

I nodded toward the door. "Maybe I want to hook up with that guy and have him do those things to me. Ever consider that?" I deliberately let it sound like I knew what those *things* were.

"You don't even know what those things are," he retorted, seeing right through me. And how did he do that, anyway?? Did I have a sign around my neck that said TOO BORING TO FUCK? Harris's face flashed across my mind. *I need more, Georgia.*

I fumed. I could be more. I was *more*.

"Yes, I do. He told me," I bluffed. "We were talking about it when you walked up."

His eyebrow winged. "Really? I heard he likes it when the girl dresses up as a dude and puts on a strap-on. You into that, Pearls? I would have pegged you for the type of girl that's only ever done it missionary style."

I sucked in a breath. Insulted, yes. Shocked, too. Shocked that he had guessed that about me.

He laughed, nodding. "Yeah. Thought so."

"Asshole," I spit out. Another first. I had never called anyone a bad word before. It wasn't something ladies did.

"Why don't you go home to your safe dorm room and forget about this place?" His look then was part pitying and part smirk. I could have handled the smirk. It was the faint pity that got to me. I wasn't pitiable. No way.

How dare he talk to me like *I* was the child? I was an adult. I came out tonight to have a good time. To put an end to my drought and prove to myself that I wasn't boring. I could be spontaneous. I could be unpredictable.

I could be wild.

Before I could stop and think about what I was doing, I stood on my tiptoes, circled his neck with my hand and pulled his head down to mine.

About the Author

Sophie Jordan is the international and *New York Times* bestselling author of the Firelight series and Avon romances. When she's not writing, she spends her time overloading on caffeine (lattes preferred), talking plotlines with anyone who will listen (including her kids), and cramming her DVR with true-crime and reality-TV shows.

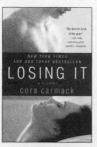

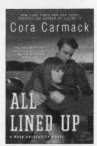